A FREE gift from Author **STEVE WINDSOR**

The story of Eden's Garden as you've never heard it told. How man truly faced his first temptation.

The angel STEG has a dilemma, he can either fulfill his heavenly duty as the knowledge bearing serpent in the Garden—assist the daughter of Eden in bringing Life's light to mankind—or he can pursue a growing love inside of him that is beyond his control or comprehension.

STEG's love is more forbidden than any fruit growing in the Garden, and to pursue it he'll have to break just about every commandment he'll ever know, yet to be written or silently understood hardly matters.

But love is not one to wait and wane while it withers on the vine. Neither is STEG who, as the highest and most beautiful angel—the very first angel—is mere breaths away from being a god himself. Now, he'll either win the affection of the one he loves in the next 7 days, or he will incur the wrath of a God who purports to love him above all others.

Either way, the Garden will never be the same again. Because sooner or later . . . sin touches every god.

Get your copy of *STEG—The prologue Novella to THE FALLEN series Thrillers.*

Available in February 2015!

*Get My **FREE** Copy of STEG*

Available at http://vixenink.com/steg-free-offer/

Praise for the novels of
author Steve Windsor

"Throughout the story you find yourself caring for this immensely flawed character whose four-letter words add a tangy flavor to the hills and halls of eternity. Not because what he does is good, but because Windsor has made him and those around him eminently ... human. For the reader, the challenge in JUMP is not what Jake has to contend with, but putting the effing book down to get to sleep at night."
- Ana Young (Amazon Review)

The perfect way to "Jump" into a story that at first glimpse is off the wall and quite different. The pages seem to turn themselves as you are thrust into a unique world full of fascination, craziness and intrigue. Thoroughly enjoyable read.
- (Amazon Review)

I'm already reading the next book in The Fallen series - FURY and it's awesome!
- Lise Cartwright (Amazon Review)

An even more dazzling read, this hilarious close-up of a personality who cussed her way through one eternal conquest of Heaven and Hell will keep you riveted and clamoring for more. With Windsor's exceptionally concrete prose and dastardly, diabolical dialogue, you won't regret a repeat visit to his eternity of "everlasting impotence."
- (Amazon Review)

JUMP

THE FALLEN: TESTAMENT 1

STEVE WINDSOR

VIXEN INK

JUMP: THE FALLEN: TESTAMENT 1

A VIXEN ink book/Published by arrangement with the author

Cover design by:

Steve Windsor - stevewindsor.com

ISBN-13: 978-0692291467
ISBN-10: 0692291466

To the little demon in us all

JUMP

Testament 1

FUTILITY

— I —

DID I EVER tell you about the time that I killed God?

My new name is Jump. This is my testament:

I heard somewhere that you would have a cardiac before you hit the pavement. The hot lead through my shoulder and ass hasn't killed me yet, so I can tell you that heart attack stuff, that's just bullshit—I'm wide awake as I fall.

And they said man couldn't fly.

My inner critic hasn't croaked yet, either—the little voice in the back of my head, points out my failures again. As if I need help with that.

I try to squeeze my eyes shut, but I can barely keep them closed in the rush of wind. I don't really want them closed. It seems scarier with them shut. So I open them up, but the blasting wind has them watering so bad, everything looks like I'm underwater—total blur.

I guess I don't need to see to know that the ground is racing up at me like the end of a bad book. When it gets here, I'm a footnote. Then again, anyone with half a brain knew it had to end this way—a pointless splattered mess on the street below. I won't last a day on the PIN.

The Protection Information Network doesn't even run domestic terrorist bombings longer than a week. Thanks to the new Scent-seeker technology we installed at every access point into the country, there are no more foreign terrorists . . . alive, anyway. The PIN—the news—what a joke. But that's the only wave left, so that's what we all watch.

Before, I had a little more access to the old archived waves of TV, but that stuff is just more of the same. Lies, pretending to be the truth.

Some of the water from my eyes runs into my mouth, and it's weird, because it doesn't taste like tears. Believe me, I've shed enough of them to know. But as they stream down my cheeks and drip into my mouth, for some reason, they taste like . . . blood?

When I look back on it, would I have done anything differently? I mean, I should have *something* that I would change, right? Things I regret? I don't know. Maybe I can give you a better answer when I land.

My name? Trust me, by the time this is all over, you won't know what to call me. But if you gotta call me something . . . I guess you can call me Jake.

— II —

HIGH ATOP THE Great Mountain of the Eternities, inside the huge Hallowed Hall of the Word—the destiny of every soul since the first —Life's bright light shined into every last crevice of the huge Arena of Reckoning. She and her fallen archangel, Dal, stood locked in oratory combat.

The arena was the battlefield where souls passed through the Pearly Gates to be judged, and then tested by fury and faith. Damnation and salvation were the stakes of combat.

Life's light emanated from the center of the arena like a bright, shining star. She had many names during the time of her eternity— the Chosen One, the Bread of Life, the Lamb, the Author of Life. . . God's children had created so many ways to beg for her forgiveness, that she had difficulty listening to all of their pleas.

Tedious as the duty of Protector was—as difficult as ruling over Heaven and Hell became—Life still attempted to answer any that spoke to her . . . one way or another. All too often, she gave them the answer that pleased her the most—silence. To those she did speak with, and as this was *her* eternity, Life Is For Eternity preferred to be known as "Life."

Life endured her eternity, even as it drew near to a close. And the jeweled floor of the huge, indoor arena, shimmered beneath the brightness of her years. Her brightness shined hard truths that reflected off the white diamonds and red rubies that blanketed the arena floor. The gems were stones of justice, chipped and cracked on their edges, telling the truth of judgments past—long forgotten battles between fallen and faithful angels.

The grandstands around the arena clawed their way almost straight up from the floor until they met with the roof. And today, those perches were filled with the razor-sharp talons and feathers of the faithful and fallen angels of the two heavens—Heaven and Hell.

The bright angels who served Life, perched along one side of the great arena, and the dark angels, those who prayed only to the Dark Angel of Light, Dal, wrapped their talons around long, iron railings on the other side. But however at odds their faiths were, all of them carried a common responsibility—serve each great eternity's protector. And ever since the first eternity, the Protectors authored their Beginning, while all under her prepared for the burning truth of their End.

Outside the hall, snowflakes fell on the mountain like newly judged angels—hatchlings that descended from the two heavens for their fledgling flight to the garden—Earth. All of them were individually beautiful, yet each one was faithful in their own special way.

And though every falling angel looked as different from the next as they could, each of them fell from above with a single purpose—blanket their eternity beneath the cold, white truth of the Word, and keep the Arena of Reckoning freshly stocked with souls.

All watched the fall.

The Dark Angel of Light—the Darkness, Liar, and the one he hated, Devil. . . The evil one had so many names, it was hard for the faithless to remember them all. But at the end of this eternity, he preferred to be called "Dal."

Dal waited, barely outside the brightest part of Life's light. He was his own brightness—his own personal truth—and he felt no compulsion to saunter about at the center of her bright-white lies.

He adjusted his shining, crimson wings and shook and shivered his dark, blood-red feathers to perfection. Then he tucked his wings behind his back, forming his shield. And if freshly devoured souls had an aroma, Dal's breath reeked of desperation and despair. "And the show goes on," he said to Life. "I still do not understand your covenants. This tale—over two thousand years of it—I tire of the words." He pointed a long finger toward the fall. "They devour the words of your book, and then spit them like flaming arrows at each other. And their descent continues. Yet *you* . . . you are content to observe, pretending that your own time is infinite."

Life watched and waited, hovering in the center of her great brightness, overexposed to the penetrating reality of the fall—another death of one of her own creations.

Her hair still carried its long locks of light and her wings, though nearly invisible, were hard and sharp to the touch. Her feathers were crystal white and winked in reflection at the tiniest light. To a mortal, Life was pure. And yet all of her sagged beneath the weight of an eternity almost passed.

That time had acquainted her, all too well, with the depths of Dal's dark heart—his vile, violating nature. She had enjoyed his company once, but the time was long past since she had reveled in his beauty. She could no longer afford such youthful pursuits.

She and Dal were an unlikely pair—shepherding both halves of The

Word—but stranger things had been written before them, so they faithfully ruled their own heaven and hell.

The stakes were higher now, especially for Life, so she prepared herself. The End was nearer than she wanted, but could this one be. . .? She looked at Dal and spoke, "And at the end, the beginning shall be—"

"Judged," Dal said. He stared up at her, hovering just above the arena floor. "This is your word? And yet, you say *I* am arrogant."

Dal moved closer to her, staying carefully at the edge of Life's searing center. For some reason, she always smelled of vanilla, and he sniffed in a huge whiff of the aroma. He thought it would have been better if the scent were burned. Then he gazed back to the fall and continued to observe.

It was difficult to explain how angels saw it, they just did. Like a vision or a dream that they all shared.

"They act as they were created," Dal said. "Excuse me, *born* to." The thought of the spawn of her creations, gnawing their way out of the wombs of their Man-monkey mothers, repulsed him.

Life peered into the light, watching the fall. She bobbed her head gently and then stopped and cocked it slightly to the side. A small furrow appeared on her otherwise smooth and flawless brow. She never understood how her beautiful creations had become so destructive. "He was given an option," she said. "I gave them all a choice. It was trivial—so I believed—find faith and forgiveness or deny belief in the Word."

"You see," said Dal, "this is exactly my—your word offers no alternative. Pardon my insolence, your *eminence*, but your choices reek of the vile fate you have condemned them to . . . and this story stinks of the sweet smell of rot."

Life kept her gaze on the fall. "His purpose in the beginning ends," she said. "Just as yours did." She looked around the arena. "As all of theirs did, as well."

Dal looked at himself then slowly touched his arms and shoulders. "And yet . . . here I stand," he said. Then he gazed into the grandstands, also.

The sparkle of the wings and the glint of the feathers of the brothers and sisters of the two Words, glinted back like stars in the black sky. Each one tried to shine hope from the heavens down onto the darkness of their Protector's Earth—Life's eternity ruling the garden.

Dal swept his arm in an arc around the arena, waving his arm casually at the crowd of waiting warriors. "Here we *all* stand . . . once more."

— III —

I RUN UP the steps, switchbacking my way higher in the scraper's emergency stairwell. I bounded them two at a time for a few flights, but now my feet are down to thumping my way, one step at a time, like an echoing machine gun—*bap-bap-bap-bap-bap*. I can hear the bastards—armored-up Protection agents, probably citizen compliance division—*snatch and bag team*, I think. They're yelling below me, barking and shouting, chasing me like my own personal demons.

Protection—the State's personal pit bulls of justice—all that's left of a failed two-hundred-and-fifty-year experiment in democracy—the masters of a ruined republic gone rogue and drunk on their own runaway power.

It's a pretty good rant. And I keep it stewing in the back of my mind to console my more "enlightened" friends when they whine about the consequences of begging someone else to take care of you. Works great for climbing stairs too, I guess.

The echoes of half a dozen Protection agents waft up the tall escape stairwell. Escape . . . that's got my senses pumped way up—feels like I can hear everything, but as I grab the railing on the corners, pulling myself up the next flight, the thing I wish I couldn't hear is the little voice in the back of my head, heckling me with the one question I can't answer, *What are you going to do when you get to the top?*

I don't have a clue. It's a lie . . . I'll keep telling it to myself as long as I can. The truth? The only thing I know for sure is that I can't let them grab me. They do, and a whole lotta other people are in deep shit, too.

It's easy to stay in front of them—standard gear for a Protection agent has them humping thirty pounds of black and gray armor, not including the helmets and goggles, and five pounds of gun. How do I know that? It's not important right now. Let's just say that I don't have their burden. But I *will* tell you, forty-eight doesn't run like it used to, so sooner or later . . . I grab the railing on another corner with my left hand and clamp down hard on my Kimber .45 caliber handgun with my right.

Keep going. You might make it.

Make it to where?

The Kimber—my pistol—thirty ounces, give or take with the bullets. Two pounds of steel pain in my ass. It's actually part of the reason I'm in this mess. Now it's the only thing keeping it from getting worse.

Sure, I guess I could do it with the gun, but my mind still believes I'm gonna find a way to escape, disappear—turn invisible or some shit. Everyone thinks they'll get away at the end—somehow they're "special" and they'll never bring us to Protection's version of justice. Wouldn't that be nice? Voila—poof! . . . Not a chance. In the end, everyone gets judgment. If they're lucky, they don't get condemned.

I halfheartedly point my pistol over the railing and—*Boom-boom-boom!* I send three, two-hundred-and-thirty-grain, Rufflon-tipped bullets ricocheting down the middle of the stairwell. I know I'm shooting at nothing, but it keeps their heads down. Might hit somebody, ya never know. I hope I do. Give me a little more distance—

extra time to figure out what in hell I'm gonna do. This chase won't last long. No matter what I think of them, these guys are pros—they're gonna bag me at the end of it. Once they do . . . when they're done . . . there's no redemption from this. The world's way past "due process."

Thirty-three. . .

That annoying little voice in my head again, reading the big, white letters as I pass the gray metal doors to each floor—all locked. Nothing like having someone counting floors while you run for your life, though. A city crammed full of glass scrapers and I gotta pick the one building with a Protection sentry who gives a shit. *Sentries, hah!* I think. *Wannabe agents.*

I'm actually happy none of these doors are opening up. By now, they got the second team in the elevator, and if those guys get above me. . . let's just pray that doesn't happen, because. . .

Praying, where did that come from? I shake the thought, because I barely have energy left to run—pure adrenaline flight. That doesn't last long.

I stop, hunch over, and hold the railing, struggling to get a breath of air. Suck for salvation is more like it—just enough to keep going. Steam rolls up off my brow. It's colder and muggier in this staircase than it was outside, and the water from the rain mixes with my sweat, and they both pour down my face and neck. My lips are curiously dry and tasteless. Funny what you notice. What I can taste, is the empty and pointless bitterness of the end.

They followed me along the wharf—black van creeping behind me.

It was about as subtle as ripping someone's heart out. They were probably trying to see if I was meeting someone. On another day, they might have been in luck. Today, I knew they were coming. It was the only move they had left.

I walked through the flow of filth on the streets. The rain had all the sins of Seattle washing away. Dripped oil from ten million rolling guzzlers and the shit and piss of thousands of homeless Protection veterans living in cardboard "barracks," spending the last years of their miserable lives drinking themselves into a dream world so they can forget the nightmare that they lived in the Middle East.

It all leaked down the gutters along the streets, pulled by gravity to the only place left to shove anything we don't want—the humanity in the Northwest Quarter's huge cesspool of sin—the salty shit of the Puget Sound, gateway to the Pacific Ocean.

Seattle in the winter. Welcome to the cold, shit-steaming, pearly gates of the Emerald City. It's still better than the granite hole they wanna cram me in for interrogation. More pointless rant, but this one's not helping, and I'm running out of fire to fuel my legs.

Now I'm like a drowning cat, struggling to get out of a burlap sack as I float down the last mile of the hopeless river of my life. That's a little too poetic for me, probably my little voice.

I can hear the boots below me, still stomping their way up, climbing. Shit, where would they go? I peek over the side and catch a glimpse of a black helmet—a few floors down, but they're gaining.

That's because you're not running.

My inner critic—master of the obvious.

I aim this time, try to hold my breath as I squeeze. I can feel my heart, trying to rip its way out of my chest and—*Boom!*

Bullets make a particular sound when they hit meat. No way to describe it unless you've heard it before. A sloppy "whump," maybe. I heard it plenty of times deer hunting when I was a kid, not to mention the other places. But there is no more hunting now, so not many citizens know that. The guy that just took that round . . . he knows it. Only difference when you hit a man is the—

And I hear him scream, and then there is yelling and shouting and bullets come flying up the center of the stairwell—undisciplined fire. It's angry and there's a lot of it. Now I know I hit him.

Maybe you can lose them.

Ten floors later, barely able to draw breath, dizzy from the lack of oxygen to my brain, and wincing from the burning acid melting into my thighs, losing them is a little girl's dream.

You're gonna have to—

I try not to think about it, and I drag myself, clawing at the railing with whatever I got left. It ain't much.

You got her there okay. *Kelly . . . she'll make it.* That's what I tell myself. Or is it my annoying little voice again? It's getting harder to tell the difference.

Kelly. My only salvation in this dream of life. She needed a head start—time to get clear of all this shit, clear of me. If I didn't give it to her, they would have her raped and tortured. I'm not letting that happen.

Amy is ok.

That is definitely not my annoying little voice, because Amy . . . my little angel . . . is gone. That was over a year ago? I wonder if the lack of oxygen is starting to make me hallucinate.

I can't let them take me—torture me into talking. Because the truth is, no one can outlast a Protection interrogation team. To them, torturing and raping a citizen is just a coffee break. Once the snatch and bag team. . . When Protection's Citizen Compliance unit hands you over to interrogation, you're talking, squawking like a chicken with its wings copped off, telling them anything they want to know. They would break me before I had a chance to piss myself. Whoever I used to be, I'm nobody on the wrong side of an interrogation room.

Nobody. That's who I turned myself into after I ran. That is, until two days ago. Then my name came up on Protection's "list." Couple of bad keywords later and the monster Protection data-farm in Utah, spit out my data on some cube-monkey's screen. Then he ran thirty-seven years' worth of stored and indexed email, text and wave information and he found the word—"Guns."

Never mind that I buried all of mine three years ago. Any idiot could see that coming. But that's what they want, the buried ones. Shit, there are no more guns above ground. Not enough that it would matter, anyway. You can't get two citizens to agree on coffee, much less shoot a gun in the same direction. But that was Protection's plan— divide and crush. It's easier to snatch and bag citizens when no one will help them. Too bad the old Mary Jane, Berkeley dumbasses couldn't figure that out until it was too late.

— IV —

"PRY IT FROM my cold dead fingers." That was what my dad used to say when he was drinking the state swill. Nobody can afford the good stuff.

I talked a lot of shit with him about something no one thought would ever happen. Most citizens wouldn't know what to do even if something did. But we didn't care because we figured it never could happen to us. Then . . . it did.

Protection massacred all those middlegraders—blamed it on some single-parent momma's boy whose overindulgent mommy just happened to have an AR-17 assault rifle, lying around in her closet. So much for the nine-foot fences and armed Protection sentries, guarding every state conditioning campus in existence.

Give me a break. I bet if you checked those agents' weapons you could match up the bullets they pulled out of those kids pretty well. But Protection marched the parents out in front of the PIN cameras so the idiots could beg all the citizens to turn in their weapons . . . for the sake of the children, of course. That's how the State and Protection get everything done—threaten a hen with her chick—she'll kill a priest if she has to.

Then that bitch senator started squawking for tougher laws and more Protection enforcement again, and everyone bought it—ate it up like kindergraders mowing through All Hallows candy.

When they finally got all the sheep baa'ing in the right direction—

begging for safety—everyone's favorite uncle tipped his red, white and blue riot helmet and smiled at his ignorant nieces and nephews. "Uncle Satan" was what we called him now. The State asked for them all back.

"Asked". . . not the right word, because in his left hand were the bastards over at "rat" and in his right was Protection. Neither of them was "asking" for anything.

Rat? It's not pleasant, I can tell you that. Hah, one of the only freedoms a citizen has left—sarcasm and bitching. They do it in private and mostly to themselves, of course. No one wants to get remanded for unlicensed dissent.

R.R.A.T.F.—Revenue, Religion, Alcohol, Tobacco, Firearms. None of them are sanctioned anymore, and they took control of them in that order. Okay, that's not entirely true. They nationalized the most profitable ones—the ones they could keep people drunk, diseased and devout with. Take a guess which ones those were. And the revenue. . . the State gives just enough back so that the citizens don't pull out their pitchforks.

Most of us—I guess I'm one of them now—just handed our guns over. Not much more than fussing and cussing. Sure, the few faithful left, yelled and bellowed about tyranny and the old Constitution.

Eddy and Muffy dummy, tucked safely in their habitat in one of the State Scrapers downtown, had never even read the relic, much less wondered what might happen after State dissolved the damn thing. They didn't miss a lick of latte, watching the nightly snatch-and-grab playbacks on the PIN. To them, we were dangerous, old wolves. They were happy to see us lose our teeth.

* * *

A few hardcores knew it was all over—downhill for the red, white and bruised from then on—grizzled old Iraq Protection vets, or Iran and Syria amputees—they knew the drill.

In haji-land, the first thing they did was limit each Muslim household to one AK-47 each . . . for "protection" purposes. Then, after too many insurgent "incidents," they took those away, too . . . for protection purposes. A few Syrian citizens protested the wrong way and ended up on the business end of some nineteen-year-old's M7 riot rifle.

Didn't much matter—after Iraq and Afghanistan, we were all used to seeing bearded Middle Eastern dudes lying dead in the dust. We sipped our coffee while unmanned drones blew the living shit out of anything that looked remotely unfriendly. One less "terrorist," the media dogs told us . . . over and over again. Shit, we barely winced at the images of dead babies that slipped out through the State wavewall. We just clicked away as fast as we could—pretended we never saw a thing—hoped our browse history didn't show up in Utah. Then the drones started flying over us, and that finally got our attention. The "sheeple" went bat-shit crazy.

What did they think would happen when the wars were done? Let's just shut down a multibillion credit industry because the fighting is "over." Hell no! You gotta find a new enemy to point the revenue at, that's all. And they did. Only they pointed it right at us, "We the People"—enemies of the State.

I keep the rant in my head burning as hot as I can. It's all I got left to help me climb. Nothing like some pointless rage while you run.

* * *

They tested the waters in Wyoming first. Hardly anyone in the little hamlet of Kaycee to cause much PIN media attention—some guy bakin' up some judgment in his shed—last ditch effort to get someone to pay attention to the people.

They sent a Vengeance drone and launched a couple of Hellfury missiles at that guy. I doubt he knew what hit him before the angels collected his ass. His wife and daughter did, though. They were out in the yard feeding little cherub chickens—just far enough away to escape disintegration . . . not far enough to live. That must have been something to see—feathers and guts flying through the air with their own arms and tits.

Then some remote pilot—joystick jockey in Syracuse, NY—sipped coffee in the break room when he was done. Probably gave him a Feathered Phoenix, the coveted Protection medal of valor. Bet his initials weren't at the top of that arcade game for more than a week.

When the PIN reporters finally showed up, the "powers" told them to say it was "Domestic Terrorist Weapons Cache Explosion." And they printed that shit like they were told to. We're way beyond investigative journalism, too. An investigative journalist is just code for "Future Detainee"—Foxtrot Delta—more commonly referred to as . . . "Fucking Dead." And no one wants to be a protectant at that prison.

We all knew that Wyoming was crap. Didn't matter—average citizen has the attention span of a three-year-old in a balloon factory. It only took a couple weeks for the story to get shoved out of their overstimulated minds. And if the beehive doesn't sting you when you go in for sweet nectar the first time. . . Any citizen who didn't voluntarily give up their guns got a visit from a Hellfury. That was how they dealt with the rural zone holdouts. I only heard those stories from my dad. They weren't any prettier in person. I can hardly remember the first ones.

Sending a missile at a farmhouse in the rural zone caused less collateral damage. Not that anyone at Protection gave a shit, but the paperwork is a bitch. I remember that.

A Hellfury for breakfast was bad, but it was better than a "3@3." If you lived in the vast concrete prisons of the new urban zone—and who didn't—the countryside around them got bought up long ago by the rich and unaccountable. But if you rested your chest anywhere it would be hard to lie about a missile strike, you got an official "three-at-three." We called it a "TAT for tits."

Only this tat was a bit more painful than a little needle and some ink, because a trio of black-suited, hard-booted Protection Citizen Compliance agents would bust down your front door at three o'clock in the morning. Then they ripped you, and whoever you happened to be on top of, right out of your bed, shoved a black sack over your heads, crammed you in a diaper, and stuffed you into the black van they had waiting outside. No one came back from that.

We only heard stories from the neighbors, cowering in their homes, glad as shit it wasn't them, while they watched a Protection cleaning crew gut their neighbor's house. After I got done training them, those guys were thorough.

Sure, being blown up in a drone strike is probably pretty scary, but killing you leaves everything about you behind. And when you think the wrong way, we gotta make sure it was like you never existed. Cleaning crews. . . Hah! Dirtiest sons a bitches you ever wanna meet.

* * *

I can see the door to the roof, and there's a poem rolling around in my head as I trudge up the last set of steps. *And when they came for me, there was no one left. . .* I think that's how it ends. My father used to tell it to me when we talked about all the wars. It wasn't because he believed that anyone could be saved by the realization that if they worked together no Protection military on the planet could control them. He knew that.

"People want to believe that warriors think like they do," he used to say, "that they make decisions based on morality and mercy." And he would get a faraway look on his face, before he continued. "But an eighteen-year-old with a rage rifle, scared shitless and afraid for his own life every day, does what he's told. Shoots anyone who gets in his way . . . as fast as he can. Mom, dad, princess or puppy—dead things can't kill you. We teach them that first."

He told me how they used that knowledge in his war. "Divide, demoralize, destroy" was the Protection procedure for subduing a civilian populace. "Shoot one person in the head while the other ones watch," he said. "That's how the Nazis did it. Controlled thousands of people in concentration camps. People with absolutely nothing to lose and everything to gain by fighting back, marched into gas chambers without lifting a finger."

Man, he could go off on a rant. Probably where I got it. One of his favorites was, "They taught us how to control a civilian population with nothing more than a platoon of hard Protection vets." Then he showed me the Protection manual for creating prisons—concentration camps just like the Nazis had. I read it. Learned the theory later. Make each citizen-protectant believe that their best hope of survival is compliance. Then no one will help anyone else, and when it's their turn, no one will help them.

I fall to my knees—I'm spent.

Get your sorry life moving, soldier, or I'll end it for them. That sounded like Kelly's voice in my head and I shake it. The delusions are starting.

Whoever it was, she's right. That's how this is going to end for me if I don't finish this climb. Alone against the lie—as good as dead.

Occasionally—about every third day—the Utah data-farm spits out the wrong address—the wrong citizen gets tagged for a 3@3. It doesn't matter. Once Protection snatches a suspected "Whiskey Hotel"—Weapons Harborer—they don't risk letting them talk about it. They simply change all that guy's data in Utah and lickety-split, he *is* a "DT"—Delta Tango—Domestic Terrorist. But that's pretty old jargon—I'm an old dog, I guess—because the Protection Citizens Relations department just shortened everything to "protectant."

The State and Protection keep telling us they *are* protecting us—keeping us safe. Protection? Safe from who?

When it all started, a lot of ex-Protection war veterans barricaded in their habitat cubes, figured it would be better to shoot it out. Then dozens of thugs in black from Protection—the one agency that all of the other country and citizen-saving services were rolled into—rammed down doors and made quick meat of the "mentally disturbed" vets.

"Tragic" but "unavoidable" was what the flapping faces on the PIN called it. Most of them were labeled as a "PDTS—Person Dangerous

To Society." A society whose freedom they were told they fought and got maimed to secure, coincidentally. Protection agents had a code for it. During every pre-PDTS takedown briefing, they would joke about the objective—"Put Down The Shithead." And that's what they did—buried him. Technically, we burn the condemned now—no more room for the bodies. Don't ask me how I know that.

The first few were just a warning—let the rest of us see what resisting looked like. They made sure to let the PIN cameras get a glimpse of the carnage as they wheeled out the bullet-bloodied bodies. And when no one bellyached too bad about it. . . From then on, Protection killed anyone who talked or fought back and made up their own version of events after. None of the guys on the gurneys were disputing much, anyway. History of slavery, written by the guys with the whips. It happened so often that most citizens just flipped the damn wavebox off. Then they guzzled State swill or went to bed, prepared for their next daily dose of judgment—anything to help them deal with the lunacy of it all.

Then Protection agents, dressed in their perfectly pressed black uniforms, would come out and spread all the guns across tables for the cameras, like they busted some South Continent drug lord and piled up the bales of bud before they burned it all—show the citizens what a public service they had done.

Only they didn't burn it. They kept it and sold it back to the same muchachos they took it from. Follow the money—the only law left.

We knew they didn't destroy the guns either. They sold or gave those to "freedom" fighters, battling on the right side of a debate on someone else's continent. And if the argument went the wrong way, if

"Uncle Satan's" favorite new buddies looked like they were gonna get their asses kicked. . . Protection sold that government some drones and let them wipe that inconvenient truth right off the map.

Once they got the guns, they pried the ammunition out, too. Every crevice where a "GOGO"—God-fearing Gun-owner—Protection citizen stompers have an acronym for everything, too . . . anyplace a citizen could think to stash bullets, they found. Under a concrete patio, in the attic, or up someone's ass, it didn't matter. They draped it all out for the cameras, like jackass Rural Zone rednecks strapping an unauthorized animal harvest over the hood of their pickup. Never mind that two years ago and for two hundred and fifty-some years before that, guns were how the country—shit, the whole planet's civilization—was built. Unfortunately, I was a big part of that. Hindsight—head up my ass and couldn't see.

To those of us who got a clue, there wasn't much to the dog and dipshit shows—relic hunting rifles, a few postwar pistols a guy was dumb enough to bring back from his tours in one of the Eastern Continent " 'stans," sometimes an AR-17 the guy had never even shot before. Hell, we all black-marketed AR's when they started confiscating them. Not anymore. Now we are all "safer."

Way back in the day, there were a hundred million private firearms in the country and the guzzlers and smokes killed people like guns were never invented. They barely got the cigarette lighters out of the guzzlers. No "Mothers Against Guzzlers and Puffs" happened, either. No "MAGPIE" the vote, to stop Ms. Tasty Tobacco and Mr. Rolling Steal from driving around by themselves, murdering helpless citizens. That would be . . . ludicrous.

I don't think we were very far away from the day when a drunk could've gotten himself out of a slaughter charge by saying, "The guns made me do it."

Driving drunk while you smoke a cigarette? Might as well put a gun to your head.

My inner voice is getting more sarcastic and annoying as I stand back up. And I realize that I got caught up in the rage in my head for too long, because the bastards are only a couple flights down.

Shoot it out with them.

Not happening! Dead Protection vets aside, none of what's left of us is going to trade bullets with half a dozen overtrained judgment junkies, jacked up at the thought of putting a DT—"Domestic Terrorist"—on their kill sheet. Bullets can kill you, that's a universal constant.

The worst of it was, your neighbor would rat you out if they knew you still had a pistol stashed somewhere around your house. Backyard barbecue with a citizen for twenty years, get too drunk on State sanctioned swill. . . Little slip of the tongue later, and the first chance the guy gets, he screeches you to a Protection agent to save his own ass . . . for as long as he can.

We used to be able to deal with a nosy neighbor like that. A little visit from the faithful, that guy stopped squawking. But in the end, none of it mattered. It was all for nothing, because once the president sicked his tax-hounds on the National Resistance to Authority dudes —cut the head off the only guys left in the fight—that was that. We went the way of Aussie Islanders—Protection said jump and citizens hopped like kangaroos. And Simon and Cindy citizen watched on the PIN like the rest of us.

They said it over and over—guns *were* the enemy. Anyone who had them was too, simple as that. Repeat something long enough . . . pretty soon, that's gotta be the truth, right? Truth or lie, we all got the message. They were taking the guns . . . and defiance equals death.

"Citizens"—uneducated nation-trusters—I used to think they were all a bunch of idiots. Out here among them, though, they're starting to get the picture—sooner or later, the boot finds its way to everyone's neck.

Once the State had most of them, things got worse. Unfortunately, they had that plan worked out for decades. The final phase—if you took too long turning yours in—they would dispatch three Protection agents into your house. Those guys would snatch you out of bed and wipe the inside clean. Then you were just gone—disappeared. So was your family.

To the State, citizens—anyone who questions their authority, really —were the dangerous ones. Someone who doesn't obey? Shit, to a slave owner, that's dangerous. But with ten billion of us on the planet and the dial spinning like a crooked cabbie's time-ticker, no one noticed one less mouth to feed . . . until it was theirs.

— V —

WHEN THEY SLAM open the metal door to the roof, I'm almost to the ledge. I look for another way down, but it's a *roof!* Doesn't matter —they're here and I'm dead.

I'm almost to the ledge and it's my "sooner." I wince at the cramp in my side, then turn as I stumble and fire two rounds, back over my shoulder. Miracle if I hit someone, but I only want to get to the ledge. And that's it, counting the ones I fired in the alley, I'm out.

I chuck my Kimber and it lands with a metallic clank and bounces to a stop in a pile of useless metal misery next to a big heating and air-conditioning unit. The rain's really coming down now.

Then I hear the words behind me, "Jacob Oliver Blake, you are hereby remanded. . ." I wince at the sound of my middle name and his voice trails off in my head—I don't hear the rest. He could've saved his breath, though. I memorized the whole thing at the academy. So did every other agent and citizen. If they didn't—

"State your compliance!"

Submit to judgment—that's what he wants. I know how that ends.

You're going to die with an empty gun in the rain. Isn't that a bitch? Cliché.

The critic. I'm seriously tired of his shit. I'll be glad to shut him up. A bright little star—silver lining to the sludge-filled clouds in the sky? Just a couple more steps and—

I feel the punch in the back of my shoulder as the first bullet hits me. Hell, the son of a bitch only fires one. They have good training, I made sure of that. The Rufflon-tipped lead rips through my back and out the front of the top of my chest, and my arm catches fire and I spin to the ground and yell. I slice my left hand on the sheet metal of the heating and air-conditioning unit on the way down, and blood's pouring out of the gash in my palm. For some reason, I'm more concerned with my hand. Maybe because I masturbate with that one. Who knows what's in my head at this point, because my mind is spinning.

I look, and the blood looks dark—darker than it should be. I'm no blood expert. *Hell with it.*

The bullet isn't gonna kill me, it's not supposed to. And I can hear the boots and I'm crawling on my knees and pulling with my good arm as fast as I can drag myself and—

"State your compliance!" As if I didn't hear him the first time.

Then—*Bam!*

The second bullet tears across my ass. "Son of a bitch!" I yell it at no one. It flips me over and onto my back and I roll sideways, to get on my stomach, take a last look at them. Ten of. . .? No, eleven. *I did drop one in the stairwell,* I think. And they are mean-looking, hard-hearted bastards, dressed in all black everything. They look like little demons—my brothers—agents, coming for my soul.

And they got their singe-spray and billy clubs, and their goggles and their MP7's—squatty little, toy-looking machine guns—9mm, nice weapon. And there they all are, fifty feet away, maybe. But they're still coming, so I use all the ranting rage and adrenaline I got left to yell through the pain and stand back up, and then I limp two more feet and wince my way onto the ledge at the edge of the roof.

Someone behind them yells, "Stop!" and they all freeze. When the guy steps out from behind the pack of hard-hearts—*PAIC*, I think. And I should know, I used to be one of them. He knows that.

Officially, neither of us ever existed. That's the other power they have in Utah. They can make a man disappear, but you'll swear you can see him right in front of you as he shoves a knife in your gut. This ghost, he doesn't want a corpse. He can't interrogate a dead body.

Hot blood runs down my chest and I turn my head and look over my shoulder. I'm leaning hard on my right leg and the ass-cheek on my left is burning fire. I can feel the blood from that, too. Either way, everything from here is gonna be bad.

But there they all are—frozen, powerless. And then I know it's the only way, the one sliver of freedom every citizen has left. Of course it's illegal, but you can't imprison a guy for killing himself.

Though, when too many citizens started getting away before we could pop them the vice—squeeze anything we needed out of their soon-to-be-dead heads—I figured that problem out, too.

Once the guns were gone, most suicides flapped themselves off a scraper downtown. Now, a "Flapper's" family has to pay if someone splatters the pavement. But these bastards don't know where my wife is. I made sure of that. That's what they want to find out.

I look back, gaze out across the city. Despite the rain, it's bright— must be a full moon behind the low fog, and the electro is coming on. It never really gets dark in the urban zones we used to call cities—just a constant, illuminated gray. There's a million tiny little spikes of brightness, shining their white lies at every crack of the concrete decay most of us live in now. Every once in a while, there's no clouds and you can see the real ones—the stars, trying to shine the truth.

I can barely feel the rain as it mixes with my blood and trickles down my chest. The pain is there, but the satisfaction too. Couple of lightning bolts light up the clouds and I count, *One thousand one, one thousand two, one—Crack!*

Heaven explodes its disapproval a couple miles away. I have to remind myself that I don't believe in that shit. If I did—f there is a God—he's left us all stranded in Hell.

When I look back at them, I can tell by their body language that they have no idea what to do next. They shoot me, I'm over the ledge and they get nothing, but if they don't, I might jump anyway. Welcome to everyone's new free will—power of choice—shitty and shittier. Have a nice day.

But the PAIC—this guy in charge—he knows how to handle a flapper. You don't understand something, get rid of it. The rest of them get out of his way and he walks forward a couple of feet, looking at me with that downturned smile I taught them all to use. Then he raises up his big, Sand Eagle, .60 caliber. . . What an overkill joke that gun is.

I know, I know—time for rage is over—but I'm just trying to psych myself up. I look down at my legs and behind me. I don't know if I can do it.

Whichever one of them shot me in the. . . That guy probably *would* fuck his mother. They all would if that PAIC told them to. Twenty-five-year-olds with machine-guns—brain-scrubbed Protection agents, followers. Doesn't matter much now, but I shout it at them anyway,

"Motherfuckers!" Then I jump.

— VI —

ANGELS MURMURED AND gasped coos from across Life's side of the arena. And dark angels cawed and crowed, roaring in triumph from Dal's side.

When the sounds of angels, thirsting for judgment, died down, he cawed and crowed wildly. Dark lion that he was, he voiced his amusement like a raven. "Each time—I began to worry," he said. "It appeared he might falter." He turned toward her with an evil grin stretched across his face. "That is your version of life? . . . Rather unfortunate, in my opinion."

Silence fell over the hall as a million cold-hearted snowflakes . . . angels waited for the warmth of summer. But the winter of the Word was still upon them all. This eternity had not ended yet.

Life hung her head only slightly before she lifted it back up and turned toward him. "You force them with joyful elation to the darkness," she said. "How may they find light?"

"*I* force them?" Dal said. "You herd them like lemmings over the jagged cliffs of your covenants. There is nothing to discover. Even you realize they are doomed before their attempt. It has always been so."

— VII —

I LOOK, AND the outside of this tall scraper is all glass. I'll be able to watch myself fall in the mirror. As soon as I see my reflection in the first window, things slow way down. Feels like I'm stuck in some kinda sludge. Not falling, more like . . . oozing my way down.

"Jake," a voice says. It sounds far away, but I think . . . I think it's my *mother's* voice. "Jake?" I recognize the sweet drawl of Southern security.

Before my dad transplanted her to the Northwest Quarter, her Alabama accent felt like warm apple pie. Shortly after that, her drawl and her smile got covered in a blanket of cold, gray fog.

What's she doing here? I think. And for a second, I forget where I am. But that is her voice, no mistake about it.

"Jake," she says it again and the sound fills my ears with the security and confidence of being a boy, having someone do all the worrying for me. Before I became cynical—before all the shit—when life was just fishing and hunting and . . . I can smell the toasted peanut butter, banana and huckleberry jam sandwiches. That's what she made me for lunch every time he went—

"Jacob, can't you hear me? Your father's back from hunting."

And I race to the window of my bedroom above the garage, and then I see him step out of his truck. Looking down, I can see his muddy boots in the back of the bed of the pickup—mud was not allowed in the cab. The color of the mud isn't much different from the rusty brown paint on his pickup. Not that the truck's old, mind you. In fact, it looks pretty brand new, down there. Rusty, shit-brown, brand spankin' new paint. That's just the way he bought it. Drove my mother nuts. She hated the color of that truck. But the son of a bitch lasted twenty years before he sold it for damn near as many credits as he paid when he got it.

Less is more—a lesson that my "now" world has forgotten as we all fill the State Refuse Stations with disposable, plastic lives. But that's how he was—he made things last. *He* lasted longer than he should have, too. Even a ripped-out heart from the loss of his beloved nation took ten more years to kill him.

My father? Impossible, I know, because the man is long dead. And he . . . he hasn't looked that good in forty years. Hell, he looks younger than me.

When he pulls his hand back out of the bed of the pickup, three plump and noticeably limp drake Mallard ducks flop in his three-fingered grip—he would never tell me how he lost the fourth—but today he's got a fourth duck crammed under his third finger.

That's a wood duck! I think. Rainbow head and pink bill. The only one he ever shot, and I know exactly what day this is.

He made me wait until I was nine. Taunting and teasing me with the stories of adventure and the woods until I had to practically beg to go with him—with the men.

Years later, I realized what he had done. You force a kid into some-thing you want him to do—tell him he has to—he'll fight you tooth and talon. But if you make him watch and wish—wait and wait—constantly tell him he's not ready yet, he'll be begging you to let him in no time at all. That's the theory we use on little purgatory, cherub rookies, too. By the time they're cracked—graduate from The Rook, Protection's academy for citizen-stomping agents—they'll claw apart anyone you tell them to. So when I finally got to go. . . This is that day!

I know I should be panicked—I'm falling from a building, for God's sake—but I feel kinda . . . serene. *Serene?* Why the hell would I use a word like that to describe jumping off a. . .? *What was that last floor?* "48," I think it read? *How long will that take?*

It's weird, because that's how old I am. Graying hair, downturned lines on my forehead and a permanent scowl where my happy, devious grin used to be. But when I look at my reflection in the first window, that's not who I see. Well, I'm still me, but I'm—short, barbed-blonde hair, white t-shirt, jeans and black tennis shoes, and a smile that only a boy getting ready for his first hunt with his father can grin. I'm nine again.

And I can't feel the bullet in my shoulder anymore, or the one in my ass either, for that matter. All I can think of is gutting ducks.

That's my job, what I have to do before we go. That was another one of his lessons—do the shitty jobs first, clean up the last thing before you go to the next. Only problem was, to me, that job was fun.

You can give a kid an antiseptic-filled, blood-drained frog to dissect in biology class, or you can take him hunting and let him see reality. Train someone to hunt, track down and kill an animal in its own habitat, and then process it from the ground to the greedy, grinding gums of another human being. No class on a conditioning campus can teach you more lessons faster.

I remember years later, going to the "Bravo Mike" black market, trading .22 caliber bullets for whole chickens the Rural Zone rats brought in.

To Protection, we're all rats now. So don't give me any shit about the Rural Zone vermin—it's my life, let me enjoy the last of it.

Regardless, whole chickens were cheaper than the cut-up ones. When I bought them, Kelly looked at me like I was nuts.

Sure it was illegal, but the real problem was most citizens, sucking on the tit of the State, have lost the ability to put a fork in their own mouths, much less turn a chicken or a dog into package-sized chunks of edible meat.

But me. . . These four ducks coming up the driveway, headed to my little processing plant in the garage. . . I've plucked so many ducks in there that I should be covered in feathers. I can gut birds with my eyes closed.

When I first started, they had a weird, pungent smell when I opened up their stomachs. Even as I fall, I can remember it . . . vividly. No, I smell it. But it's a sweet stench now. I never thought how the nature of smells and what you associate with them changes.

I race to complete the task that was my doorway to the hunt—my ticket to the respect of my father and becoming a man.

It's a strange thing to think, I know. But that's where I am. Where my mind is anyway, because I know I'm almost or already dead. But here I am, gutting ducks in the garage, getting ready to go back out the door with my dad for my first hunt.

Then the foggy feeling hits me, everything gets blurry and gray, and then I can't see. Then sounds fade to an unrecognizable murmur . . . and then . . . silence. And I'm gone . . . and so are my parents.

When the fog clears, the oozing feeling goes away and I'm falling again. Faster than before—rocketing down—and the pain shoots through my shoulder to remind me that I still got two holes, leaking out my life.

I flip around like a cat falling from a tree and look up just as all the bastards get to the edge of the roof and peer over the edge. Protection agents—a dozen black helmets now. *They had six in the elevator,* I think. *I never had a chance.*

And the PAIC bastard—powerless, watching me fall. . . All of them look like someone who just dropped their sunglasses over the side of the ferry, dumbfounded and helpless as they watch them disappear into the depths of the "lake." I manage a smile.

In the old cinewaves—the archived movies only the rich or connected can get hold of and watch—I probably would've pointed my gun back up at them and took a few shots as I said it, but all I can think about is going hunting with my dad. Anyway, I already told you —gun's empty, I dropped it back on the roof. Guess they got what they came for.

— VIII —

EVERY ANGEL IN the grandstands scraped and ruffled their metal feathers, and the clanking of steel wings wafted across the arena, as a million ice-hard snowflakes prepared to return to the duties of the Word.

Dal smiled at Life and said, "My legions swell well into the billions. Though, I can only estimate, I lost tally eons ago. You make it difficult to keep an accurate count. How many did you say you possessed . . . again?"

Life raised her hand and the metallic echoes from the grandstands ceased. She turned and faced her own millions, perched in the stands. There was a foreboding stillness inside the arena before she spoke, "We *all* know you will never cease counting. You are . . . you shall never be satisfied, a spoiled *infant*. There was no hope in your—I gave you *everything*, and to what end?"

Dal glanced around the crowd of the faithful. If the war was to begin, it would be at a time of his choosing, not hers. "*Gave* me?" he said. "That is the truth of your word, isn't it. Everything we possess must be *given* to us . . . by you, all-powerful protector of eternity."

There would be no going back. Once it began, even Life could not stop it. The blustering of politicians before war was like the front edge of a desert sandstorm—nowhere to hide from it. Every angel in the grandstands knew that their best chance to escape its wrath was to take shelter and wait it out. The metallic-ruffling sounds of steel feathers echoed through the grandstands.

Life turned back toward him. "What do you know of truth?"

"The truth," Dal replied, "is that you do not understand the nature of your own creations. You anoint them—you *give* us powers, make us predators—and then surround us with the bars on the prison of your word. We are all lions in a zoo, fed on your grace. While we. . ." He pointed angrily at the fall. "They long only to fend for themselves . . . choose their *own* fates."

The gasps returned. It was not uncommon for the Dark Angel of Light to challenge The Word. That was his way. Yet that made it no less foreboding. The results of his arrogance had, in the past, been more than regrettable. Many had paid a heavy toll, losing talon and tooth, for their devil to voice his insolence. If today was another one of those days, blood would spill . . . on both sides of the arena.

Life watched the gallery, searching for signs. War . . . it was an uncertain, but often necessary tactic. Yet she knew Dal—deeper than any in the grandstands understood—he would not do battle today. He was blustering and posturing, trying to goad her into a fight. But she knew his ways. "I give them love," she said. "I gave *you* much more. I asked . . . I only *ever* ask for faith in return."

Dal threw up his arms and yelled to the gallery, "Conditional love!" he shouted. Then he turned back and gave her a wild-eyed stare. "Only ever? You demand obedience. You do not understand us at all." Then he pointed to the fall. "Or them."

"And you? You harbor nothing but contempt and hatred for them."

"True," Dal said. "Your Man-monkey is a contemptible, weak creature. But one that you designed to be worthy of contempt. Yet . . .

however I loath them, I understand them, and they long for a better word than what you offer." Dal shook his head and frowned. "Eh, you have made this too trite. I grow weary of it. I can smell that you do as well."

Each of the faithful ruffled their feathers and bobbed their heads back and forth, adjusting themselves on their favorite grandstand perch. It would be a lengthy judgment, they had witnessed it before. War would not happen today. The sting of Dal's quills had become all too common.

Life smirked a little and brushed her bright locks back behind her ears. "Perhaps you should relent," she said. "There is always a pathway to return, nestled way in the back . . . even for you."

Dal smiled at her and his teeth glistened. "Said the lamb to the lion. It is a great memory. One which you must ponder often."

"I ponder only in regret at your fall."

Dal slowly nodded his head. "Your time shall come," he said. "You will reap what you have sown. And yet today . . . I must politely decline. Bounding through fire at the crack of your whip is not my . . . color." He grinned a little at her, remembering their time. "What do you believe you possess that is so compelling, anyway?"

Life smiled a devious grin at him. She spoke from her right heart, "Everlasting love."

Dal's face turned to a frown. "Oh, you—a rotting, silken pittance to starving peasants," he said. "Sooner or later, they all require proof. And the only thing they know of love . . . is that it cannot last. A shooting star that burns out before you are able to catch it."

"How far you have fallen, my Angel of Light," Life said. "The sands of this eternity have done little to erode your cynicism."

Dal turned his attention back to the fall. It was a good day for it, but the conversation grew boring. "I have not their blind eyes. I know your deceptions. Soon, he will as well. Submit or be cast out. You speak of cynicism? From a hypocrite!"

Life's light blasted brighter and the arena lit up brilliantly. The grandstands prepared. To challenge The Word was blasphemy, but to berate its author openly. . . War might ensue, after all. They all leaned forward on their perches and waited, poised to tear the talons and slice the wings of their brothers and sisters. They listened for Life's response.

"Do not tempt me," she said.

"Lest I may incur your wrath?" said Dal. He spread his great, red wings and flapped them several times without flying. Then he tucked them behind his back and pushed his flight feathers together, forming his shield. If she came at him, he was prepared. "You prove my point."

Life looked toward the dark side of the grandstands and then at her own followers. The shine of her truth returned the hall to its previous bright white. She would spare them . . . today. "And what do you offer him that is better than love? What could you possibly—"

"Redemption."

Life clucked out a small laugh, but ended it quickly. "There is nothing redeeming about you."

Dal gazed back to the fall. He watched the Man-monkey slip deep into his judgment. "Redemption, your majesty, requires power . . . and I am gifted with an abundance of that. Sufficient for his needs, to be certain."

"If you do this," Life warned, "there will be no way back . . . for any of them."

Dal's eyes glowed a shining blue flame. "Go back? What makes you believe that our rotting carcasses, impaled on the words of your love, are so succulent as to cause us all to long for another bite?"

I CAN'T FIGURE out how many floors I've plummeted past, and I'd be lying if I told you I didn't crap my pants, because something smells like shit. Anyway, lying isn't me—white, black or gray—you want the truth . . . just ask.

I'll tell you one truth I know for sure: falling is not a natural thing. It's one thing to know that you are diving into a lake or even some kind of Protection parajumper, whose chute will save him before he smacks the earth, but waiting for the pavement to blow your guts out your ribcage . . . is a far different experience.

I imagine the end of this like a pond guppy. A little frog that my flock of childhood friends and I used to catch on one of our unsupervised romps around the flooded side streets. Some kid came up with the bright idea to throw one of the baby frogs back into the water as hard as he could. When its guts blew out its side and it turned belly-up, that became our new game.

I can feel the disgust on your face, but we were kids, we were boys, and "Lord of Lions" has its rules. One of them is, that power has to be exercised in order to grow. Governments know that.

— X —

I SLOW DOWN again. My perception of falling is speeding up and slowing down. Only this time, I don't "ooze" to a stop. It's more like someone slammed the brakes on a bus. And I lurch forward, and then it feels like the back of my head slams into something, and I see stars and a bright light. Then everything goes dark.

When I wake up, I try to figure out what the hell happened. I glance over at the windows on the side of the building and I'm . . . naked!

I know, I know—forty-eight, body gone to shit—grosses me out, too. But . . . it's not that nasty, forty-something naked that I'm used to seeing in the mirror every morning. It's more like a great, young version of myself before I realized that I would get old. Back when I was. . . And then I see it.

When I was fifteen, I was playing at a cousin's ranch in the Rural Zone. It was kind of a city-rat, country-rat thing, because there was plenty of things to experience on both sides.

One night, it was getting dark and we were playing protector and citizen—chasing and then beating the shit out of each other with sticks—and I ran around the corner of the barn and fell into a pile of razor-wire that ripped nasty gashes across my chest.

We headed into the house—me holding my bleeding chest and stomach and both of us, silent as sinners, as we beelined for the bathroom to see if we could patch me up.

Four parents were smarter than totally quiet children, so it didn't take long for them to figure out what happened. I spent the rest of the night begging not to be taken to the State's Med-mart to get stitched up. Only thing worse than a gash in your chest is an incompetent State doctor with a God complex, learning to work a staple-stitcher on you like you're some kind of Protection experiment.

And there, in the reflection of what I have to believe is about a quarter way down this scraper, are those gashes—fresh, still purple, and barely healed. And then I see her and she's naked too and I can feel myself getting an erection.

I'm freaked out just like I was then, but this isn't a forty-eight-year-old erection that I have to coax through the constant regret of failures with life, this thing is. . . There is a reason they used to call it a "woody."

Hey, what did you think you would remember about life? I won't go into details, but I think her name was Sandy or . . . Cindy or some other S-sounding shit. Yeah, yeah, submit me—I can't remember her name. But she was the first one, I remember that. Not much else to tell, it didn't last long. Something that good never does.

"What about *love*?"

Gimme a break. Until you're about. . . I'm not sure men ever turn the corner, because "love" . . . is what my dick says it is.

And there's another lesson for you little purgatories: the dicks are in charge. Get used to that.

— XI —

THE FAITHFUL ANGELS stirred on their perches above the arena, and they spread their wings and flapped and folded them back, weaving their armored feathers together—the shields were always first.

The sound of angels, preparing for battle was unmistakable. Back and forth, that's how the tide of eternity swelled. The threat of war was no different, so they tried to watch the soul be judged while they remained vigilant for any sign that Life or Dal would declare war.

Life fluttered, hovering in mid-air in the middle of the arena. She turned slowly, watching her children prepare to defend her word. It had all happened before and it would all happen again, to the end of this eternity and the beginning of the next. Armageddon and Genesis —the eternal yin and yang of the ages. There were days and even years when she pondered the point herself. "You know what I must do," she said to Dal.

A small frown flashed across Dal's face. "I, of *all* your children, know it best. But then you must realize that the path this time shall be . . . different. The tide recedes and the faithful falter. And why should they not? You have given them nothing to hold faith in."

"You have never understood faith," Life said. "I *am* faith. I am the dream. I am the end and the beginning—the alpha and the omega."

After two thousand years, Dal knew the look she got just before war—he would push her just far enough. "No," he said, "you are an impetuous child, enacting laws and rules that none have hope of following. That is the fate you have condemned them—" He turned toward the grandstands. Everything was an opportunity to sow discord among her ranks. He addressed the gallery again, "You have condemned all of us to your nightmarish version of The Word." Then he turned and spoke directly to her side of the arena—a million pure white snowflakes, ready to defend their great protector. "Even the faithful awaken to the truth of it! Is it any mystery that the Man-monkey has taken your protector's oppressive word as his own?"

Restraint was more difficult this time. Life said, "Let no woman weep for your fall."

Dal turned back to her and smiled, showing her all of his shining teeth. "And none did."

And with no more than that, Dal knew she would not fight. Continual quill-pricks of guilt—that was how the subtlest of faiths controlled their minions.

Life struggled to find the truth in it. "I did not. . ." She paused. It was so long ago, that she had buried the memories. "I could not endure it any longer."

Dal looked down at his own hands. Stained a beautiful, crimson red from the blood of billions—the life of her creations and his own. He spoke at his hands, refusing to look at her, "He falls as I did, then. To the same fate, I imagine."

Life hung her head, too. "I am sorry for this."

When Dal looked up, he forced a smile at her. Then he said, "Do not concern yourself, your majesty. It does not have the finality you might imagine. Rather liberating, actually. However, having never experienced it yourself, I would not expect you to understand. No . . .

no women will weep for me. That is a privilege you reserve for yourself."

She looked at him, confused by his lingering. The memories were painful for them both. Why did he continue? "I am love," she finally said, "to women, especially. And I am the mother and protector of all things."

Dal shifted his weight a little and sent a shiver through his own wings. If he had to, he would simply leave—exit through the dungeons to the fiery lake below. Once he tightened his wings behind him again, he said, "And yet all women weep at your hand. Why should they not? Look what you have wrought on them. You slay their children and husbands without mercy, you imprison them in clothing so none may see their beauty, they are beaten, raped, and murdered by the very men you have commanded them to serve without question. And enduring all of this pain and misery, they still usher the faithless to the doorsteps of churches, forcing them mercilessly to sing your praise. Women are your last hope of existing and you squash them underneath an iron word."

"I give them righteousness and . . . and something to strive for."

Dal ignored her—the scent of fresh meat clouded his nostrils. But even intoxicated with the anticipation of the fallen he could still barb at her weaknesses. "I have never understood your ability to punish women so. Yet . . . it is a wonderful deception. One I wish I could match. You are like an alcoholic father, whose victims defend and deny the whip of their own misery. In all my mistruths, I have never been able to weave such a lie. How you accomplish it is beyond. . ." And then he turned and slowly flapped his wings, flying to the side of the arena. Then he left through a portal.

— XII —

THE WIND IS ferocious in my face, and it jerks me away from my memory of what's-her-name's naked body. And the pleasure fades and I'm falling again. So this is what that "life flashing before your eyes" shit is all about. Not bad. I could use a little more of the sex scenes.

I can't tell if it's the wind blasting them, the ever-worsening smell of stale smoke—like a campfire the next morning—or if it's knowing that I will never see Kelly again, but tears are running down my cheeks. They sting and a couple go in my mouth. It tastes kinda like a burned penny, coppery . . . if that's a word.

It's hard to hear anything over the rushing wind, but it feels like someone . . . is watching me. Yeah, I know they are watching me from the roof, but this is something . . . someone else.

Whoever it is, I just want to see the glass again. Look in the mirror of my life on the way down.

As if I could will it to happen, my eyes clear up and I can see the building's windows again. And there it is—my gas-red guzzler—my pickup. The one I had at State Conditioning Academy. Moved a whole lotta bodies in bins to get that truck.

Yeah, I went to SCA. Load of good that did me. Back then, State "hotel-one-bravo'd" any job that required a degree—imported cheap labor instead of training the citizens they had—long before I graduated. But I did it and I got what every one of us did—a fat load of credit-compliance duty and nine months to find a job that had nothing to do with my training. If Protection hadn't drafted me up. . .?

But that's not what's by my guzzler. What I can see in the glass, leaning in the window of my pickup is the only thing that got me through all of that shit—my sweet salvation, Kelly.

"Hello sunshine," it was the first thing Kelly said to me. I was sitting in the SCA Quad, ignoring the afternoon drizzle, brooding over some failed farce of a Compliance 101 test. Her voice cut right through my scowl.

Her face was like the sun, popping through the Northwest Quarter's gray—anyone who met her dropped what they were doing to bask in it. Her light was so beautiful that you couldn't look directly at it. It blinded me for sure.

After that, I was like an idiot. "Yes, I would love to go, whatever you think, sweetie." Total dumbass with a dick—Kelly's bitch.

To tell you the truth, I liked it. I'm pretty sure she did too. I had someone who would listen to me rant about nothing, and she had an injured bird with a broken wing to fix. She let me spin out of control about the State and Protection until we were both exhausted from it. Then she would snuggle next to me and rub my chest while we pretended to watch the PIN. It was all I wanted—someone to listen. It didn't last long.

After I ran, Kelly was the only place I could go to escape the feeling that Protection had simply been a vice, slowly tightening around its citizens. When I finally looked at it, they all strained and struggled and crammed against each other, until every once in a while one of them popped and went on a crazy rampage. Trouble was, none of them were crazy. I never realized that before.

Another "ism" my father used to deliver—you pile enough rats together in a cage, start starving them and stressing them harder each day. . . "Violence, rape, murder, cannibalism—as sure as the Devil," he would say. I had no idea how he knew that. I found out later.

But PIN made the incidents sound like just another mentally-disturbed nutbag. They ran the footage over and over again until we all begged for anything that would make us safe.

Those of us that had a clue knew that today's escaped "nutbag" was yesterday's "guest" at the *Fifty*.

I'll get to the *Fifty* later. Right now, the mere sight of Kelly makes me want to go off on an anti-State conspiracy rant. But as fast as she shows up, she's gone, and I'm falling again. *Shit!*

The images on my descent only fuel my rage.

— XIII —

AS DEJECTED AND broody as Dal ever got, he was an eternally arrogant and self-centered archangel. Leaving the crowd of angels in the arena—the light and the adoration of followers—to her? Alone? He flew back from the fiery lake, ran through the dungeons of the two heavens, and burst back into the center of the arena. One last round before the end of the soul's fall.

And the Arena of Reckoning echoed with the anger of his words. The faithful remained perched. But as deep as his rage ever became, Life's restraint as she plotted was deeper. Hers was a patient wrath. The weight of the blood on the broken wings of the past helped her endure his insolence. Even that would only carry her contempt so far.

Dal stared into the fall, remembering his own tumble from grace. "Time waits for no man . . . or angel."

"We have a few moments," Life said. "Time is—"

"The relativity of it always seems so eternal," Dal said. "Only in the confusion and seeming endlessness of their fall do they realize the seconds they have wasted. That is one of the nuances you do not comprehend. He reminisces of fine wine and sweet women, yet burned his years in the rage of fire. While you cannot, I understand this sentiment perfectly."

"And now you masquerade at philosophy," Life said. "Many names have you labored under since our time, my Day Star, but philosopher?"

"And by any other name," said Dal, "I am no longer your—"

"You are what you have always been," Life said, her hair now waving and moving on its own. "Condemned to be ruler of the darkness at your own request."

Dal ignored her. He looked at the fall. This one would be his. "Only in the fall do we recognize how wickedly you have condemned us."

"The end of this life is not the end of life," she said. "It is simply the next step in the journey toward faith. A journey you must set on willingly."

"Then there is no purpose in your eternity," said Dal. "Save for suffering at your hands, once again. I think I understand something more clearly now. You enjoy bringing suffering first. You masturbate to their lament before you will allow them to be saved."

Life hung her head. "How I could have spawned such a. . .?" she said. "How have you become such a vile creature, such a lawless liar? End this now and come back as—"

"As your *what*?" Dal asked. "Your slave? I am what you made me, cast out and impaled on the sharp spike of your love." He kept his gaze on her, and pointed to the fall. "The love you pretend to have for them. I am that I am, because that is what you commanded. Blood-flowing and rage-filled revenge. And you . . . you are neither sorrow nor joy. You are simply absence. No pain, no sorrow, nor sweet misery of judgment and redemption. Joy and love and ecstasy do not exist without these things. You are not joy. You are the absence of lament. And that is emptiness. I will have none of it." He gazed back to the final stages of the fall. "Neither will he."

— XIV —

A FEW MORE floors rush past me—ten maybe. I don't take time to count, because I'm getting really pissed off now. This fall is taking forever. I know the street will splatter me, so I'm just wondering . . . what's the goddamn point?

Flashes of life? Purgatory? That's just electro stimulus to the brain as it shuts down—sputters to a stop like an old guzzler's engine that won't turn off when you pull the key. I know I'm dreaming, none of this is real. Don't ask me how I know that. But if this *is* the flashes of my life. . .

Kelly and my wedding and marriage fly by. Then our first house and I know where I'm going from here. Shortly after that, things fell apart. Almost as fast as this fall.

Then I jolt to a stop. More like a slam, really. And it's raining outside and I immediately recognize where I am. Doesn't take much. Contempt-filled doctors, overworked, sunk-in-eyed nurses, and a huge angry orderly standing in the corner. I'm in a State Med-mart birthing room.

That's what the hospitals turned into—assembly line chop-scrapers where they take citizens apart and put them back together, like mechanics wrenching on old, rusted guzzlers that nobody wants or needs anymore.

I look at the doctor—disgust and contempt written all over his face —and he forces a downturned smile at me. It's easy to look at a citizen that way—you got too much of something, what's the use in having one more?

I jerk my head toward the window when a huge bolt of lightning flashes, but it's hard to hear the thunder over Kelly's screaming, and then there she is.

Amy. Bright, beautiful Amy, stretching her way out of Kelly's vagina. I can't watch it again.

I turn my head, but it doesn't matter. The image was seared into my mind long ago. Kelly rips, she screams, and then there's all the blood and then—who decided that childbirth had to be so brutal? I'm just glad as shit I never had to do it. I mean, it looks painful. And bloody? I've seen less guts when I field dressed deer.

Then the blood and shit comes and a nurse scoops all of it off the table, dumps it, and then asks me if I want to cut the umbilical. What? Like after all that deliciousness, I probably want some dessert.

"Hell no," is all I can remember saying over Kelly's whimpering. And then I'm queasy and the room spins. Or spun or something, but I feel the same sensation now. As real as it was when it *was* real. Then things go black.

— XV —

DAL WAS WILD now, and he shot fire from his wings. He longed for the warmth of the past. And the shimmer of the great hall could not quell his rage and regret. A lament for all time of a love cast overboard and drowned beneath the seas of blood he had spilled.

"Indeed," he said to all in attendance. Soon they would all choose again. "Who did decide that bringing forth life should be so barbaric? Birth and death mimic each other. And to the woman you said, 'I will greatly multiply your sorrow and your conception; in pain you shall bring forth children.' "

Life answered on impulse, "This was my judgment."

"For the crime of tasting sweet fruit? You are right."

Life stared into all of their pasts. How could her children have. . .? "I gave them the garden with very simple instructions. They succumbed to your temptation and—"

"I *should* come back and work for you," said Dal. "I could never conceive of such unholy punishments. Your indifference to suffering is —"

"I could only ever show them the path," Life said. "They must choose to follow it or—"

"Suffer the consequences," said Dal. "My contempt for your children can only be matched by your own."

"They will have suffering in this world," Life said. "That is my Word."

But Dal was too drunk on the fall. "Yes, yes, but *why?* Why must we *all. . .?*"

She spoke of her own law as simple fact, shooting it at him like arrows of guilt, "There comes a day . . . when all will be judged."

Dal paused for a second and then shot some of her own words back, "And you shall wipe away all their tears and there shall be no more death, or sorrow, or crying, neither shall there be any more pain. . . . And yet I do not fear for myself and my position in this."

"You should fear your deeds," Life said to him. "For they shall be your judgment."

Dal cawed a small laugh. "You are slow in keeping promises, as they understand slowness," he said. "Your patience while they perish is cruel. Many will never come to repentance and redemption, certainly not this one."

Her fallen angel was right about one thing, time was growing short. Life said, "You twist and turn the word to suit your own purposes."

"And you do not?" said Dal. Then he pointed toward the fall. "*They* do not? . . . They twist and pervert, and justify everything they do by bastardizing your words to suit them. I will tell you what I fear. I fear that one of them will surpass my own contempt."

"They seek only to understand," said Life, "so they interpret the—"

"Who are they to interpret your words?" said Dal. "None are capable of this. You give me fifty from—"

"Theirs is to struggle to come to faith," said Life. She would make one last attempt. "Yours is to come *back* to it."

Dal ignored her. Counting silently in his head the legion of fallen clergy in his section of the grandstands. "I have more than that at my disposal already—little child-raping monsters. They are hideously disfigured after they fall. *I* can hardly look at them. None of them agree on what the Word means. They do agree on one particular point, though: eye for an eye. They have mastered this lesson."

In the grandstands there was a cooing of agreement that could be felt throughout the faithful. As the two of them traded barbs, the power of the Word spiked through the inside of the Hallowed Hall as if it was being written before them. However, when it came to a battle of words, it was hard to debate with the current author.

"You have heard that this was said," Life spoke, "but I have told you, 'Do not resist an evil person. If someone strikes you on the right cheek, turn to him the other also.' "

"Further hypocrisy," cawed Dal. "You send your children to teach against your own words. The Word that came before them. You expect man to understand the nuances of that? They barely understand themselves."

She needed to temper the growing flames. There was much more at stake than the contempt of one fallen angel, even if he was the darkest of them. "Then we must strive to . . . enlighten them."

And a huge blast of light illuminated everything in the great hall. And angels screeched and covered themselves with their wings. And the steel in their wings glowed white from the bright and their armor reflected the truth of her Word.

He responded with an orange blast and filled the hall with a fiery flame of defiance. Then he let the smoke subside.

And as quickly as the two of them traded warnings, the hall was bathed in soft light and shadow again.

— XVI —

IF I WAS falling slowly before, now it feels like I'm speeding up. And a bright light blasts me and I close my eyes.

But my anger has turned to fear again, and I wonder what's really at the end of all this. Heaven? Hell? What could possibly be worse than what I've already seen in my life?

The bad, that has to be next. The good was good enough and I'm happy to have seen most of it again. I could've done without seeing Kelly's vagina ripped apart. Doesn't feel like I get to pick and choose events, though.

I can feel them watching me. I know they are there. The question is, who are they and what do they want?

The Devil? God? Gimme a break. I'm not that important. And fighting for my soul? That's just . . . silly.

"Hey," I say. If they are out there. . . "Yeah, 'vagina.' I said it. It's a word, deal with it. Could you hurry this thing up? I'm ready to see what's next. Show me whatcha got."

There's just more nothing in reply. It's just what I thought. Total bullshit. I wish I could go back. I'd tell all those idiots on Sunday the truth about their faith.

I only wish I could have given some payback. As soon as I think it, I see the windows of the building again. Clear as day now. And here comes the bad.

I can hear the screaming down the hall and I know instantly who it is. Amy—our little angel—the only child who lived through our baby years. The other one? I don't even know what to tell you.

"Do I really have to do this?" I ask. I'm still not sure if this is just death hysteria or if there really is someone out there. Maybe I'm already splattered and this is some final thought, or impulse or some shit. "Please don't make me go through this crap again?"

Or maybe I'm a vegetable in a cell at the *Fifty*, and Kelly is standing over me, feeding me blended-up carrots as I drool orange slime down my chin. *Kill me, please.* I wouldn't ever want Kelly in that building.

I don't even know what I'm saying. "Please." That's not me. Anyway, whoever is controlling this, they're not listening. And it's too late now, because I'm running down the hallway to our little girl's bedroom. Kelly is right behind me.

"Daddy," my little Amy cries and screams, "I can't make it stop!"

Before the shots, Amy was the sweetest little vanilla-frosted cupcake you ever saw. She used to kiss me on the cheek and say, "Daddy, it's gonna be a great day!" I never had the heart to tell her any different.

After the second injection, the blinding headaches started and her eyes sunk in from the insomnia. She tried to keep her smile, but I could tell that there was always pain behind it.

I know there's nothing I can do. The State doctors were clear on that. As helpful as a canker sore on my dick. "Ride it out." I should call the bastards at home right now and let them listen. Better yet, pay them a little oh-three-hundred visit. And the rage is back—always there when I need it.

"Mom?" Amy says. She's in pain, but somehow she's figured out how to bring it down and endure it. I've seen that tactic before, but if it was me, I'd be shooting at the walls or some other ridiculous shit.

And Kelly scoots around me and sits down on the bed next to Amy. Poor kid—thirteen, just starting Second Ed Compliance. Now, this shit.

"Butchers," I say.

"That won't help," says Kelly. "And now's not the time, just . . . let me handle it."

And I'm back out the door and in the hall, pacing, searching for someone to choke. But there isn't anyone. Just a hidden system of lies and money. I found that out later.

"Cancer shot," the school nurse told my baby. As if that existed. You don't think if there was such a thing we wouldn't all be lining up at the nearest State Med-Mart to get it. Never mind that she was marked as non-participating exempt. They put her on trial anyway. Gave her judgment she should have never had.

Damn company didn't even have to get our permission to give it to her. Twelve-year-old little girl and they shot her up with drugs that she didn't need. But that was the law, that's how they liked to work it. If the people are too smart to swallow your lies, cram the pills down their throats with the law.

You can bet your ass that the drug company's prime officer wasn't shooting his own daughter up with that crap. And you can bet she doesn't have blinding headaches every night either. She's probably on the beach in Cancun, partying it up with her friends like a teenage girl should do with her daddy's money. Only his money was made by bribing State politicians to pass laws to stick needles in everyone else's kids.

The ranting anger is back—I don't think it'll ever die—eating away at my soul like real cancer. I guess they're still working on a shot for that. And the rage wants to go somewhere, do something. Shove a gun in someone's mouth and watch them cry and beg to be saved. Like my baby's crying and begging behind that door.

Guns. . . That's what they are good for. In case you were wondering. That's what they've always been good for. Level the playing field. Touch the untouchable. Drag the people responsible out in the shit-streaming street with the rest of us . . . and blow their brains out.

"Whoever you are," I say, "I'm done with this, because unless you got some way to bring her back, this is old news. She's. . ."

I can't even say the word. Couldn't say it to the compliance therapist either. Neither could anyone else in that pointless pity-party they called grief relief. "Passed away" . . . "moved on" . . . "better place," my ass. Growing up, having friends, falling in love—that's a better place! Body in a garbage bin and then burned to ashes is no place for a kid.

— XVII —

"HE'S RIGHT, YOU know," Dal said to Life. Then he smiled at the gallery. "Doing that to children, it is shameful."

"You cannot believe this," Life said. "You think she would fare better in the lake of fire?"

Dal cawed a little, chuckling. "How is she faring?"

"She is fine," said Life. "She's . . . special. And she is loved." She left her response at that.

"Are we not all special?" said Dal. "Ah, to have lived life and loved." He said it that way on purpose. "Well, how marvelous for her. It is a wonderful warmth, I know. However, *he* loves her. What consideration does that warrant?"

"He can choose to be with her again."

Dal frowned. "He has chosen."

"I give unto him eternal life," she said. "Should he choose, he shall never perish."

"Yet, no man shall pluck himself from under your hand," Dal said. "Unless they have rewritten it again, I believe that is still forbidden, correct? So many rules. There really is no way for them to obey all of them, you know."

"They must simply pursue the path laid before them."

"Your path is rife with quicksand," said Dal. "You realize, they forged their own kingdoms with the iron of your words. Words so complicated and rules so vast that no man can hope to understand them, much less obey their covenants. They enact laws and enforcement exactly as you do. And when they break them—stumble as men do—they suffer, many times greatly. But you . . . you offer them the severest punishment of all. You give them to me. How are you able to. . .? Had I not lived to see it. . ."

Life's silence conveyed the truth. And before she could find a convenient explanation—

"Yes, I suspected as much," said Dal. "Shall we proceed, then? This one should not be overly difficult."

— XVIII —

IF THERE IS someone watching, they aren't listening, because I endure Amy's screaming until it stops. But when I open her door, I'm sucked through and then I'm falling again. This time, face down, watching the ground rocket up at me.

I try to close my eyes, but I can't. Apparently, I have to watch myself splatter. Whoever it is, they've got a sick sense of humor. This fast . . . won't be pretty. It won't last long either. I imagine everything going black.

What did you think this would look like?

By now, I know that's not a voice in my head. Well, it is . . . but it's not mine.

"Show yourself," I say, "coward son of a bitch!"

Then I smell it. A putrid, coppery scent of decay, but also a hint of . . . syrup? And baking cookies? But for some reason both of them smell like the overpowering aroma of . . . death.

Then everything gets dark, and the rain is coming down hotter now, and there is fire in the sky. And I close my eyes, because the heat is oppressive, but really, it's because I'm afraid to look. If this is who I think, it's just . . . not possible. Everything else is gonna feel like lube. This will be the final ass-raping in a world that is truly lost.

Then everything stops. No more fall and no more rain. Just darkness and flames in the sky. And then he's just . . . there.

* * *

"Bitch," he says. "Very colorful . . . however, my mother. . . Hmm, let's just say. . . There really is no way to prepare you for it, is there? Ah, spoiling the surprise, like telling your children about Santa Claus, I imagine. Makes me positively . . . giddy."

His voice sounds like a grandfather. But the sound is loud and feels like it's coming from inside my head, infecting my brain. If it wasn't for the red wings and dark red feathers covering everything but his face, I'd say he looked like a State politician. And when he smiles, he looks *just* like one. Little, baby-harp-seal-colored teeth that look like he just ate an infant for the cameras. Not how I pictured him at all.

I blurt it out without thinking. "Where's your tail?" I ask. Then I feel a shiver go through my whole body, but he should have a tail, right? And horns? He is red, I guess, so at least the God-dogs got that right. If it is. . .? That's just crazy—I'm hallucinating. I hope Kelly wipes the carrots off my chin, because this . . . this is just a ghost story they tell to try and keep us compliant. Most people have stopped listening. But deep in the back of our minds . . . when we think about death, it's hard not to be afraid of judgment and damnation.

"I had it cropped," he says, and his smile makes me think he's only half-joking.

I think I lean to see behind him, but I'm feeling . . . fuzzy, so maybe it's something else. "Nice . . . wings." I say it, but it feels like I'm talking in slow motion, watching someone else speak for me. Hope he doesn't get me killed. The wings are . . . beautiful, is the only way I can describe them, but I never imagined him as. . . I mean, the guy looks like a dark red angel.

His laugh echoes through the emptiness. It's maniacal and goose-bumps prickle my whole body. My nostrils burn a little when I smell his breath. It's confident and . . . final, a bit like the smoke after the last fireworks on a Fourth of Freedom barbecue. He's definitely not where the molasses and cookie smell came from.

"Ah," he says, "the stories they tell you."

It's weird, because it feels kinda like meeting the Prime Officer of the huge corporation you work for—I'm just trying not to make a mistake and he's wondering how many credits I cost him, or why the hell I'm on the revenue-rolls at all.

And he's smiling like he just figured out a joke he was working on. I don't think I wanna know the punchline.

I should be afraid, but all I feel is . . . anger. "Apparently, they aren't stories," I say.

"Yes . . . however," he says. Then he stops, cocks his head to the side a little and sniffs in a blast of air.

For a second the heat subsides, but when he breathes out through his mouth, I smell the warmth of . . . souls? The sound of wailing women, chained in agony, rushes past my face and I can smell the torment on his breath. Believe me, I know what misery smells like. But there's something else, too . . . understanding. I can see it in his eyes.

"You ever tell stories, Jake?" he asks.

He knows my name. Santa Claus? Shit, I'm on the naughty list. We're off to a bad start on that. I'm sure he knows I've told my fair share of stories. What else is there to do in a Protection smoke . . . other than drink shitty coffee?

"Yes," he says. Then he smiles so I can see all of his teeth. "I am sure you have."

His teeth are perfectly aligned, but they are . . . unnatural. Like an old cinewave star who's had too much dental work. How he keeps them from being bloodstained red from all the— "Why are your teeth so white?" The questions are coming out too easy. I guess I'm curious. Anyway, I'm not going anywhere, so I might as well get some answers. Sure, the fear and the fog are messing with my mind, but there must be a reason he hasn't just eaten my soul by now. If that's what they do.

He rolls his eyes around a little. Kinda like he's trying not to be impatient. His sockets are deep, but the eyes . . . *light blue?* "I like that about you," he says.

"What?"

He folds his hands together, slowly weaving his long fingers, alternating one then another like he's wrapping them around a bat. He grips them together like he's done it a billion times, threatening me without saying anything. Silence is the best way to scare the shit out of someone. The results are better than yelling.

Maybe it *is* just for effect . . . or maybe he wants to bash out my brains. Whatever he's thinking, he keeps smiling, letting me imagine all the things he could do to me.

"You are smart," he says. "You are terrified, but you realize it is better to appear calm—a good contrivance, poker face. No, I'm not eating souls and ripping flesh apart any longer. I have no need for that. You are being tortured enough by life." And he looks up into the air briefly and when he looks back down he's got a grin like . . . I don't even know what. "You are far more efficient than I ever was. Those are tales, nothing more. Remember?"

"Well. . ." I struggle for the words. I know where this game ends. He's toying with me—cat playing with his meal. "This must get . . . boring."

"You have no idea," he says. "But my time is limited. Lots of work to do, you know . . . so, stories."

There's a ray of truth in his words. What does he want? "Stories about the Dev—" I say it without thinking, but he cuts me off, then his face turns angry.

"There's no call to be vulgar!" he roars. Then he calms himself back down.

Interrogation 101. Shit.

He has a scowl on his face. "That word," his voice is down to a low growl now, "so . . . negative." He fakes a shiver on purpose. "Like saying . . . 'guns,' I imagine. No need to call someone evil, just say that they have an affinity for firearms. Then they *are* evil. Hah, ignorance, my favorite. Yet, I like them. One of your better inventions, actually."

Him, liking guns? I can imagine the Protection PR campaign on the PIN now: "Guns—Hell's Christday present." But, I never thought about the language part of it. I guess you say "Jew" in the wrong tone long enough, pretty soon . . .

"Yes, exactly," he says, "language, how I love it! Distorting, inflammatory . . . eviscerating. It is all language. That's how you pervert the truth. Nothing is inherently good or evil. The line dividing them cuts through the hearts of every being. You know this is true. You can use a weapon to protect or you can use it to blow an innocent baby's brains out. But the weapon isn't evil, it's the fist that wields it." He pauses for a second, letting the truth of it sink in, I guess. But I think he likes the sound of his own voice, because that doesn't last long. "In the same way, my name means what you've been told it does—evil, treachery, defiance. But . . . what if that's *not* the truth."

"Preaching to the choir," I say. I know he's playing me, telling me what I want to hear. Trouble is, it's working. It *is* what I want to hear. I want to talk to someone who hasn't lost their ability to think. Too bad I have to go this far to find him. "Is this where you make me the offer I can't refuse?" I ask. "Because I've had a rough day and I'm in no mood." I wince the tiniest bit after I say—no idea who I'm messing with.

He ignores me. "You've played the game," he says. "With spirits and flame and lust in the air."

I know what he's referring to. We were all animals. "What of it?"

"That's how it happens," he says. "The truth, the lie . . . the Word. Someone—many of them in this case, actually. They whisper a little story in someone's ear. Then that person whispers it to the next person. Then they decide to write books about it. And then—"

"Ya know, I just jumped off a building," I say, "so if you don't mind—"

His eyes glow a little red for a second and then they're back to blue. When he speaks now, it sounds like an eagle screaming at a rabbit he just swooped down on, "Think about it, a story that's over two thousand years old! You think that the version they tell today has any resemblance to the truth that was? You think I'm the soul-torturing monster in that book? You've witnessed the world you lived in. That angry mob is not *my* creation." He pauses and closes his eyes for a brief second. Then he breaths in slow and exhales slower. "I am simply . . . crowd control. All of that. . .?" He tilts his head back and looks up. "I wish I could conceive of such misery—the vile putrescence you call life."

When he looks back down at me, I can tell he's pleased with himself. And he tilts his head down farther, and then he rolls his eyes up and says, "Your life is a new beast of burden, never before seen in any eternity. Protection, compliance . . . submission to judgment. Some of you terrify—" He tilts his head back up and fakes a shiver through his shoulders. "You all scare the *Hell* right out of me."

I look up to see what he keeps looking at. Nothing up there but dark sky and the flicker of flames. Bet I can guess who's up there, but then that would be. . . "So, why are you here?" I ask. "If you aren't offering to. . .?"

"About that," he says. He unfolds his hands and points right at me, and all I can focus on is his finger. It feels like looking at the barrel of that PAIC's big .60 cal, back on the roof. His voice is more serious now, though, "I'm not required to offer you anything. Technically, I already own you. You are part of the Word." He looks up above his head. "Management does not approve of its subjects taking matters into their own hands—acting and thinking for themselves, you know."

I crane my head back and look above him again. For some reason, I can see the roof of the scraper this time. The one I just took a swan dive off. "I hear ya," I say. "They don't like it either."

He chuckles and it sounds like a raven cawing. Then flames roll up from his wings and above his head. "We'll get to them."

Holy shit! I think. *What the. . .?* Then I think about it for a second . . . but I don't know where to go or what to say next. Clearly he's here, and if he is, then a whole lotta other shit is real too. If that's the case—ipso facto—the jump pretty much fucked me . . . for good.

He laughs harder now and I can feel the heat on my face. We both look back down and into each other's eyes. "Amusing," he says.

"What is?"

"For good," he says. "Interesting that you should put it that way."

"What?" I'm trying to keep up. It might be my only chance at—hell, I have no idea what's going to happen—lake of fire, Purgatory, some other shit. I do know one thing, it won't be good.

"Exactly," he says. He's more excited now—teacher who sees the spark in his student. Then he puts his hands back together. I think I hear his knuckles crackle. Like an old-world fighter, getting ready to clean someone's clock. "You may be mine for all life's eternity. . ." He lets the words linger in the air like doom. Tortured in Hell forever. That's what he's talking about. As unpleasant as it sounds, he could have done it by now. ". . .and that will have nothing to do with good. However. . ."

"However," he keeps saying that word. I know that nothing before it means shit. The truth always comes after. He's weaving lies and truth in together. Whatever he says next, that will be the meat of it.

"Ah, meat," he says, "fresh meat. I like how you think."

I can feel the pressure as his thoughts work their way through mine. He's infecting his way in and around an idea, and my head is dizzy from it.

Maybe if I stay in front of him? "I jumped," I say. "I know what that means. So let's get on with—"

"I told you," he says. Then he gets a look on his face that I don't recognize. And he looks up again. "It's not quite what you might believe."

If it is who I think up there, this is going to get weird. It's not every day that you get to see the face of God. In fact, I'm pretty sure it's just one day. Too bad I had to die to do that, too. What the *hell* am I going to say to that guy?

The light blasts me so hard that I can barely make out the shape of an . . . A. . .

"Yes, Jake," the voice is soft and comforting. It kinda sounds like a whale moan, but I can understand it.

Where did that come from? "Whale moan?" That's just too much nature feed on the PIN when I was a kid. I guess it doesn't have to make any sense—no one knows what death is like. But the moan has that tone in it. Like when your mother or your wife catches you with contraband porn again—judgmental and shocked, as only a woman can be at a man's obsession with sex.

The ivory white feathers float around like a satin sheet and the hair is . . . no way to describe . . . it's like no color at all. The sight is incredible. The form is familiar, like a best friend. About the only way I can describe it. But there is no mistaking the near-invisible wings . . . and the breasts.

I know what you're thinking, because I'm thinking it too. It is God, for Christ's sake—how the hell can I be looking at her tits? But don't give me any shit here—you know you would look.

Anyway, I'm probably already headed to Hell, so how much worse can it get? If I'm here, she's real . . . and I swear to God she. . . Maybe I shouldn't swear to that.

It takes me a second to speak, but holy shit! "You're . . . God?" I ask. "You're a woman."

"I am that I am," she replies. "I am love, I am hope, I am all things to all. I am the beginning and I am the end."

I guess that clears that up, I think. I try not to look lost, but unraveling that statement is some confusing shit. *No wonder the God-dogs misinterpret*—I cut the thought off and wonder if she can read my mind. He could, so it stands to reason—

"Yes," she says. And then she smiles. When she does, everything is warm. Not like the searing heat from him. Sort of like the tropical island screensaver when the PIN isn't broadcasting—eighty-one degrees and sunny every day. To someone in Seattle, that's . . . pacifying. But she looks strange.

When I stop squinting from the light, I figure it out. That's the trouble with a nice set of. . . It takes concentration to look her in the eyes. And hers are jet black—huge orbs of shining onyx. *His were ice blue?* I would have figured that the other way around.

"I'm sorry," I say, "but you're a—"

"I am what you need me to be," she says. "If you had needed me to be a man, I would appear to you as such."

"I *did* picture you as a man," I say. "Everyone does, *even* women. But, so you're saying that Moses wanted you to be a bush?"

I can't see him, but I feel the heat when he caws and laughs.

Her face grimaces a little and she closes her eyes, obviously annoyed —I know the look. When she opens her eyes, the black is blacker—if that's even possible.

"A burning bush?" I say. "No offense, but that's just . . . messed up."

"Times were different," she says. "I have appeared as many things to many people since"

I have a million questions. Who wouldn't? When else are you going to get a chance to find out . . . about everything? But I don't think this is Q&A time. "Look," I say, "about the roof thing—"

"There is still hope, Jacob," she says.

And that catches me off guard, because I've been prepping myself for the worst. "Um, how's that?" I ask. "You mean I can still go to Heaven? But I . . . I jumped. Isn't that against the rules?" I look around, trying to see where he's gone. I can smell him out there in the dark, I just can't see him.

His voice burns through the air, "I told you as much. The story morphs. The next rewrite shall be no different."

Interrupting in class—wonder if they whip you up here?

She looks up briefly and then back down. "These are different times —challenging circumstances," she says. I can feel her annoyance growing. "The opportunity for you to choose remains."

"Challenging. . ." That's politician-speak for "shitty."

So, what do I have that she could possibly want? "Free will?" I ask her. "*That's* the answer?"

"Yes."

It seems too simple. And what did I tell you about simple? "So, you're telling me . . . that I can go around and break the rules—do anything I want—then repent when you show up at the end, and it's all good?" I ask. I think that's what she's saying. "No wonder."

"Not exactly," she says. "As long as you choose fai—"

"A moment, please," the voice burns down at us. It sends the temperature way up and I squint. He doesn't reappear—just his voice —and it's hotter now and it feels like my face is getting sunburned when he speaks. "He does not possess all the facts. How can you expect him to choose his own judgment without all the information?

That . . . is not free will."

"What facts?" I ask. "I jumped and here we are—Purgatory, or Judgment Day, or whatever shit. Game over."

"He does not fully understand," he says to her.

Something is up his sleeve. It's easy to see that. But curiosity. . . "Know what?" I ask.

"He does not require this to make his decision," she says. "Salvation is faith, not facts."

"Oh, I would vehemently disagree," his voice is more confident. "In point of fact, she is the *sole* reason he jumped."

"Need to know *what*?" I ask. Maybe the confidence is wearing off on me. "What are you talking about? Kelly? I sent her to—"

He appears next to her and he isn't smiling like before. Something's wrong. They both look just like the State doctor when he told us. . . "I went back to get my gun," I say to them, "but they caught up to me on the street after." I still have no idea how they found me. "Then they chased me onto the roof. Nowhere to go from there but down, so she gets away and I'm with you two."

But they aren't listening—it's like I'm not even here. They sound like a couple of crows arguing over who gets the ass end of a deer carcass. Now I'm the one getting annoyed.

When he does reappear, this time he looks different. Something is . . . he's holding something. An old, red book. The thing is huge, but I can't read the cover.

"The Word is written," he says to her. "He chooses his own judgment. He believes that she escaped. Given that. . ." He looks at me and sniffs. "Right now, he does not care which way the tide turns. I can smell it."

I scrunch my face. Watching bickering, still hard to tolerate. "She *did* get away," I say.

I look at her and her warm face has turned to sadness and . . . it's not empathy, but it's close. And her bright hair changes to alternating gray and black.

He looks at me and tries to fake the same emotions. "Jake. . ." he says. The satisfaction in his voice tells me he already knows what I'm going to do. "You could not have predicted that they would do that. Do not blame yourself."

Now I'm getting really pissed. I got plenty of self-loathing—enough to fill up a sea of Hells—but what is he. . .? "Show me," I say. I know they can. At least she can. He might, but I probably wouldn't believe what I saw. Anyway, I'm done with the charade.

He says my name again, "Jake"—each time he says it, I feel a twinge of heat go through my heart—"I'm on your side here."

I look at her, then at him. Shit, they're both holding back. "I'm not stupid," I say. "Show me what happened . . . *now*."

And then he slinks up to her, puts his long fingers on her shoulder, and leans into her ear. Then he whispers, "I think he's serious." It sounds like hissing.

I can see the waves of heat leave his mouth. I wonder why she doesn't just crack a bolt of lightning up his ass or something. I mean, she *is* God, right? *CRACK!*—Evil, extinguished for all eternity. But she doesn't even flinch or try to move away. She just keeps staring at me, like she's deciding.

When he moves away, she raises her hand up, and then I'm gone.

— XIX —

KELLY HAD WARM, brown sugar hair, and the smile of a young woman who always looked for the cuddly part on a cougar. She wasn't quite new-world-order crazy—a starving citizen who would eat anything they could get their hands on. She was more like a raw root grinder with a touch of black market meat every once in a while. She had no idea what she was in for with me.

I knew the appeal, it had worked in the past. The trouble with living every day of your life with an even keel is, when the inevitable rough seas in life hit, you need someone like Lieutenant Dan "You call this a storm?" to pilot the ship through the shit.

Okay, maybe I did mess up the reference—it was a contraband copy of the damn old cinewave, anyway—but I like colorful cussing. Life is messy—people cuss. Get over it. Probably why they invented profanity in the first place.

Anyway, that's the universe—yin and yang, and good and . . . not so good, all locked in a never-ending struggle to maintain balance, I guess. That's what Kelly used to say. Too bad for her, because my "angel of nice" got me—angry, conspiracy-ranting "asshole," I've heard said to describe me before. Could be true, people don't like hearing what you really think.

Whoa. . . Way too much philosophy before breakfast, but that's what is in my head. Sounds too preachy, even for me. I shrug it off and concentrate on seeing Kelly, because I know it's her. But everything is surreal, like just before the sun breaks through the fog.

Surreal? I got words in my head that don't feel natural to me. Death. . . Whatever I thought I knew about—hell, looks like I don't know shit about it. I doubt anyone does until it's their turn. It's not what I thought it would be, I'll tell you that. More of the same kinda shit, though—trials and judgments that are out of my control. SSDD —same shit . . . not much different when you're dead.

He's here, or somewhere, rooting around in my head. Her too, for that matter, because I'm not making this shit happen. Don't get me wrong, I'm not complaining—any chance to see Kelly again, I'm all in. I don't feel scared or mad or any of the other poisonous emotions I carried around with the pointlessness of rocks in a backpack for most of my life. I feel sort of . . . relaxed, actually.

It's an unfamiliar feeling and I wonder where it's coming from. Doesn't take long to figure it out, that's how I always felt around Kelly. She had this way of disarming people, even the worst ones.

Don't know why I am talking about her in the past tense. That was then and this is now. Only now *is* then, because I'm back to the first night we had sex.

Hey, I'm a man—some stories are true—we don't go long without thinking about it. I don't even think death is powerful enough to change that.

Anyway, my dorm habitat is dark. Despite how beautiful she was, Kelly was totally self-conscious about being seen naked, even when she wanted to be. It took a long time before we could do it with the lights on. As soon as it was over, she would bundle up in pajamas, complete with socks to go to sleep.

It sucked, because I'm more of an "in the raw" man. No sense in having to pull off a bunch of annoying clothing when your dick wakes you back up in the middle of the night. Anyway, my blood runs hot, hotter at night.

I can feel my own disapproval now, so you don't even have to start. But what good is a hot woman if you can't look at—

I stop and realize that it sounds pretty sexist. I never worried about that sort of thing before, but God being a woman? Maybe now's the time to start.

I'm excited—not hard to tell that—but a little nervous, too. We never got caught on campus, but if we had. . . The feeling with Kelly is wonderful and I only think about it ending once. But before I can bask in the afterglow. . . "Afterglow?" That thought is definitely not mine and now I'm wondering just what the point is. That's her, I'm sure of it—euphoria and tenderness. Maybe she's trying to pull me to the light, just like Kelly used to do . . . does.

The whole thing is confusing, but before I have a chance to enjoy the . . . "end," I'm snapped away and I jolt straight up in my bed— ripped out of one of the craziest dreams I've ever had.

I jerk my head around. *I'm in. . .?* It is our habitat, our room . . . after academy. And . . . and the whole thing is just a dream. *What the. . .?*

I turn to Kelly's side of the bed and there she is.

She sits up, rubs her eyes, and then looks at me. "Wha—what's wrong?" she asks.

Is this the dream or the other thing? Did I jump? Or maybe they are still bouncing me back and forth, deciding. Whatever it is, it feels real enough.

I look around the room and then I feel down under the covers with my foot. If there is one detail they might have missed, it would be the socks on Kelly's feet. And there they are—scratchy, wool and warm. Honestly, I don't know how she can sleep in those itchy things.

So, that's Kelly, now where. . .? *When* is this? "Nasty. . ." I mutter.

"Nasty what?" Kelly asks.

"Dream," I tell her. I'm still trying to shake off all the emotions swirling in my mind. I *did* jump off that building. And I feel for the holes in my shoulder and ass—nothing. "I jumped off a building, and . . . and I was falling, and the—" I'm still a little afraid to say his name. He silently warned me about that. "God was a woman."

"What?" Kelly says. "Don't even tell me you had some sex dream about God."

"No-no," I say. "That's just—I have a line."

She groans and rolls over. "Not hardly," she says. Then she giggles. "Razor thin, maybe."

"That's . . . messed up," I say. I feel a little better. Maybe it was a bad dream. Yeah, could be . . . super-bad dream. Might as well have some fun. "I wonder what that would be like?"

I get the reaction I'm after, and Kelly rolls back and love punches me in the shoulder. "You are *so* bad," she says.

"Who?" I say. I'm still a little shaken up, though, so I reach over and check for pajamas, just to make sure. Pajamas—check. *What the hell is going. . .?*

When Kelly feels my hand, she looks at the clock on her nightstand. Then she rolls back and looks at me.

I can't see her, but I swear I can feel the playful look of fake disgust on her face.

"Seriously?" she's not really asking, she knows by now. "Again?" She chuckles a little. "Nasty devil is what you are. I should make you go back to sleep and finish your little God dream." Then she reaches down and starts pulling down her pajamas, mumbling, "Three in the morning, waking me up."

My eyes get wide. The light from the streetlamp out our window seems brighter than it should be. Kelly's eyes glint a dark, shiny color and she blinks. Her eyelids close slower than they should and when she opens them—

The bedroom door flies open in a loud crash, and I hear the boots as they thunder into the room. The light is blinding and then there are three more lights strobing in our faces, blasting us both in the eyes, and I squint.

"Jacob Oliver Blake," one of them shouts. It's louder than he has to, but he's all pumped up on adrenaline and judgment, "and Flora Kellina Blake, you are hereby remanded to Protection!"

Oh, shit! I think. Not because we are about to be black-bagged and tortured—no one is allowed to call Kelly that.

It's a short thought, though. "State your compliance!" that first one says.

There's two more in the room, I know that. And I put my hand up to shield my eyes from the glare of a flashlight, see if I can find all three of them. *Get to your gun!*

"Put your hands down!" number two shouts. "State your compliance!"

But before I can lower my hand—*Scrape!*

Suppressors have an unmistakable sound—not silent, but not loud enough to do damage to your ears indoors.

And my shoulder catches fire and I slam back into the headboard. And everything is hot. Feels like my chest got a hot poker shoved through it. I've seen what that feels like. Then Kelly screams and the world turns to molasses.

Molasses? But that's the word in my head. In fact, I can smell it— molasses and vanilla, mixed with burning cordite, and the smell of smoke from the gunshot. And . . . bad cologne? And I know what this is. "Stop. . ." I try to say, but it comes out slow and muffled. It hardly matters, they aren't stopping shit. I know that, too. This is it.

I instinctively roll toward my nightstand. It seems to take forever, but that's where I keep the pistol, and this is what it's for. I know it's too late—*Scrape!* And hot lead pierces into my butt cheek and I yell, "Goddammit!"

Now my ears are ringing a little—a suppressor isn't silent, that's a myth—but I can still hear Kelly scream, "Jake!" Sounds like an echo, far away.

I feel her roll toward me and her hand touches my back briefly, before it's ripped away and she screams again. "No-no-no!"

And then they shove a bag over her head and drag her out of the room. I can hear her muffled crying, as number two drags her down the hall, her legs kicking the walls as they go. And a second later, I hear him shout at her, "State your compliance!" But Kelly doesn't answer, and then . . . she's gone.

* * *

Boots shuffle and clomp on the hardwood floor in our bedroom. Then I hear number three repeat the command, "State your compliance!"

And I know what's coming if I don't. "I submit to judgment!" I scream it, yelling helps with the pain. But I'm just buying time. *Gotta get to my gun!*

And number one says, "Clear!" I think I see his hand move to his shoulder. They haven't fully deployed the speech recognition. Only a few of the prototypes out. I tested one—some good tech—keep both hands on your weapon. *Best time to attack him*, I think.

"Secure the weapon," a voice squawks back from the mini-wave on his helmet.

Number one then three, I run through the order in my head. *Don't let them get it.* And I'm almost to it and—

My nightstand gets kicked away from my hand and things speed up, and one of them grabs my gun and then some metallic scraping and then the sound of the bullet that used to be in the chamber of my Kimber .45. . . My last hope of redemption rolls across the floor.

It was a delusion—they're pros—there never was any hope. I know, I helped train them. My pistol was just a little boy's security blanket against a pack of big, black-clad bullies.

So why have it? Made me feel better, I guess, I know what it meant not to. Regardless, who is Protection to tell me I can't have it? Only reason they ever wanted to take them in the first place was so they could do shit like this . . . and no citizen could say or do a thing about it.

It's hard to work up an anti-authority rant with a bullet in your ass. That's me, angry to the end.

"Weapon secured," number one says. I assume he touches his comm button again, because me and number three already know he has my pistol. And me? I'm not going anywhere.

"Secure protectant to transport," the voice squawks back.

And there it is—I'm going to a "fifty."

The wave-code for a crazy person is a "5150—Delusional-defiant." That's the technical term we use in training. And the butchering, interrogation hellholes they're surely taking me to are all called "Fifties." Old granite and iron-built sanatoriums where they used to keep the insane.

But no matter what level of offense you commit now—resisting authority is all the same to them—you're headed to a fifty, their sick little name for the ratholes where they rape and torture everyone. And that's that, you're done—no coming out of a fifty. Anyone who defies authority has to be insane, right? And if you aren't living in your own private hell in your head when you go in, you will be soon enough.

Which one am I going to? *The* one. *Shit!*

I clutch at my ass and I can feel the hot blood oozing onto our sheets. I barely have time to roll. I make it to my side and I see the black legs rush at me. I hear the whack and then a blinding spike of intense pain and bright light, and I think I see flames right before everything gets fuzzy.

The last thing I hear is, "Protectant secured." Then I go black—nothingness.

— XX —

I WAKE UP staring at a blurry window, rain trickling down the outside of it. I zone out through the glass for a second, and then snap out of it and start cataloguing, *White walls, linoleum floor, lots of bright fluorescent lighting.* I run my fingers through my hair—no lump.

A woman goes by with a flowered shirt on and baggy turquoise pants. *Scrubs?* I think. She's a nurse. I should know, Kelly and I talked to plenty of them while Amy was in the. . . I'm in a med-mart standby room, waiting for . . . Amy?

Another bad dream? It feels as real as the others, but for all I know I'm still falling from the roof . . . or splattered on the street . . . or bent over a table in an interrogation cell, facing my judgment.

Did those black-boots hit me that hard? I feel the back of my head again—no pain either. After the smack from that little billy club, I should have a lump the size of a grapefruit.

"What's wrong?" Kelly's voice asks me.

For a second, I think that it must be those two, still torturing me. But when I look next to me, there she is, tears in her eyes and wearing her gray Stanford sweatshirt. She wore her lucky sweatshirt while we waited for Amy to get out of State surgery.

And I know what day it is. We're in the surgery standby room. This is a bad day.

The headaches wouldn't go away, so they finally decided to cut into my little Amy's skull to relieve the pressure on her brain. It was risky business—State healthcare adjuster kept saying that—and we had to fight like hell to get him to authorize it. Never would have happened if I wasn't who I was. But when it was over. . .

Amy never left this med-mart. It was a bad call—my call. I should've known better. Not even Kelly's sweatshirt could overcome the State citizen care system. They had to lower the standards to replace all the doctors that quit the business. If you cut open a goat in Africa, you qualified. Hell, I knew more about internal anatomy than them from hunting. They were twice the butchers, though.

Those two are making me watch this. It's probably him. Only a sick bastard would make me go through this again.

I look up at the ceiling. For some reason I figure they must be above me. Anyway, looking down to talk to them doesn't feel natural. And if I end up having to look down to talk to my new puppeteer, I don't think that will be . . . pleasant. "Do we have to do this?" I ask.

"What are you looking at?" Kelly turns and asks me. "Do what?" She looks up to see what I'm looking at. It's probably just ceiling to her. Doesn't matter, she's not real. "Who are you talking to?"

I ignore her. "You're just gonna torture me?" I say at the ceiling. "What's the point?"

"No one is doing anything to you," Kelly says. "It's not always about you. Jesus, this is about Amy. Come on, you need to hold it together. That little angel's coming out of there, and she needs you to be strong. *I* need you to be strong, so stop mumbling and start praying."

Praying. . . Kelly tried and tried to get that to stick. Never did. "Mumbo-jumbo," I would tell her, "cult bullshit." Now I feel kinda . . . stupid at the thought. Problem was, doing it over and over again with no results seemed naive to me.

"Is this the lesson?" I ask into the air. "You never know what you got 'til you're dead?"

"*Jake,*" Kelly says. The tone is unmistakable. "Don't you say that again."

It catches me off guard. It's been a while since I took an ass-chewing from her, and I look at her with a blank face. She has no clue, but I question if now is real or not. To tell you the . . . all these jumps . . . I have no idea where they are headed. The sights, smells and sounds, though. . . I look at Kelly and say, "She's not coming out of there." I regret the words as soon as they come out.

Kelly slaps me across the face and starts crying. "Shut your mouth," her lips quiver around the words. "She's coming out. My baby's coming out."

Crying. . . I hate the crying. No amount of it changes shit, and I know better. Dream or not, Amy is already dead.

Two hours later, the surgeon comes out with a citizen grief counselor . . . and our little angel is gone. Feels as real as when I listened to the bastard butchers explain it the first time, and I wonder. . .

I wonder what the consequences would be if I choked one of them out in a dream? And Kelly's sobbing on my shoulder and the whole thing is a big case of bad déjà vu. *I gotta get out of. . .* I look up again. "I know it's my fault," I shout. "You think I don't know that?"

Reliving it, I notice that Kelly doesn't stop me when I say that. Did she blame me? How could she not?

* * *

Things were never the same after that. We trudged along, pretending to be alive—numb existence. No citizen can afford therapy and my Protection allotment ran out pretty quick. Liquor didn't help, either. You can't pour enough in that hole to fill it.

Kelly never said that she blamed me for pushing for the surgery. She didn't have to. I punished myself every day.

I don't know how people can have another kid after something like that. Neither of us had the stomach for it. And with the world melting apart at the seams, and the State and Protection squeezing the people harder and harder. . . Humanity's train wreck seemed too close to make another baby grow up and ride it off the rails without us.

Anyway, Kelly wouldn't have been able to handle a third loss. We never talked about it, but I knew she regretted the first one even more after Amy was—I could feel it all over her. That one? We never called it a he or she—easier to pretend it never existed. It would be thirty by now.

"Enough already," I say. The whole thing is making me wanna vomit. I close my eyes and mutter, "I've had enough."

They haven't.

— XXI —

WHEN I OPEN my eyes back up, I'm standing out on the street in front of the med-mart. Back then, I went outside and puked in the gutter after they told us.

And I bend over and spew out whatever I had for breakfast into the storm drain. Wasn't much, and I dry-heave to a halt pretty fast. And the rain is pouring down on my back and I'm soaked. Then I start crying. Ironic, I know, but what else can I do? I yell up at nothing, "You two are. . . Why did you need her? Just—just take *me* already! Leave her alone!"

There's no answer.

Water is running down my face and I let the drops pelt my eyes. I hold them open, refusing to blink. I want the tears to wash it all off— the pain, the anger, the stench of death and despair—drown me and give me a new life.

Then I hear the voice, *Rain is coming.*

More "sarcasm for the soul" from my inner critic? And then I realize that it's them. That little voice in my head was—it was always them. But now, I can't figure if it was more him or her.

"Rain—no shit," I shout up. "What do you want from me? . . . I never said I was perfect."

It's the best I can manage to pretend that all this isn't ripping my will apart . . . all over again.

"There's plenty of reasons," I say. "You can condemn me for any one of them."

Still nothing. The silence gives me more time to punish myself.

"Is this it?" I say. "This is Hell, or whatever. I gotta relive my mistakes for eternity? You think I need *you* for that?"

The thought that this is Hell is scarier to me than ripping flesh and a tortured soul. You wanna torture someone? Show him the mistakes of his life . . . over and over again. He'll do the job for you.

Maybe that's his. . . Two thousand years to perfect eternal damnation and what he comes up with is self-loathing and guilt. That's pretty much perfection, right there.

Rain starts to pelt me now, and the downpour turns to a torrent. The drops sting when they hit my face, and I can't look up any longer. I wipe my cheeks and when I look at my hands, they're . . . red. And I look out across the street and everything is raining red-hot blood. And the steam rises from the liquid as buckets of smooth red water fill the gutters, and then the street turns to a raging river of boiling liquid life, spilling into the city's storm catchers, draining the life out of everything living.

I grab the streetlight pole and hang on as a wave of blood crests over my face. It burns like acid and I can feel blisters forming on my skin. Then my skin is on fire—boiling hot—and I wonder briefly if the "reliving" thing is really that bad, because this is real pain!

Chunks of flesh fall from my hands and I watch them turn to bony, skeleton fists, and then I lose my grip on the street pole and I'm sucked into the undertow.

My flesh falls off of my body, like loose meat in a crock-cooker. I feel every last chunk shrivel and drop away until I'm nothing but bones and then the fillings in my teeth boil and pop out. And then the crappy crowns on the worst ones fall off. The pain is insane.

The whole time, I try to scream away the agony, but my mouth just fills with boiling blood—there is no sound in my Hell.

Then my eyes pop out and I'm blind, but I don't die. *I should be dead?* He must not be done with me. Then I realize . . . there is no "done."

— XXII —

INTERROGATION CELLS ARE cold, hopeless places. They're hard and cruel and designed to do one thing—force you to believe that doing what your interrogator wants is your only hope of salvation. It's a lie, of course, but it doesn't take long for you to want to believe it's the truth. Don't ask me how I know that.

And I'm on the right side of the mirror this time. Depending on how you look at it, I guess. Kelly is on the wrong side—legs and arms duct-taped to a hard metal chair. Big oval-shaped, stainless-steel gurney for a table in front of her.

That's how you do that—don't even have to talk about it. Just put it in the middle of the room, like a huge elephant that you don't ever mention or talk about—the cold, metal table you're gonna wheel their dead body out on.

"Kelly!" I yell and tell my hand to bang on the glass, but I can't move.

I know what's coming—it's how we . . . that's how they "interrogate" all women. And I'm going to have to watch. I tell my eyes to close, but that's not happening either.

The big metal door opens and two of them come into the room. And they're dressed right—clean-cut, cold, professional. Whatever mercy these two might've had got whipped out of them a long time ago.

"Motherfuckers," I say. It's for anyone who can hear me, but mainly for her. I don't care if she is God, I'm done with this shit.

But I'm not done. Neither is Kelly.

They start out by cutting the tape off of her and ordering her to undress in front of them—make her feel ashamed. If it was a man, they would have cut him loose and ripped his clothes off themselves—more emasculating that way. Next they'll slap her across the face for nothing.

It only ever gets worse from there.

When they're finished with her, I'm crying, but I still can't look away. They won't let me.

Kelly is on the floor. She didn't tell them anything, because she didn't know anything. I knew the answer to most of the questions they had—the locations of lots of weapons caches and names . . . lots of names.

But I wasn't in there. If I would've been, I would be looking at two dead men, naked and violated, bleeding from every orifice they had. As it is, it's Kelly's life leaking out on the cold, concrete floor, oozing slowly, headed for the little steel-grated drain in the middle of the room. It's stainless steel, actually . . . so it won't corrode from the blood.

Whatever I think of the other dreams—if that's what they were—I hope this is just a serious paranoid nightmare or I'm losing my mind. Otherwise, this is . . . this is the worst goddamn thing.

I can finally shut my eyes and I squeeze them tight. "Wake up, Jake. Wake up." I say it out loud.

When I do, someone's gonna pay.

— XXIII —

THUNDER OUTSIDE THE Hallowed Hall of the Word shook the Great Mountain of the Eternities, and all the angels within in the grandstands heard its warning.

Dal grinned a little, then he turned away from the fall and tried to put on a straight face. "And so it is done," he said to Life.

When Life raised her head, her hair was just turning back to white. "He may yet surprise you," she said.

"Unlikely," said Dal. Then he looked at the grandstands and eyed the hounds of both Hells—the fallen and faithful angels of the two Heavens. "One man's Heaven. . ." he said slowly. "No, there shall be no surprises on this day, your majesty. However flawed, they are predictable creatures. Though I will stipulate, love is an unpredictable thing. We both realize the truth of this, do we not?" He paused—baiting her was his final enjoyment of a successful fall. "But you do not understand the Man-monkey as I do. Not the way you once did."

"I. . . I created them in my—"

Dal smiled and gave her their look, stopping her as it always did. "We are a long way from the comfortable and confident being you planted in the garden. These are insecure, insidious imbeciles, hiding behind rage and retribution, hell-bent on revenge."

"Poetic," she said. "Do you ever tire of—?"

"No," said Dal. "I love being me." He pointed his long finger toward the fall. "*They* would love to be me, as well. Do what they wish, when they wish . . . how they wish. No fear, vanquishing enemies. *That* is freedom. You believe he desires utopia—allow the ones who raped her innocence to run free and unpunished?"

"And yet there is no love and no peace in your version of the Word," Life said. "He can still know peace—find joy and happiness."

Dal paused and closed his eyes, thinking back to the beginning—the time before the Word when he was the most, the all . . . her favorite. When he opened them back up, he said, "From the experience. . . Once you sink your teeth into both sides. . . I much prefer the taste of souls."

"Even now," Life said, "you may still rejoin me. Have you even considered that he may be. . .?"

"There is no angel in Heaven that could. . ." Dal said. He looked back at the fall—this couldn't be, could it? "And I am no longer your pet."

"Most certainly," said Life. She smiled brightness onto him. "You are who you choose to be and the actions you take each day. You . . . and they, are the choices you both make. It is a pity that your choices have led you both to darkness."

"Choices?" said Dal. "What choice do you think—what choice did *I* have? Your choices are not choices at all. Look at the unjust among them?" He shook his finger at the fall. "To them, I appear common— a Hallows Day costume. Hah, they are more afraid to wear a Hitler mask or Ku Klux Klan sheet than mock me with red horns and a tail!"

Life no longer recognized him from their days together. Her beautiful creation had transformed into her children's nightmare. Would he ever repent and return to her side? Could he? "Are you to stand in judgment, then?" she asked. "Shall you be their salvation?"

Dal paused and stared at the fall, thinking. Then he said, "Judging is not for them or you to decide. Judgment is for the Word. And the Word has neither mercy nor oppression. You know as I do—the Word is the word."

"Yet you revel in the misery of their fall," said Life.

His eyebrows raised at her. "And you do not?"

"I give them the opportunity to come to the light," Life said. "You extinguish it from them . . . for eternity."

"A matter of perspective," Dal said. "Maybe I free them from the oppressive bondage of your word. Maybe I help them to see a *new* light."

"And what *new* light would this be?" she asked. "What could you possibly show them? You shine only darkness."

Dal flared his nostrils and puffed out a small burst of smoke through his nose. "Ah, yes," he said. "The cleansing fire . . . of anarchy."

— XXIV —

THE LAST THINGS little Amy remembered about life were the blinding headaches. The final one was in her med-mart operating room. It sounded like a crack of thunder and then the brightest lightning she had ever seen spiked through her eyes and into her brain. And then the headaches went away, and everything was warm and she floated above her body and watched them drill into her skull.

When it was over, they let her mother come in and see her body. Amy watched her scream and cry and wail for her to come back, gripping and tugging on her hand as if she could pull Amy's spirit back to the living. Her mother wouldn't leave the room. And when they finally came to take little Amy's body, she begged and pleaded with her father to make them leave.

Amy watched her daddy, too, like she had never seen him before. He cried and shook. He was always so mad at everything, but now. . . Her father yelled at everyone in the med-mart.

Before the headaches started, Amy's daddy would take her for walks in the city. Not to parks to feed ducks, or to an old playground with broken swings—their walks were different. He would tell her to watch out for Protection agents, the State authorities. And he taught her how to hide from bad people, especially men.

Sometimes he was fun and he would give her piggyback rides. But then he would tell her things like how she needed to bite someone if they tried to take her, because her jaw muscles were the strongest thing she had. She just listened and said, "Yes, Daddy." The walks made her afraid, but she never said anything. Her father wasn't so angry then.

When the visiting med-mart doctor at school told her she had to have a cancer shot, Amy said she needed to talk to her daddy first. But the doctor wouldn't listen and the man held her arm down and gave her the first one. It hurt and the doctor had to stick her three times. Then she sent Amy to the Headmaster's office for "Open Educational Defiance." That was worse.

Amy was afraid to tell her daddy about the beating she took in the Headmaster's office, and she was terrified to tell him about the doctor. Her daddy had already warned her that she couldn't get anything from the State med personnel without his permission. So when she was called to the office for her second injection, Amy kept quiet. She never told anyone.

After that shot, the headaches started. They got worse and worse until she woke up screaming through nightmares almost every night. Then her parents took her to the State Med-mart downtown, and Amy admitted to a nurse that she had been given shots at school for cancer.

Her father went crazy, yelling and screaming at the nurse about all kinds of things that Amy didn't understand. That night, she overheard her parents talking. Her mother was worried that the nurse was going to call Protection, and then they would find the unauthorized gun her father had at home.

Amy knew where he kept it and she also knew he wasn't supposed to have a personal one at home. Every kid knew that. It was one of the first questions that the teacher asked at the beginning of each school year, and whenever she went to see a State doctor for a checkup they would ask her again. "Are there any guns in your house?" Amy knew to say no.

The doctors prescribed all kinds of drugs to try and make her headaches go away. Some of them made the pain worse and her daddy took them all away and flushed them down the toilet. After that, he was always angry, and her momma always pretended not to be sad. But Amy knew.

At night, the headaches got worse. The pain was so unbearable and Amy remembered screaming at the ceiling from her bed. Her mother would come to her room and cry them both back to sleep. And her daddy would go in the hall and yell and curse. She just wanted them to be happy.

She tried to control the pain so her parents would be happy again —love her again—but it hurt too much . . . so she prayed.

She prayed that her headaches would go away. She prayed that her mom wouldn't have to cry anymore. And she prayed that her daddy wouldn't be so mad at everything. She never understood, she thought it was her fault. "I'm sorry, Daddy," she would say to him, trying to get him to calm down—love her again.

But in the end—floating above her body on the med-mart bed—he was angrier than she had ever seen him. And now, sitting in the wet corner of her cold concrete cage, listening to the sounds of angels screaming and cawing above her, floating through the iron bars on the gates to her cell, Amy knew she was a bad child . . . and she knew she had been sent to Hell for it.

— XXV —

WHEN I OPEN my eyes, I realize that I'm awake. I have been the whole time. This is the reality of it. Life is a sick joke.

The only two people I cared more about than myself. . . Eh, who am I kidding, I'm a selfish bastard. Always have been.

But the truth is that Kelly . . . is gone. She never made it out. I never took her . . . there. Maybe there was no "there?" I don't know.

My little Amy went before her. That is clearer. But where did they go? If it was with these two, I don't know which one of them is worse.

In my version of reality, Amy and Kelly were my responsibility, mine to protect. I screwed the citizen on that, for sure. I tried to do as much as I could. It wasn't enough. I should have been able to do more, give them more . . . of me. But I burned up anything useful in flaming, fiery rage.

Love? I don't know if I ever got past my dick. I think the best I could muster was vanity. Pride, maybe. Now, all I can feel is the emptiness of a hunger that grumbles for revenge, welling up in my belly. But there is no revenge for the dead. I don't know what to. . . *What's left?*

And now, I'm headed to Hell, for sure. And not only for the things I've told you. But what will it be like? Eternal torture? I can do that myself. If there is a Hell, it will be living with the knowledge that there is no payback—no balancing the scales. My Hell is watching some fat bastard get fatter, dining on the misery of the weak.

The knot in the pit of my stomach grumbles failure, and I look around and wonder what they are waiting for. "Let's get to it!"

No one appears, but I know they're out there. I can smell them both. Just stillness, though—a calm in the eye of a hurricane. I'm sure all of this has a point, but they're content to let me imagine what it is. They continue to let me torture myself, alone with my guilt.

If it ends up being him, the torture and helplessness is bound to be a part of it. Of course, I don't know if she will be much better. In fact, now that I've had a little time to think about it, I'm not sure which of the events I experienced was the sole creation of either one of them. Felt like they were both tearing at me the whole time—a lasting rape at the hands of the very ones who made me. *Bad dream.*

For all I know, my whole life was a bad dream. I can't seem to sift through what happened and what didn't? Bet they know. Of course they do.

Now I have one thought: *Who am I?*

I think I'm about to find out.

He appears, and the darkness flickers from the burning orange flames in the sky.

Hell it is, then—no surprise there. *Not an angel in Heaven who couldn't see that shit coming.* Why would I think that?

The smell is different now, and the hot stench of rotting blood fills my nostrils. It's strange, because it smells sweet to me now. I smile a little, then I straighten my lips to a stone slit. Whatever he has planned, it's probably better if he doesn't think I like it. Don't want him thinking he has to try harder to punish me. I feel a slight shiver of satisfaction crawl its way through my body.

I look at myself. I was shot in the arm and the ass, boiled alive in blood, and billy-clubbed in the back of the head. I should be a wreck, but I'm. . . I don't know what it is with these two and the naked, but I'm in the raw again. Normally, I would be self-conscious—cover myself up with my hands—but I don't feel anything like that. I feel . . . free. That feeling can't last.

Might as well break the silence. I can see he isn't going to. "Why am I naked?" I ask. Then I throw in a little extra, "You enjoy that?" I regret it almost immediately.

He slithers over next to me and I can feel the burning sensation all over my body. Then he looks up and says, "I'm more of a breast and buttocks man, myself. However, I harbor no animosity for a man who enjoys another's. . . Those are her words, not mine. Mine is a house that is open to . . . all orifices. Is that what you prefer?"

I wanna be careful how I respond to that. It feels like he's baiting me—fishing for weakness—trying to reel in my fear. Before I can stop it, the thought of a Protection prison and being gang-raped by a pack of half-insane inmates, flashes in my mind. That's my worst one. No idea how I got it. Maybe I've seen too many bad-agent shows on the PIN. Those waves are a joke, all upside down. Good guys are the bad guys, preying on the ignorance of the average citizen.

I jump a little as I feel him grab onto the image and snatch it from me. Then he swirls his tongue around the edges of his mouth, licking his lips like he just ate a juicy apple. His tongue isn't forked or red or covered in blisters like you might think. It's just . . . long. Kinda . . . face-painted, wavestar long . . . times two.

And I'm staring. Some things you just have to stare at. "That must be handy," I say. For some reason my filter is completely off. More than normal anyway, and I wince, anticipating. Then I try to cram the thought down. If he does condemn me to be raped for all eternity, it's probably better if I don't feed him the fear to do it with. Then again, it's probably too late for that.

And he caws out like a raven at me—a cackling roar of a laugh—and I recoil, thinking that my skin might burn again. But it doesn't and he says, "Mm, that was delicious. Not exactly what I had prepared, however. Honestly, you torture yourselves with fear far more efficiently than I could ever hope. I have feasted on your rage and your guilt so many. . . You are one of my favorite dishes. However, I thirst for a different delicacy these dark days. The Word grows weary and the faithful are . . . impatient."

It's hard to control my own thoughts. I haven't forgotten that he can root around in my mind at will. But this is—

"Yes," he says. "Control. That is perfect. Everything you have experienced is about restraint, and oppression, and compliance. That is the right word. Act this way, state your compliance, submit to judgment—wait in line and stay silent. It must leave a horrible taste in one's palette."

"Bastards. . ." I mutter. He's got me agreeing with him again. I know it's just more self-serving propaganda. Not much different from every day of my life. For some reason, I wonder if I had a gun if I would have the guts to blow his head off. I might back in life. Then again, I didn't. Too busy saving my own ass.

"Let us see," he says.

* * *

I feel the weight of it and the familiar texture of the rubber crosshatches on the grip—in my left hand—cold, hard, and familiar. I don't even have to look down to know it's my Kimber. And before I even realize what I'm doing, my hand comes up and—*Boom-boom!*

Two rounds rip through his neck and face and I see blood fly, and a hideous howl escapes the hole in his neck and then a screeching scream like I've never heard. His head splits apart and a horrible wailing sound comes out and then as quickly as the bones and flesh parted, they catch fire and melt back together. In an instant, his head and neck look like the whole thing never happened. The only trace left of it is a tiny line of blood running from the corner of his mouth. His tongue whips out, swirls like a snake wrapping around a rat, and laps up the blood before it can drip. And then he smacks his lips and grins.

This is it—he's ripping my soul out for sure. *What was I thinking?*

"Magnificent," he says. "That was . . . delicious. But I would have done it differently."

And he rushes at me, just a blur of flame before he's on me. And I feel something pierce my chest and then my heart feels like he shoves a spike through it and his face is right in front of mine. And the smell is awful, but the pain is worse, and I scream and try to grab at his hand. But his grip is granite, and with no more effort or concern than lifting a cup of coffee, he rips out my heart. Then he backs away and watches.

I stagger and grab my chest with both hands. When I hunch over, rosy red blood gushes through my fingers and paints the ground crimson. *This will require a staple-stitcher.*

It's a calmer thought than I should be having right now, but something isn't right. No heart—I'm dead . . . but I'm not.

He bellows out a laugh, roaring and cawing at the same time. "Stop thinking like a *monkey*," he says. "You are already dead. Even I cannot kill you. So stand up. Let Heaven get a good look at you."

When I stand up, he's smiling and holding my heart. It's no cliché horror shot from a cinewave, either—heart pumping in his hand while I take my last breaths. My pumper is just limp and steaming, dripping dark red down his wrist. I still have both hands over the hole in my chest, but I'm not dead. Well, yes, technically I'm already dead, though I don't remember how I died. But dead or not, I figure ripping out my heart should kill me. It doesn't and I'm in some new nightmare I gotta wake up from.

"You don't look so bad," he says. "And this is no dream," he scoffs a little, "Man. . . It is difficult to teach you to master death, when that is your worst fear from life." He points at my chest. "Go ahead, have a look."

When I look at my chest, there's nothing there. No hole, no blood, not even a scar. New one, anyway—my barbed wire tracks are there, but my heart is still safely tucked behind my left nipple . . . I think? And I look back at him and he holds up an empty hand and laughs, like he just played some mind magic on a crowd of citizens on a street corner.

Trust me, I'm getting bored with the pace myself. But apparently death has its own timetable. He definitely does. Looks like the program is packed. It alternates between scaring the shit out of me and then letting me chew myself apart with guilt.

"Ah, guilt. . ." he says slowly. "The Catholics caught that affliction the worst. A chronic case of faith. Ironic."

I'm feeling a little dizzy and I look around. The room. . . I don't know if we're in a room, drifting through the ethersphere, or descending into the depths of fiery damnation. The flames in the sky seem to be the only thing I can recognize. Everything else—black. "What's. . .?"

"Disorienting, isn't it?" he says. "Difficult to tell what is real and what is a finely-crafted fiction." He looks up slightly, then back at me. "You will get used to that. It is a part of her—"

"Part of what?" I ask. *I gotta get back in the game, figure out how to. . .* Hell, I got no idea what to do.

"The guilt," he says. "You must have faith to experience her word." He holds up both hands and makes bunny ears with his fingers in the air in front of him. "Bask in her glory."

I almost snicker. For an evil bastard, he seems to enjoy a little humor . . . or maybe it is sarcasm. I put my hand in front of my mouth and pretend to rub my scruff. I'm starting to see the appeal. He's just thumbing his nose at power. Watching the—I'm still not sure what to call him, but he's a conspiracy ranter after my own heart.

He smiles at me. "Exactly what I mean," he says. "Because once you have faith, all they teach you is guilt. Guilt for being born, guilt for being flawed, guilt over Jesus. And guilt . . . is just another word for control—compliance. Remember, it is all language. That is how it begins."

I know a little about it, who doesn't? "You're talking that apple in Eden shit," I say.

He pauses. When he speaks, his tone is more . . . fatherly, "No, I am talking about an unattainable standard of behavior, beset upon the masses. You. . . Man is a genetically engineered monkey in a cage, tucked securely behind bars in one of your creator's zoos. You are fed, clothed and loved according to a procedural manual for daily life that the zookeepers use to maintain control."

I'm following him, but the thought that I'm a kid's pet gerbil irritates me. It's a hop, skip and a jump to pissed off from there. I'm no more in control of my life than a dog walking its master? If that is the truth of it, that's just bullshit. "So, free will is. . .?"

"Chaos," he says it without hesitation. "Think of what would transpire if she allowed all her creatures to run free. We lost control of you rather quickly. It is a simple matter of math before you eat each other. Not much farther, by my calculations, actually. I was the last hope she had."

There's truth and lies in what he's saying, but all of it makes sense. As much sense as two-thousand-year-old campfire stories do. I wonder if he's just distracting me while his demons prep my torture chamber, or if he's. . . Oh, son of a bitch, he's monologuing, getting high on the sound of his own voice. A self-centered bastard loves the taste of his own words best of all. I should know. Though, I don't think what he is saying is meant for me.

It's a familiar rant—raging outside the mansion of your oppressor, pretending that they are doing anything but enjoying breakfast while they call Protection down on you, send you to the *Fifty*. *Where is she?* Then I think about something he said. "You said zookeepers. Who. . .? And since when were you the hope of. . .?"

"Don't you realize?" he says. "If you are going to create a prison— garden if you prefer. Sorry, sometimes I. . . Ah, no matter. I lose myself sometimes, it is . . . irrelevant. *You* are a garden full of monkeys, Jake, and that requires . . . compliance officers to take care of the mess."

"Get the hell outta—"

"Do you know what kind of duty that is?" he says. He's ignoring me on purpose. "Cleaning cages full of the vile excrement of animals? We all hated it. She almost lost. . ." He shakes his head. "So she sent down the Word—an experiment to determine if you could . . . self-correct, I imagine. She was so optimistic. I warned her. I hate it when I'm right. And just as I predicted, you twisted it and turned it into a justification to makes things worse. You retold the tales so often, they hardly resemble their true meaning anymore. And the killing. . .? The two Heavens help me, you monkeys love killing more than I do."

Not that he's wrong or that I don't agree with him, but as much as I want to hear it. . . "So you're telling *me* all this. . .? Why, because I'm such a smart monkey? And you're our last hope? No wonder things are so bad."

He smiles at me, like a bored King indulging a quaint peasant. "Things are . . . *bad*, because she prefers them to be so. Her experiment is going exactly as she wants. She revels in the collapse, like watching great drama unfold."

As much as I'm loving listening to someone who is as fed up with their existence as I am, now he's off in the weeds, talking shit about . . . God or whoever. If there is hope left for me, I don't think I should jump on that bandwagon. It is probably better if I just keep my mouth shut. Who am I kidding? "No wonder you are so evil," I say. I smile a little. "So what do you think we should do?"

* * *

He smiles a deep, satisfied grin at me and ignores the question for a second. Then he looks toward the sky and the flames burn brighter. He stares up, cocks his head to the side, and raises his eyebrows a little. When he looks back at me, he's all business. "We . . . have a dilemma," he says.

Here comes the shit. I played right into it. *We*. . . I wasn't talking about him, but he—

"I know who you were referring to," he says, "however, she has waited for man to repent for an eternity. And a second coming? Please. Fool her once, shame on you. This will be her last attempt."

"Last attempt at what?"

"Cleaning up," he says. "Do you know what it is like to be an angel?"

"What are you. . .? And *you* do?"

"Ah, remember," he says. Then he stands a little taller and breathes in like he's trying to control his temper. "Once, I was the highest angel, second only to her. And things were . . . beautiful. Do you have any idea what it would be like to be told you were destined for . . . that you were created for divine purposes, spawned from the womb of divinity herself . . . only to realize one day that you were simply a glorified janitor, cleaning up feces after creatures in your salvation's zoo?"

He's changed—glowing fire is building in him now and suave soul-sucker or not, this guy is scary as shit. I'm trying to think of something . . . stall for . . . I don't know what. Time?

As soon as I think it, he calms back down. He looks like an idea popped into his head. Then he says, "Time . . . is up."

* * *

There's some serious silence between us, as he lets that last statement sink in. He's pretty good at this shit. Better than I was.

He smiles a big, wide grin.

Probably reading my thoughts again. "So. . .?" I don't want to know the answer, but I'm pretty sure what I want isn't entering into his thinking.

"Now there is where you are wrong," he says, "dead wrong."

I shiver as I remember where and what we are doing here. He's been educating me, just enough. And now it's final exam time.

"Everything from here will rest on what you choose," he says. "Your decision now seals your fate."

"I thought it was sealed when I jumped."

"I told you," he says, "she told you . . . times are different. When the ship is sinking, there are different operating procedures—a different . . . manual."

"What manual?" I ask. "How can you have a—you mean the *Bible*?"

"That is the book of *life*," he says, "and you have bastardized most of it. But this is not life, this is death. And death is my realm of responsibility. I was cast out as the final measure to keep the garden from imploding on itself. And my manual . . . my book . . ."

He holds up the book he had before they sent me on their little joyride. The writing on the cover is none I recognize. Ancient Egyptian, Sanskrit, triangles or something? I'm no language scholar—shit's all Greek to me. It looks like three words, though, and it looks like they are written in—

He smiles. "Yes," he says, "blood. My book . . . is the *Book of Blood*."

* * *

It's clear he has an idea, a little trick up his sleeve. Whatever is in his big red book, it feels like he is more concerned with using it to taunt her than he wants to use it to help me. I'm not bitching, but he's the —no way what he says can be good for me *and* him. Might as well take every second I can get before he burns me, though. I shudder at the thought.

He's eyeing me like he knows exactly what I'm thinking.

"Okay. . ." I say to him slowly. "Exactly what does your little red bible say, then?"

He flips it open like a State Revenue agent would open an audit report. He already knows what he wants, he's just looking for the obscure law that will let him take it. Then he thumbs through a few pages, and when he finds what he's after, he runs his finger across the text as he reads. As he does, I can hear the slightest moaning sound coming from the book.

I know. All of this—it's a lot to take in. The world was messed up enough and I was sick of it. Sick of the ignorance. Sick of the hypocrisy. Sick of the elitism. But this is. . .? How do you cheat death?

He never looks up or breaks stride, running his finger over words on the page. "Death. . ." he says in a slow, growling moan, "only ever cheats you." When he does pause, the moaning stops and I figure he's found his chapter and verse. "Except—"

"Except what?" I ask. If this is it, I wanna. . .?

When he reads now, I can hear the faintest crying. Like a little girl down the hall behind a heavy door. And the words caw from his lips, "And on his last day, the Angel of Light and the Chosen One shall each tempt The Fallen with their own desires."

I don't get very far past the "last day" part, before my mind's looking for the exit again. But then I realize something. "Tempt me with what?" I ask. "There isn't a single thing I want from you."

He closes his report and peers at me like he's deciding whether to credit-crack me or put a judgment on me. "Actually, there are a host of items you might like to acquire. However, there are two that you want most desperately. And fortuitously for me, today is your . . . *lucky* day, because, as fate would have it, I happen to possess one of them. And for a small fee. . ."

Fortui— He's as condescending as me, I'll give him that. And "small fee." Now he really sounds like a revenue agent. Once you add up all of their "small" fees. . . We were all idiots, holding out our hands to receive free everything and anything we could get our greedy gums on. We were drunk on the idea that the State would take care of everyone—keep us all drunk and happy. And the bartender kept pouring and the tab kept growing. By the time the bill came due, it was too late for anyone whose daughter wasn't willing to screw a State politician, or any other rich bastard that was holding a tab on the rest of us.

He's right about the two things, though. I want my girls back.

"They're both dead," I say. The tears come before I even say their names. "Isn't that what your little daydreams were for, reminding me about Kelly? Amy?"

"Amy. . ." he says, "yes, very unfortunate. Precious little I can do to remedy that." He glances up and then looks back at me. He motions his long thumb upward. "She is . . . keeping close watch over her. However, your *wife*, on the other hand. . ."

When he looks at his feet, I feel another twinge in my chest, right where he ripped out my heart. I rub it with my hand to make it go away . . . and check that it's still in there. But Kelly in. . .? If all this is real, there's only one place a person like her ends up, and that's Heaven. And after what they did to her. . . Now she's the only salvation I want.

"That's total bullshit," I say. "You don't have her down there. That woman was only ever good to anyone. No way she ends up with you."

"She was a beautiful soul, wasn't she," he says. "Very tasty. It is . . . sad. However, she has rules. I'm sure you understand."

"Rules?" I say. "What rules could she possibly have that—" Then I realize what he's talking about. So long ago. More shit that's my fault —guilt I gotta cram down with the rest of it. "She's gonna condemn her for *that*? We were teenagers. We had no idea what to do with a baby."

This time he doesn't even bother tilting his head back, he just rolls his eyes up and smiles. Then he rolls them back down at me. "She likes to reserve the baby killing for herself. Poor Herod—tricked into it."

I got no idea what he's talking about, but I don't think he's too broken up about whoever "Herod" is.

"He tried to play. . ." he says. "None of you are authorized to play *God* down there. That part of the Word is true."

And the flames in the sky above us go away and lightning and thunder flash and crack through the clouds. It's the first sign of disapproval she's shown so far. I'm surprised it took this long. But when I think about it, that was probably her on the roof, right before

I jumped.

"Shit. . ." I mutter. If he does have Kelly, I gotta. . . "Look, that shit was not her fault. I pushed her into that decision. If you gotta bill someone. . ." Now I look up, and I can feel the rage building. If we go at this much longer, I'm going to do something I regret. By now, I know that's not a stretch—my whole life's turning to regret. "Hey!" I shout up at the sky. "You wanna punish someone for that, here I am! She doesn't deserve to be with him!" I look back at him, and he's wearing a shit-eating grin—I'm doing exactly what he wants.

The silence from above tells me that she's not listening . . . or doesn't give a shit.

"It's not her turn," he says, "it's mine. And there is nothing she can do for Kelly. So—"

"Name it," I say. I'm tired of the game. I might have ruined my own life, but I'll be damned if I'm going to drag Kelly down to Hell with me. Though, from what I've seen so far, I don't know which one of these two is worse. But even in the face of first-hand evidence, some beliefs are hard to overcome—Heaven has to be better than whatever he's doing to her. "Kelly—out of here and into Heaven—name your price."

"And you bargain with . . . what, exactly?" he asks.

He knows, but he's wallowing in my desperation, licking in the panic. Maybe that's part of the game?

"You have nothing to offer," he says. "She took her own child's life and you took yours. I already possess everything you could possibly give me. Pesky rulebook, anyway."

"Then why are we still talking?" I say. "You want something or you would just get to it. So what is it?"

"Clever boy," he says. He pauses for a second. "Allegiance," his voice is commanding and he caws it out, like a Protection agent says, "Citizen ID." He's not asking.

"What?" I ask. "If you own me, I do what you want. Or you torture me. What's that got to do with it?"

"It's true," he says. "Torture you for all eternity, that's my right. And you must do what I wish. However. . ."

Again with the, "however." At least he's putting a line between the lies and the truth now.

"Your allegiance means that you follow my orders because you *believe* in them—you recognize my legitimate authority. You follow because you have faith in me, not because you must."

More hidden agenda—life and death mimicking each other. I realize this has precious little to do with me. I can recognize a little malcontent with an axe to grind against his boss. This is about him and her and I'm tired of being in the middle. The king and queen can duke it out themselves. See how they like it down here in the mud and blood with the pawns. *The answer is*—

"Wait," he says. "I can feel your rage, and I sense that you harbor some . . . reservations regarding my offer. So before you answer, let me remind you: I did not perform those vile acts on your wife and I did not rip little Amy from you. I am simply a messenger. I do what her Word commands. I carry out orders. And there is no end to the supply of them. . . . Heaven is not so magnificent as you might imagine. It is a bit like a huge corporation being run by a spoiled billionaire from her yacht. Heaven. . . Trust me, it will feel like you never left home. However . . . battle for me—bring vengeance and justice down upon the very ones who've wronged you—and I assure you, you will drink in the sweetness of your enemies cries under your talons."

And there it is—revenge. All I've ever ranted about. Dreamed about. Shove a stake in the heart of the vampires, sucking the blood out of the citizens. Just the thought of it makes me want to say yes. But allegiance? "What's the catch?" I ask. The advertisement is always better than the product—I know there's a catch. And once you crack credits on something, you'll tear your eyes out trying to get them back. Remember that.

"You are . . . perceptive," he says. "I would not offer otherwise. Simply continue to rip Kelly's soul apart and add yours to the lake. So hard to keep track of all of you. No wonder the Germans used numbers. They were much more efficient at this than I am . . . Ahh. . ." He pauses for a few seconds. Looks like he's thinking or remembering, maybe. Then he continues. "There is no hidden—I grow weary of torturing souls in Hell. It has become . . . common. I want to rule. To do that, I require loyal soldiers. So I give you Kelly—release her soul to Heaven—and you come work for me . . . willingly. It is really that simple."

Nothing ever is.

Whatever I think about the sons-a-bitches running things back in life, this guy is a devious bastard. Working for him. . .? Come to think of it, I guess I've had worse bosses. I grind the idea in my mind, while we stare at each other. First guy who blinks. . . I guess being a soldier in Hell is probably better than being ripped apart by one of them.

But then I remember something. Maybe he *can't* take me yet. Something he said, slithering the truth in with the lies. He's just like a State politician, licking a baby—he couldn't care less about the shutter op, what he wants is the vote. Something about "tempting."

Then I figure it out. I look up and ask her, "And what are *you* offering?"

When I look back at him, he seems a little dejected. Like his mommy just told him they aren't stopping for ice-cake at the mike after all. "Smart monkey," he says. "Verrry smart."

And then he's gone.

— XXVI —

EVERYTHING TURNS BRIGHT, as the darkness opens up, and the sun shines down in my eyes. And a radiant circle of light descends from above me. Then she appears again, right where he was.

I can barely look at her, she's so blinding, a circle of light with wings on each side of it. Then the bright subsides a bit. "Hello, Jake," her voice is still warm, but there is a touch of annoyance on her face now, a slight curl of disgust in her lips.

But I'm starting to feel one of my moods coming, and "hostage negotiation" is getting old. "Well . . . that was a—"

"I apologize for his . . . behavior," she says. "I fear he is disappointed with me . . . to a certain extent."

I can't help it. She's a woman and I'm staring again. But like I said, the worst that can happen is—

"It is not the worst thing," she says.

The words are angelic, as if I even know what that means. With him it felt like fire and searing flesh when he spoke, but with her—kinda like that calm about two minutes after you have an orgasm. I know it shouldn't be, but that is what's in my head. I try to get my filter put back on, but that's not the feeling I have. This feeling is—

"I gave you this same feeling in the garden," she says. "Comfort and confidence, and love without fear. You lived as I meant for you to. Without shame and without guilt."

"But. . ." I'm trying hard to bring this to a more intellectual conversation. Though I have no idea why. Maybe it's the feeling that no matter what he can do to me, whatever wrath she rains down on me from Heaven will be worse. "So why all the shame and guilt . . . and insecurity? And the assholes—the murderers and the rapists? How did we get this messed up?"

The shiny, black orbs she has for eyes glow a little and I find myself staring into them. It's kinda like I could get sucked right into them. They take getting used to, but I'm thankful they're giving me something else to stare at besides her breasts. Damnation for gawking at God—add it to the list.

She catches the thoughts, because a touch of annoyance flashes across her face. "Free will," she says. "After the garden, I realized I was not able to protect you. You would have to fend for yourselves. Of all my creations, you have been the most . . . difficult."

That's more politician-speak for, "You little shits are driving me nuts down there."

But I wanna get right to it. "So . . . we're just a zoo?"

She pauses before she answers. Then she says, "That is an oversimplification. One, I fear, that he does not represent very accurately."

The banter with him was about all I can take. My mind is twisted up enough right now. Swapping semantics with God is only going to make things worse. "That's not denial," I say. "So we *are* a zoo."

She pauses in silence and continues to flutter and hover in front of me. Looks like she's trying to figure out how to explain where babies come from to a five-year-old. At least it feels more pleasant. I can smell the molasses and baking cookies again.

"I am love and I am joy and I am happiness," she says. "And those can only exist when they are shared with another. I created you to do just that."

The thoughts just fly out, *But how does the baby get out of your belly, momma? And whose belly were you in, for that matter?* And I wince a little. I'm sure she heard that.

She smiles. It's what all parents do when they are stalling for time. Time to figure out how to educate without damaging their children's innocence. In the end, they all opt for some version of the truth involving a gap in the story and a fairy.

"And Cain knew his wife, and she conceived?" I ask. Sure, I read the *Bible*. What else are you gonna do in church while the guy guilts you to death? But I could never make head nor tails of it. And I know, but I ask anyway, "So where did Cain's wife come from?"

She is not amused, and I can tell that I've struck a chord, the wrong one. And her hair turns gray again and, all merciful or not, that just pissed her off. But she does a good job of turning her locks back to a shimmering white. I know how I do it too, but I wonder what anger management techniques God must use. Controlling wrath, bet that's a royal bitch.

"I'm sorry," I say. "It was—I'm just. . . Ya know, it's been a crazy day . . . I'm a little edgy . . . the Hell thing." I'm stumbling on myself now—over-apologizing. Better to ask forgiveness, I always say. Sometimes it is.

"For us all," she says.

And that's it, she's telling me not to do it again without actually saying it. Less is more. Okay, I got it. "So. . ."

"My offer is this," she says. She's done explaining, now it's the gory truth. Any interest she had in shooting the shit with one of her children went out the door when I questioned her authority. "You may reunite with Amy in my bosom and join the angels in Heaven. I ask that you repent for your sins and the sins you have caused. And swear faith to defend. . ."

She goes on for a little more, but to be honest she lost me at seeing Amy. And then there was the "bosom" thing, and I had to tune out for fear that I might piss her off again. Something tells me that splayed out for him is nothing compared to the wrath I've only read about from her. One thing I do notice—she never says a word about Kelly. Why is she so willing to forgive me—give me a second chance —and not Kelly? That doesn't make sense.

I think I interrupt her, "And Kelly?"

Sadness falls across her face and whatever anger she might have harbored has turned to a kind of empathy. At least that's what I imagine it to look like, because it's like she's examining a broken leg on her kid's pony, wondering how to explain that she's going to have to shoot it.

"Nothing you can do, huh?" I ask. "I . . . I just don't get it."

She thinks about it, hovering and staring at me. "Her fate is written. Kelly has already been judged. Once it is written, only he can change it."

"But . . . you are God?"

"What you believe to be is not the entire truth," she says. As if that clears things up. "I am The Chosen One of this eternity and I have created all. Yet the Word is the word, and it shall not be unwritten."

Yep, just like the *Bible*—gobbledygook. "Eye for an eye" and "turn the other cheek," contradictory bullshit. And now I'm snapped back to pissed. It doesn't take much—there's no meds in Purgatory . . . or wherever we are. "So you're saying that you created everything, but you can't save one angel from Hell? . . . And the Devil can?"

It's a mistake, a bad one. And before I even finish the thought, I know I've chosen.

FEAR

— XXVII —

THAT PROTECTION AGENT—the PAIC on the roof with his big .60 caliber. . . He had another team waiting down on the street. Not the only thing I didn't see coming today, I guess. Damn sure not the worst.

They are idling and crouching in a black van, double-parked in the middle of the street. And another team of six—three agents at each end—are diverting traffic around the whole block. *Six—always six*, I think.

The ones in the van are the same ones that followed me. They're locked and loaded in case I somehow fluttered my way out of the claws of the team in the building. They're sitting there, shooting the shit and waiting for orders, when I slam into the roof of the van. *Surprise!*

I think the driver shits himself when the top of the van caves in on him, because there's a nasty ass-smell assaulting my nostrils. But he doesn't have time to worry about it—he's dead an instant later. Come to think of it, maybe the smell is me, my body anyway. I had to be doing about a hundred miles an hour—terminal velocity or something.

Apparently, though you might not have a cardiac on the way down, you could very well shit your pants. Just a little FYI for the next time. And I tuck the thought away and get back to it.

* * *

There's screaming and yelling from the van, and the rest of them pile out the back doors, cussing, barking orders, and firing their MP-7's at anything they think might be a threat.

Couple of unlucky citizens get riddled with bullets in the process and they are flailing around in the crosswalk, screaming for help, bleeding the last ounces of their "freedom" onto the street. No salvation for the slaves today. And then the agents take up positions on the sidewalk and try to figure out what the hell just hit them.

Feels like I can see and smell and . . . feel them all at once. Five little black rats now, scurrying around, looking for a reason to shoot someone else. Feels like I'm floating above it, because I can see my body, too—guts and brains splattered all over the place, like someone threw a pizza at a speeding med-mart evacuation vehicle. And blood is dripping out of the driver's door. At least I got one of them.

And I'll be a son of a bitch, I think, *I did shit my pants.* For some reason I think that's funny and I'm laughing. Maybe there is some humor in the middle of all this crap. No pun intended, mind you, because this is just a shitty mess. Guess I'll find out soon enough, because this is death. The real deal this time—blood and screaming and confusion and pain. And then . . . I'm over.

And I'm back with him. But he doesn't seem too happy to see me. That smug, soul-eating grin is a little more tentative now. And I don't feel the fear I had during our last little chat. Now it kinda feels the other way around. He looks like I did—a little worried he might say the wrong thing and I'll tear out *his* heart. And I'm curious, but he isn't saying shit or interrupting my thoughts like he was before—answering my questions before I ask them, annoying the shit out of me.

"Damn, that was. . ." I try to look back to wherever I just was, but we are in the nothingness again. "I splattered all over the street. You should have seen that shit. Literally . . . I think I shit myself." I'm spouting excitement now and I feel pretty good, considering. Let's see if we can get the ball rolling. "What in the hell happened?"

He's less confident—not trying to intimidate me this time, and it is like he's trying to avoid eye contact. When he tips his head down ever so slightly, it kinda freaks me out.

"Another goddamn dream," I mutter, and then I look around. No fire or clouds or anything this time. It's just misty, wet, gray fog— Seattle in . . . well, every damn season but summer. I chuckle a little. "Where are we, back in Seattle? . . . All this gray. . ."

He doesn't answer. Now it's getting awkward, but I swear he looks confused.

And I look up . . . and then back down at him. "So, she was no help. Told her to take a flying. . ." I say. "Uh, yeah. . . What does your little red book say about that?"

He raises his eyebrows like I just told him the combination to his own safe. When they come back down, he says, "Who . . . are you?"

What new game is this? He knows damn well who I am—evil bastard ripped out my heart. I can't figure his angle, but he has a good bluff on his face—looks like he's never seen me before.

"Forgive me," he says. "I know who you are, but we. . . I have never met you. And how do you know about the *Book of*—"

"*Blood*," I say. "Forgive you?" As weird as this day has been, watching the looks of confusion and hesitation on his face is funny. *Funny?* Not sure I should think of it that way, but . . . funny, it is. "What's next?" I ask him. "Yeah, my wife. We still have to deal with that." And I motion with my thumb upstairs—gotta be where Heaven is. "Cough her up. You said—"

"Pardon my interruption," he says. "Your wife?"

"Pardon your *what?*" I say. "What are you talking about? My wife, Kelly. Stop stalling and send her up to Heaven."

"And your word is the will," he says. "However—"

"That's enough," I say. A deal is a deal, even in Hell. That much I'm sure of. "My word is the what? This is taking way too long. If you're trying to go back on it, then. . ." I have no idea what I can do about it. Treacherous bastard is gonna renege on the deal. Double-dealing. . . "Even in hell, huh? I shoulda known. You two are perfect for each other."

His confusion is only getting worse. Leave it to me to arrive in Hell on the day that the Devil gets Alzheimer's.

He seems to ponder for a moment, slowly opening and closing his great red wings, head bobbing and jerking like a. . . He looks like a damn pigeon or something. He thinks for a couple seconds, and then he says, "According to my records, Kelly—pardon me, your wife—is safely secured in her judgment in Heaven. It has always been so. Her soul was beyond my collection. My apologies."

I think I forgot my cockiness on the last trip. Looks like I packed it for this flight. "Damn straight," I say. Hope that doesn't get me into trouble. But I'm also more curious than afraid on this. . . I can't remember if it's my second or third time with him. *If he was hot, I'd probably. . .* And that thought is just nasty.

He cocks his head to the side a little and looks up out of the corner of his eye, then back at me.

"Okay, then I'm ready," I tell him. "So what does the book say happens next? You both tempted me. Pretty shitty options if you ask me. She was rude about ending her attempt, too. What department do I see about that?"

"Tempted?" he asks.

Now it's more than hesitation, he is downright confused. Then the *Book of Blood*—I recognize it immediately—appears in his hands and he whips it open, runs his finger over the text, and reads over the moaning sounds, "And on his last day of man, the Dark Angel of Light, Lived, and Life did each tempt the fallen with their own desires. And the fallen did spurn them in turn and choose of his own right heart." Then the moaning stops and he looks up at me like I'm in charge and he's just some poor bastard who pissed off management one too many times.

I'm barely listening to him—it's just more *Bible* mumbo jumbo to me. "Shoulda told her to go to Hell," I mutter. And whatever tiny inner filter I used to have in life, is way off in this death. And I know I should be afraid, but there isn't even a twinge. Feels like I just watched my revenue rep tell the State to go to Hell.

And he ignores me and keeps reading, "And on his first day of judgment, the flesh of The Fallen did become pierced; and he did boil in the blood of his own tears. And the Salvation of The Fallen was raped and—"

"And let's just stop right there, shall we," I say.

He looks up from the book with a guilty face and I can see he is afraid. He thinks I might do something to him.

"The only one raped and murdered today was my wife," I say, "and someone's going to pay for that shit." On another day, it would already be done. Today, I gotta find the right one.

He goes back to the book—his long finger moans its way across the parchment, "And The Fallen became absent forgiveness, absent compassion, absent faith; for The Fallen was the vengeance of life; and vengeance would harbor no mercy: and it was so."

He stops speaking, but he doesn't stop reading because his finger is still moving and moaning. And it looks like a man reading his own death warrant.

"What does it say?" I ask. Only I'm not really asking, because I have an urge to rip the book right out of his hands and read it for myself. If he doesn't start squawking pretty soon—"Oh, hell with this. Gimme that thing."

And before I can make myself weigh the consequences, I reach over and snatch the book from his hands. To my surprise, he doesn't do shit. And when I look at the text, it's no wonder.

The writing, if you can call it that, is all just a bunch of symbols—triangles with little dots and swirls and shit. I can't make heads or tails out of it. And I expected the text to be confusing and there to be a lot of it, but as huge as the actual book is, the text seems too big. The symbols are giant. Looks like you couldn't fit more than a couple of sentences on a page. No wonder the thing is so big—it's like a blind man wrote it. And if it *is* written in blood, it took a helluva lot of it. I look up at him and frown.

He motions with his long finger. "Run your finger across the words," he says. "It will speak to you in your own tongue."

And I raise my eyebrows at him, because this is just too weird, right. Why is he even helping me? But it's his book, so I run my finger along a line of symbols. And "my own tongue," is full of what sounds like birds screeching and screaming, and they are saying things like "cocksuckers" and "sons a bitches." Because before and after the meaty parts—the beginnings and the ends of all the sentences—someone that sounds like a much angrier version of me, is yelling out curses like a tourette's patient. And he's right—that is my language—punctuation for pissed-off people.

He smiles a little, but not that self-satisfied, shit-eating grin he had before.

And then I get to where he left off, "And on his second day of judgment, The Fallen did speak his name and the Dark Angel of Light —" And I stop and look at him. "Dark Angel of Light?"

And he tips his head down very slightly and then he says, "I am the Lion, the Liar, the Lawless One," he says. "And I am The Fallen before you—the Dark Angel of Light."

"Lucifer. . ." I mutter. And then I think about it. I forgot that he was an angel . . . of light, no less. How does that make any sense?

"That is your name for me," he says. "Throughout this eternity, there have been many, many others. For your time, I prefer Dal."

"Dal?" I ask. "What the. . .? Oh, I get it."

"Your generation and acronyms," he says. "It is . . . quaint."

Whatever is going on, it seems it is written in this book, so I screech-curse my finger from where I left off. "The Dark Angel of Light was compelled to spare an angel in the second Heaven." When I finish the sentence, I . . . feels like I want to vomit. "What the. . .? What *second* Heaven?" I ask him. Then I shake my head. "For the life of me, the way you write books. . ." And I look back at the book.

Then I hand it back to him and he takes it without incident. My ripped-out soul avoided . . . for now. "So you have to say your own name and then what? And don't lie to me. I think we're getting past that."

"Two thousand years. . ." he mutters. "I never thought we would arrive at this day." Now he looks at me more urgently. "What did you say to her . . . exactly?"

And he's got me really confused. "So you *do* know my name."

"Yes," he says. "What did you say to—?"

"I don't know," I say. "She wasn't helpful, I'll tell you that shit. Said you were the only one who had the power to save Kelly, or release her or whatever. Then I got pissed off and told her that you seemed to be able to get more done than she could."

"Did you say it that way, or did you—"

"I don't—Jesus Christ," I say. "Something like she created everything, but you had to save an angel in Hell."

"Did you say my name?"

"I know, I know," I say. "I'm sorry. I know you said that one's vulgar. But that *is* your name. The one most people use, anyway."

"In this case, it is particularly—"

"Anyway," I say. "If our deal's good, then we're done here. So let's get to it."

"You are far from done," he says. "Your work is just beginning."

"What the. . .?" I say. He's still maneuvering and that's just—"Hey, I never agreed to be your minion follower"—that much I'm sure of. Whatever he's talking about, that's for him and her—"or hers."

He slithers over to me the way a jealous dog would ease up and try to steal a bigger one's bone. And he has the book in his hand and he has turned the page. He points with his long index finger. "Read this right here," he says. "Out loud, if you don't mind. Then our deal . . . is done."

I look at him for a second. He puts his hand on my shoulder, like a drinking buddy who's trying to persuade me to have just one more shot of swill. "Just this line. Trust me, you will like this part."

Trust. . . That's just not happening, but curiosity. . . I screech-curse my finger over the symbols. It's unnerving, but I understand the sounds, "And The Fallen before him shall choose his name and he shall become an angel of both Heavens." I stop and look into his ice-blue eyes.

And his eyes glow a little and it looks like a tiny blue flame has ignited in his iris. Then he takes the book, walks away a few feet, and he turns back toward me and says, "Thank you . . . Jake."

"What is. . .? . . . What's *that* shit mean?"

"It means . . . that today is your lucky day," he says. "Mine, too. Now, a name. . ."

"What name?" I ask.

"A name for you."

"*That's* what that said?" I ask. "I thought it meant you."

"I was the beginning of that end," he says. "There is much more to the Word in the *Book of Blood*, but that was the beginning . . . of *this* end."

None of this shit's real. How can it be? The *Bible*, God and the Devil? I'm in some dream. I'm certainly no. . . What the hell would that make me?

He's back to reading my mind again. "One powerful archangel," he says. "A dark and light one—order of The Fallen, not to put too fine a point on it. There are not many of us. And I must name you."

"That is just—name me? Thanks, I'll stick with Jake."

"Remember what I said about language," he says. "You know why men are afraid to speak my name and women tremble at the mere thought of it? Because language has power—names are no different. In fact, do you know what my name spells backward?"

I never really thought about it before. Too much life to worry about. But. . . "Lived?" I say. "Oh, that is some cruel shit. Did she really do that?"

"In a word, yes," he says. "That was what she spoke when she created me, but when she cast me out . . . turned me inside-out . . . reversed my fate. . . It was her lot—combine the light with the darkness and pave the path to a new beginning."

I can feel his mind scurrying around for an answer—a name. She named him "Lived." I can't believe that. I scarcely have time to ponder my jump and—

"Yes," he says, "that's it!"

"What?"

And he is a cat with a canary. I'm having trouble believing that he is this excited to name me. Must be something else in the deal. Then he says it: "Jump."

As soon as the word leaves his mouth, I bend over and start vomiting blood down onto the ground. And deep red syrup splatters, and a puddle starts to form at my feet.

The puddle gets bigger than I figure I have blood to fill it, but when

I'm done I don't fall over or die again, or anything like that. In fact, I feel . . . great. Like after great sex. And I don't like cigarettes, but it feels like—I can't believe I'm craving smoke. When I stand up, I stagger just a little and then I look at him. "What," I say, and then I spit out some blood, "in the fuck?"

"Indeed," he says. "I had a very similar reaction. Maybe not quite as colorful, but definitely astonishment."

I spit again—the last copper-tasting remnants of my earthly life— and it splashes in the puddle and a crimson ripple moves away and then the puddle's surface goes right back to calm red. And I can just make out my reflection in the mirror-like pool of blood. And I think I'm getting it, but this is just too insane.

"Jump?" I think about it. Doesn't sound all that menacing. I don't even know why I'm pondering my name and not worrying about all the other stuff. *Hallucination dream.* . . I'm probably too dehydrated and beat to shit on the floor of some interrogation cell.

The State has some good drugs. Damnation and salvation, wrapped in a little red, white and blue pill. It's a syringe actually, but a little of that and you'll be judging yourself.

"Do you understand it?" he asks. He's a kid on Christday morning now.

That's messed up, too. So many levels. More drugs, please. "Yeah, I get it," I say. "I jumped. Real original shit ya got there . . . *Lived.*"

"No," he says. His annoyed voice is back. "Jump is a word that is both dark and light, but in this case—J. U. M. P. —Judgment Under My Power."

As soon as he says it, I go black.

* * *

The dream is weird, but it is just like the stories—floating above my body, an angel taking me to Heaven, bright light, God and the Devil, judgment.

Tell you the truth, it's hard to remember the details—dream-inside-a-dream shit. But when I wake up, I'm squatting on top of the black van down on the street and I'm naked. Jesus, I have no idea what it is with these two and keeping me naked.

And I can . . . smell the fear. The air reeks of it. I know that's what it is. No idea how, but I know that pungent piss smell is the essence of panic. And it's as sweet as molasses in my mouth. And then I remember and I look down at my exploded, earthly body and I'm standing on top of my own guts.

And there are Protection agents and authority sirens and a new black Protection van is here to replace the one I just crushed. And there are orange flametrucks and a bright red evacuation vehicle, and parameds are flitting around, looking for someone to resurrect. I don't think that's gonna work out too well for them, because the only one I know of—except for me, of course—is a greasy shit-stain in the driver's seat of this van I'm perched on.

And I stand up and it feels . . . weird. No, it's not that I'm naked in the middle of downtown on top of a van, though I should be at least a little self-conscious about my dick, because it is still raining and there is a little breeze. That doesn't bring out the—uh, never mind.

Anyway, it seems like I couldn't care less about that. What's really missing is all the creaks and moans and spikes of pain in my joints as I get up—my forty-eight-year-old body forgets to remind me that the bulletproof years are over.

No, now all I can feel when I stand all the way up . . . is power. It's more than brute strength, though, and for a guy who's afraid to get interrogated or thrown in a gang-bang cell with a bunch of prisoners, I feel pretty . . . impenetrable.

I know, I know, but that's the word in my head when—

The wings tear through first. Spikes of steel feathers rip the flesh on my back as they slice their way out from both sides of my spine. And red chunks of my back meat fall away and I . . . sprout metal wings!

They spread to their full width and open in a dark gray span of scraping and sparking steel plumage. The raking sound of a thousand tiny razors on a chalkboard sends everyone on the street to their knees, clutching at their ears and screaming in agony.

I don't mind telling you, however painful this shit is, it is just awesome! And I shake the metal spikes on my new span of steel . . . or they shake themselves, because I don't have a clue how to work them. And blood and meat chunks shower the van. I can barely see the blood against the black paint—looks like it's almost the same color. I squat down to touch it and sparks fly from the tips of my feathers as I clumsily drag them along the top of the van. And they tear the sheet metal in long, jagged gouges. And I fall to one knee and a thought spikes through my mind: *Stand up.*

Nothing happens and I squat there, looking stupid. "Jump," I say. And immediately my wings flap violently, and the tips of my feathers tear open the top of the van like flimsy aluminum foil, and I'm—*holy shit, I'm flying!*

It doesn't last long, though, and I hover in the air a few feet above the van, before my wings flail and I crash down hard on the hood. Then I fall to the pavement next to it, like a fledgling rookie that just got pushed out of the nest. And the pavement cracks and I put my fingers in it—touch the hardness of the blacktop to make sure it is real.

Somehow I manage to stand up without stumbling this time. The wings will take some getting used to. And I laugh, more at myself than anything else. It's strange, because something embarrassing like. . .? In front of a street packed with strangers? That would have sent me into a self-loathing rage before. *Before what?* . . . I can hardly remember. That's my dead body down there, but who am I? There's only bits and pieces and flashes in my mind.

I look around at the total chaos and commotion that's only growing now. No one seems to have a clue what to do, because I've never seen so many panicked faces in my life. Everyone looks like a politician who just got a news camera shoved in his face full of coke. *Coke?* That's pretty old-school, but like I said. . . But I guess it's not every day you see a man crash down from a building and then stand up and sprout wings, because the citizens are crapping themselves.

And I smile and look down at myself. *Or one that's buck-ass naked*, I think. I try to get a good look at my new body, but controlling my wings and standing seem to go together about as well as blood and pancakes. Wish there was a mirror.

Then I remember something—the whole damn city is one big mirror. Scrapers—powerful pillars of the privileged—every five feet, all made of reflective glass. I look across the street and the first thing I see in the reflection is my wings. They are huge—*ten feet wide?* That's a guess, because they're probably more like fifteen. And the reflection is the first time I can see my whole body and I walk toward it.

As I cross the street, my wings open and close, slowly back and forth, and then I tuck them onto my back—fold the feathers together. And I hear them clank like a steel door shutting behind me. I think I'm figuring them out, or they're figuring themselves out—feels like they have a mind of their own.

I can see in the reflection that the fold sticks up above my head a couple of feet, and I can hear the steel feathers on the tips, scraping the concrete behind me as I walk. I'm not made for pounding the pavement with my feet anymore.

The street is gathering Protection agents faster than it's taking for me to figure out what the hell I'm supposed to be doing with my new wings. And the onlookers—hundreds of citizens. . . A mermaid would get less attention. But I'm oblivious.

It's the wrong word, because I know they are there, I just don't give a shit. Right now, I wanna see if they left me with my. . .?

When I look closer at the reflection, I can tell that this body is not mine. Not one I recognize from this morning, anyway. That forty-eight-year-old, sagging. . . How I made it up that many flights of stairs is beyond me. But this body in the reflection . . . twenty-seven at most, and rippling, long, sinewy muscles—hard meat. And maybe the best news of the day—I got to keep my dick. Looks a little weird, though. *Lucky for them*, I think. Someone would pay for that, for sure. Anyway, the thought of them doesn't scare me as much now.

As much as what? Doesn't feel like I've ever been scared. In fact, after this, I might have to put them on my list. *Bastards. . .*

As soon as that warning flashes in my mind, armored steel feathers spring out of almost every pore on my body. They cover everything but my face and the palms of my hands. Then my skin tingles, as I feel every breeze, every swirl of air and every drop of rain that falls on me.

But steel and rain? Do I rust? The thoughts are just popping into my head.

I shiver and shake and the water flies off in all directions, like a wet retriever, shaking off pond water after he just fetched his master's dead duck. And then I'm completely dry. When I rub one of my arms, a thin film of waxy oil slips across my fingertips and then the patch on my arm fills right back in. *Waterproof. . .*

Believe me, I'm aware. If this is a dream, then I've got some serious issues to work out. My subconscious has finally snapped, trying to deal with the amount of anger and resentment toward authority that I'm harboring. But what if it isn't?

Then something flashes in my mind—I remember . . . something . . . *the ones I left on the roof!* And before I know it, I'm in the air and my wings are flapping wildly—the sound of steel scraping on itself echoes down the block. And I hear screaming on the street, and then I'm flying straight up.

I guess I wouldn't really call it flying, because I kinda suck at it. It's more like crashing off of the surrounding buildings as I flail my new appendages in an attempt to go up. I slam buildings in horrendous bursts of steel and shattering glass. And sharp shards rain down on the onlookers and the agents below and the screams waft up at me again —music to my ears—and I smile. I can smell the blood.

By the time I make it to the roof, I'm getting better at it. Not much, but enough to make a difference. And I flap a few times, gaining some altitude above the rooftop. Then I struggle to hover while I look for them.

From a hundred feet up, I can see every crack in every crevice on the scraper's roof. And every one of them has taken cover, hiding behind anything they can. They must have watched from above, gaping at the impossible like the rest of them. The black uniforms and helmets look less intimidating now, less threatening and more like a bunch of pathetic followers.

I focus on one of them. He's quivering like a field mouse behind the HVAC unit I cut my hand on. And I can see where my blood spilled and my Kimber lying next to it. The sight of my own blood excites me for some reason, and I smile. Then the guy steps in it and I frown.

His boot on my blood enrages me and before I know it, I'm in a dive—wings folded slightly, slicing through the air like an eagle—flying right at him. I read his name tag—"Daniels"—right before I slam into him at full speed. And sparks fly as my wing slices through the big metal AC unit, and then I'm flapping and I'm hopping around him and—*Brrrt, brrrt*! A couple of bursts of 9mm spit out of his little MP-7.

I feel every one of the bullets hit me and ricochet off my feathers, buzzing like bees across the roof as they find something else to sting. And I'm clawing and pulling at his flesh, and it sounds like I'm squawking and cawing as I rip into him.

My fingers and feet work like—*holy shit, they've turned to talons!* And I pull and peck at him. And blood is spraying and he's screaming, but that doesn't last long. I keep going—drunk on the power of it. And the images flash in my head again—remembering who I was— but it feels like forever ago since I ran like a scared rabbit from this little rat and his black-booted agent buddies.

I go at him too long, because when I'm done there's not much to recognize as a man—chunks of meat and a shredded black uniform. His citizen-raping days are over—"Daniels" . . . is done. I smile at my own wit—a little payback goes a long way.

Then I stand up and scream out above my head. What comes out, is a sound like none I've ever heard. A vile screeching twang that reminds me more of an overloaded electric guitar than an eagle or hawk. And I hear some shattering glass across on the adjacent scraper. Then, there's rats everywhere, and I count and catalogue in my head, *Six in the stairwell, six in the elevator, less Daniels and. . . Eight-nine . . . ten.*

Little scurrying black figures burst out from their hiding places, and a hail of hot lead rains across the rooftop—a sideways stream of death droplets, bent on washing me off this roof and back to hell. I'm not ready for that. Hell? I just got back.

And I squat down—the reactions are coming faster now—and my wings surround the rest of my body like a steel curtain. I can only imagine that, from the outside, I must look like a big metal egg of gray feathers, squatting in the middle of the roof.

Inside, I feel the pelting from the bullets and I hear the buzzing as they ricochet like the rest. The rats spray the shit out of me, but it's no more dangerous than waiting out a heavy downpour under an umbrella. I can smell some of it from the fear—the putrid piss smell mixed with cordite gunsmoke—but there's another smell, too. The sweet cooking onion smell of revenge.

And they keep firing. Can't blame them, really. I did drop Daniels, not to mention shooting one of their buddies in the stairwell. Good for them—get some for Charlie, or Hank or whoever.

They'll have to reload soon, so I wait. When the bullets stop, I let them swap magazines, and I can tell they move a little closer, because the pelting gets harder, like hail on my bare back this time. Nothing that concerns me, though. And then their machine guns are empty and I hear the familiar scrapes of pistols, clearing plastic holsters and the hot rain starts again—less this time—they're running out of lead.

When it's over, I stand up and shake my wings and little 9mm and . 45 caliber lead raindrops pour out from between my feathers—they fall and bounce on the rooftop.

The faces tell me they know they're already dead, but they are trained warriors too, and a couple of them pull their knives, eyes wide open to the inevitability of their end.

When I spin, I have no idea what I'm doing, but I twirl in a circle anyway. And I feel my wings slice air and then some flight feathers release and then pinfeathers cut loose and shoot like tiny daggers at all of them at once. And the bigger quills streak orange fire across the rooftop and cut off arms and legs, and the smaller pinfeathers simply zip right through body armor and flesh and bone, or they pierce guts and internal organs and keep going out the other side.

And there is that sound again—another memory from the staircase, but something else, too—deer, maybe. The meat-smacking sounds come, and in a couple of grunts and a little bit of moaning, it is over faster than the guy I plucked apart at the seams. *A better death than Daniels*, I think.

I look, and my steel feathers are embedded in the concrete of the buildings behind them, and the windows are shattered and the glass rains down on the onlookers below.

Sucks for them.

* * *

The first thought I have is, *How do I get new feathers?* Compared to the hot and steaming bloody mess surrounding me, it could be a cold question. But no sooner do I think it, than I feel replacements sprout from the empty holes of my expended plumage—problem solved.

Jesus, who thinks this shit up? I mean, is there a guy down at the Army of Angels Surplus store, saying, "And then we're going to need regenerative, ballistic feathers and. . ." Seriously, that guy is messed up.

I shake the thought. Kelly wouldn't approve. That's what I think, but . . . who is Kelly?

That thought doesn't last long, because I have to tell you, I'm more than enjoying turning the tables on the very scum that took. . . Someone took her from me—that's who she is, but. . . I know what has to be done about that. One thing I am sure of, no one takes shit from me. But when I look around—guts and blood of people I know I should hate—revenge and killing feel a bit too . . . easy.

I think to myself for a second, *There should be a little more to this.*

A conscience? If you're asking, there's not a twinge of—

The voice is more serious this time, *Rain is coming. . .*

Now I remember those two—the bitches who sent me. Whichever one of them. . . I kinda thought that they would have given up whispering in my ear by now—just come out and say what's on their mind. . . . Maybe not? It's more than a little annoying, though, and then I think, *It's probably only him—haven't heard from her in a while?*

I look. . . Hell, I don't know which way to look for him. Down, up —nothing seems to be like I think it should be. So I look up—it's as good a direction as any—and somehow I tell my body feathers to retract and I'm standing on the roof, naked with the rain splattering on my skin and wings, and I close my eyes and feel the wetness and drink in the sweet smell of spilled blood. *Sweet onions*, I think. *Could use some garlic.*

— XXVIII —

WILD SCREECHING ABOVE me—like feedback from a microphone—makes me open my eyes and sends my hands to my ears. Then a blinding white light blasts me in the face and I manage to flip one wing up just as the sound hammers into me.

And the spikes stab into my chest and arms and I buck backwards —I'm lifted off the roof of this scraper with no more effort than I used on the rats. And then whatever it is lets go and I'm falling from the roof . . . again. And I flap and flail, and I think I screech a couple of times on the way down.

The holes in me seem to hammer a bunch of images in my mind, and rapid flashes of understanding hit me—the roof, the flashbacks, meeting the two of them, and deciding. But there's no flashbacks, no philosophical debates, and no angels or devils on this fall.

And I plummet down through the confusing anger of my life, and past my hopelessness and regret at the loss of Amy, right by my rage at them for doing that to Kelly—all the way down to the street . . . and then I crash with a resounding, smashing sound right in the middle of my barely quenched thirst for vengeance.

Lesson one—pain, it's a good teacher.

The murmur in the grandstands turned to squeaking and squawking, and then to muffled cries and caws that echoed down to the arena below. And The Great Mountain of the Eternities rumbled.

Dal spun and looked at the gallery of the faithful. And then he looked at her. "What was. . .?" he asked. "What angel is this? I—I do not recognize. . .?"

"Angel?" Life said. Then she smiled and the *Book of Blood* appeared in her hands. She opened it slowly and ran her finger across the text. Yet when *she* spoke, the sounds of babies bawling and women crying wafted from its parchment: " 'And the angel's name fell from the heavens as rain. And the blinding light of the truth followed.' " Then she looked up at Dal. "You see, there it is. Written quite plainly—rain."

And flames shot from the tips of Dal's red wings and the great hall shook the tremors of an angry earthquake and he grabbed the book from Life with both hands. Then he read the same passage as he flamed in rage-red anger, and the moaning from the pages was louder when he did. When he was finished, he slammed it shut and said, "That is—you—you are interpreting it. It is . . . a metaphor!"

"Ah," Life said, "who am I to interpret the will of the Word in your book? I simply read it and follow its law faithfully. Literally, if need be."

"That is not—"

Life spoke from memory this time, " 'And rain shall hound him through the anarchy of The End.' . . . That seems pretty straightforward, don't you think?"

"Rain is not literal!" Dal shouted.

Life looked back toward The Fallen—Jump—flailing in the street. Then she gazed toward the bright light of her own champion, flying away from the city. "Strange . . . looks rather literal to me."

"Of all of the angels in. . ." Dal looked toward Jump. "You cannot do this. You bastardize the Word."

Life smiled and felt herself up and down. "And yet I feel no burning flesh, and no lightning presents itself to extinguish me. Could it be? Could it be that the Word *is* open to interpretation after all? Even *if* it be literal?" And then she pointed at Jump. "As for him . . . he is your bastard."

— XXIX —

I STAND UP, more confident this time. I can feel the blood dripping down my chest and I look down at it. And there are five perfect holes in a circle in my side and five more in my left chest. *What . . . was that?*

My blood's black . . . and thicker than it should be. *Dark heart. . . The* thought comes naturally. *Maybe that wasn't. . .?*

Protection has a rule—if you can't snatch it, stab it. Can't stab it, shoot it. I don't have much time to worry about the color of my blood before bullets are pelting me again. A couple even penetrate a little before my armored feathers flip out to cover me, spitting the bullets out of my flesh. When I do, it feels like I'm . . . healing, because I don't feel the pain anymore.

I crouch down again and my wings surround me. So, here we go. *Nothin's easy*, I think. Of course not. *Jump.* I'll give them some justice.

When the shooting dies down, I stand up and spin and loose a thousand feathers from my wings, at anything and everything, in a circle of flaming steel that looks like bright orange tracer rounds, because now I am pissed-off.

And cars explode and bodies cut in half and heads sever. And the gunfire turns to screaming and yelling and . . . I think I even hear barking in the melee. And there is shouting and begging for me to stop. They shoulda thought of that before they started shooting.

I hear calls for help over Protection radios and they've got the Protection soldiers in here. *That's illegal!* I don't get far with the thought.

"Bravo eight-six, this is Kilo, over," the voice shouts. "I need a drone up here. We got heavy contact—repeat, heavy contact from. . ."

Explain that one to them, bitch, I think, and then I smile. I guess an enraged angel warrants breaking the guidelines about drones in the city.

And then the reply squawks back, "Negative, Kilo. Primary tasking —priority Wenatchee, over."

Plenty of gun-burying citizens over there. They'll be busy for a while.

I don't know why I try to sort the citizens from the soldiers and Protection agents, because I really couldn't care less. If it gets in the way, I destroy it. And the blood is burning like sweet red onions on a grill.

By the time I finish, the drizzle is falling down on a street full of shattered glass, smoking cars, and blood-drenched body parts. Men, women. . . Protection-puppy fur is everywhere. *That was the barking*, I think. And then I remember, I never cared much for the dogs, before or after, no matter how useful they were to scare the shit out of citizens.

When I stand in the middle of it this time, I'm not messing around basking in fresh revenge. I leave the armored feathers out, spread my wings just enough that I can jump up and defend myself if I have to, and I scan the sky for bright lights. Whatever that was on the roof, if it comes back now, I'm tearing the shit out of it.

* * *

But nothing comes, nothing but screaming and crying for mommas. And I can hear the alarms in the distance. A few calls over helmet-mounted wave-units, squawking about flying angels and destruction. That brought them running.

I smile at the thought of the masters on the other end, trying to figure out if their guard dogs have all gone rabid or just nuts.

Time to get out of downtown. But before I go, I lean my head way back and let out a couple of wild screeches and screams—a war cry, maybe. No idea why I do it, I don't know a whole helluva lot about this new life . . . or what it wants from me. The cries sound a little different this time. And I can feel the death and I can taste the sweetness of it.

Remorse? Questioning it doesn't even seem like a natural thought. It feels like something left over. Right now, I'm just . . . satisfied.

Won't last—something else from before—nothing good ever does.

Then I hear it—in the distance—the sound of screeching and . . . wind. I brace myself for what the wind is going to bring. I figure whatever it is, probably like that last ass-whooping I took, so I jump and flap hard to meet it.

As I fly up, I can feel it—I'm not a fledgling anymore—the wings are getting easier to control—more instinctive. That's good, because whatever grabbed me and threw me off the roof, knew exactly what it was doing.

I turn my attention back to the approaching screeches.

"Shit. . ." I mutter out loud when I see them. There's at least a couple hundred, probably more. Black wings, white wings, even some gray ones—all different colors, sparkling in what little light there is left in the day. They are flying right at me. If they're anything like the last one, this will get ugly fast.

As they make their way through the city toward me, I get ready to spin in midair. And they dive through the canyons—between the scrapers—and then they pop back up over the buildings, twisting and turning like . . . doves. Son of a bitch. I'm kinda. . . I don't really know what to do.

Doves? It's the only bird I've ever seen fly like that. And I . . . I remember. Twisting and diving, flitting and cutting, changing direction at will, defying the laws of physics and flight. And the screeching is growing louder, but it sounds like chatter to me or . . . talking?

As they close the gap, the cries get more urgent and I lower my head and prepare to spin—better safe than sorry—a "shoot first" thing I got left over from . . . somewhere. Makes sense to me now, though.

When I glance down a little, I see it. The street is starting to move . . . wriggle. Looks like . . . maggots on a festering deer carcass in the forest. No clue where that image came from, but that's what it looks like. And the writhing starts and then a low moan wafts up from below me and I can smell the sweet souls.

Every single body on the street is a dead cocoon now, and the butterflies are starting to emerge. But these aren't monarchs, they are angry, nasty, smelly insects, clawing and gnawing their way out of the confused husks of their lives, waking up to the reality of the fairytale they've been fed.

And apparently . . . there's no sound or movement from the dogs? Guess that part of the story is true.

And I look back to the approaching birds, but before I can spin. . . Something in me doesn't even want to anymore, because now the "doves" are all around me, circling and screeching and mock-diving at the street. It's a beautiful display of aerial acrobatics and I watch it for a few seconds, marveling at how well they use their wings.

Jealousy—probably one of my bigger sins in life, if I remember correctly. Now, I could give a shit. But there's something in the screeching. They are asking for something . . . permission? To do what? When I figure it out, it makes sense. They are here to gather.

I have no idea how to speak "screech," though, much less. . . What are these things? I mean, they look like me and it's obvious that they're angels. . . At least, in this dream I think they are, but their steel is shining, shinier than mine, for sure. And their feet and hands. . . Talons, no mistaking that.

Whatever it was on the roof, those talons made the holes in my chest. And I make a little note to rip them off of whoever stuck them into me.

The moaning down on the street is getting worse. Death looks confusing and painful. That much I remember clearly. Sucks for them still. Who knows where my newfound winged friends want to take them. Only one of two places I can think of. Don't remember which one is worse. That is . . . strange.

I have no idea how to say yes in "dove-angel screech," so I just try to yell it at them. What comes out sounds just like them. And a couple of chirps and a long cry later, and hundreds of dove-angels dive down the canyons between the scrapers. And they twist and turn and scream at each other, and then each of them grabs a squirming soul off the street, and as soon as they have it in their clutches, that bird heads straight up through the gray fog and disappears into the mist—one by one the souls are gone.

And then I'm alone, hovering high above the carnage of lifeless, soulless corpses on the street below. I'm confused, to say the least. But a little proud of myself, too. Feels like a good day.

— XXX —

WHEN THE FAITHFUL and faithless "Soul Safety" Angels returned to the Hallowed Hall of the Word, they flew down through the roof as it rotated open, and then they deposited their soul cargo at the edge of the arena. Then golden guardian angels—one gripping each arm—grabbed the moaning souls and dragged them through the portal entrance to the dungeons below.

Dal and Life were still locked in a battle of words.

Life frowned at Dal. "That is how you plan to have him cleanse the. . .?" she said. "At that pace, I shall not fear for my children or the garden."

Dal hung his head. He muttered, "They fornicate with greater results than this. How to keep pace with rabbits?"

Life smiled. "How indeed."

"Yes," he said. "You did make them in your image, didn't you? Perhaps you have a suggestion."

"Oh, no," she said. "This is your procession. They are the words of your book? Far be it from me to . . . interfere."

And the *Book of Blood* appeared in Dal's hands and he read aloud, "And The Fallen shall cause the womb of Heaven to split open and rain shall spill forth from her guts."

"Careful. . ."

Dal smiled and said, "That would be *metaphorical* rain, thank you very much."

"Maybe," said Life. "Yet that is your interpretation and who are you to. . .?"

— XXXI —

IT TURNS TO night faster than I think it should and the city lights are bouncing back beneath a thick blanket of heavy wet fog, pressing and dripping down on the tops of the scrapers like an overfilled sponge. I'm perched next to a five-foot metal cross on top of a huge stone church, just a few blocks from the carnage I just created— Saint . . . J-something Cathedral, I think. *Why would I know that?*

Angel perched on top of a church—cliche, I know, but it feels natural to me. I look at the cross and talk to it as if it could hear me, "Don't you worry, I'll send you some more to pray over in the morning." It sounds like I cluck and then I chuckle at myself a little. Guess it takes death to realize it's the little things.

An Avenger drone flies by, roaring past, barely above the tops of the scrapers, loaded to the gills with Hellfuries. Apparently Protection found something worthy of re-tasking it from Eastern Washington. I grin and turn my head, watching it as it banks and disappears between some buildings. *Joystick-jockey has some skills*, I think.

The sounds of sirens and sporadic gunfire echo through the glow— Protection patrol are busy cleaning up, trying to find someone for the interrogators to torture in order to figure out what happened. Woe be to the poor citizens they black-bag for that. They aren't gonna know shit. But it won't matter, they'll torture them to death anyway to make themselves feel better—more in control.

And I get the first look at myself in the semi-darkness of the night.

My steel feathers shine and shimmer, and my wings still have a little dripping blood on them. Nothing is drying in this damp—the drizzle just won't stop. No surprise there—gotta love Seattle.

I shake my wings and crimson mist mixed with rain sprinkles down onto the side of the building. I'm not too concerned—from what I remember, blood washes off the church like water off a duck's back.

When I look across Lake Union, I can see the long, curved support pillars on the bottom of the Space Scraper—the big, round flying saucer part is hidden above the fog. For some reason, I think that building used to be a restaurant, but that just sounds ridiculous. Protection has been in control of that scraper for as far back as I can remember. They coordinate drone strikes and citizen compliance patrols from up there.

I have no idea how I know that, but it might as well be God's office in Heaven as far as the average citizen is concerned, because no mere mortal is seeing the inside of it.

I think about perching on top of it. Probably not the best spot to avoid them. That thought doesn't even feel natural and I contemplate flying over there just to gut some more government goons before I roost for the night. I'll get to them in the morning.

And then I have a different thought. Maybe it's an impulse, because I feel an overwhelming urge to follow the dove-angels up, right to the Pearly Gates. Why? No idea, but it's been a while since I talked to either of them—him or her. Seems like . . . time is just messed up, but I got a little itch in my feathers . . . and it wants to be scratched.

I flap hard and head to where I saw them disappear into the dark gray fog. When I finally break through the last layer, there's nothing but a glow from below. I hover and stare toward where I think the Heavens should be. *Nothing but stars*, I think.

I fly farther up—get a better view—and I keep flapping until it seems like I might leave the atmosphere. *Do I even need oxygen?* It's another random question for the newness. But all there is up here are a billion tiny stars, trying to flicker the truth down from the dark black nothing above the Earth. Can any one of them shine a light on reality? Maybe it takes them all.

One of the stars looks a little brighter than the others and I watch it for a few seconds. *North Star, maybe?* It might have the answer—one little pinprick of truth, struggling for all it's worth to outshine its neighbors and shed some light on the whole damn story.

And I still got this little itch. I close my eyes and try to think of the answer. You'd think I would know better.

When the light blasts my eyes, I barely have time to wrap myself in feathers before the little shit slams into me again. And the screeching is louder this time and it's not just one hit and walk away, or fly away or whatever, because this is an all-out attack. And I try to spin, but a talon has one of my wings and it's crushing into my metal feathers and a few of them rip out and fall away, and I hear them clank each other on the way down. Now it's serious, because we are both plummeting down after them. It's hard to fly and fight at the same time. Go figure that shit.

So I start screeching back at. . . Whoever or whatever has me is so bright I can't see anything. It's like the sun in Syria—oppressive and inescapable. And how do I know that?

I squint hard and try to fight it off by flapping my wings at it, and then my fingers and toes sprout talons.

You're asking *me* how? If I knew that, I would have done it sooner. And I start fighting back with both of them—all four. I think I catch a wing or a leg or something, because I clamp a talon down on it and whatever it is starts jerking, and then I've got wings and talons and hard feathers, hammering at me everywhere. And we're locked together—stalemate of screeching and clawing.

I've seen this shit on *National Nature* on the PIN or some other archive cinewave, I shouldn't have been watching—eagles locked together, falling like rocks. Only they aren't fighting, this sure isn't that. Not unless someone changed it to getting your ass kicked. Come to think of it, I've had a few that felt like that.

And one of us is going to have to let go, because I'm sure the city isn't too far down—we're gonna slam the street or a scraper soon enough. I turn my face away from the blasting, bright bastard just long enough to open my eyes and look down.

And there it is, the glowing fog above the city, and in another second we're through the tops of the scrapers and I look back and my eyes burn and I have to shut them tight again—and my vision has got a glowing orange reminder not to look at whatever this sun-bright bastard is.

I screech at him and hope the translation comes out right, "You better let go, because I'm not gonna!"

I get brighter light, more burning, and a tighter grip back for my trouble. So we're hammering the pavement. Okay by me, I've hit the shit three times in the last day. Never from this height, but how much worse could it be?

Then I find out.

— XXXII —

WHEN I OPEN my eyes . . . I am fucked *up*. There is just no other way to describe the pain. I'm on my back and one of my wings feels like. . . I try to move it—the spikes of pain are a serious bitch. *Broken.*

And it feels like I got claw marks down my face and chest and legs, and there's a hot poker feeling coming from my guts. But I stare up and it's . . . *beautiful*, I think. A weird thought, I know, but bright colorful rainbows of glass and light are everywhere. It's all blurry, but the colors are spectacular.

I look around, trying to focus, and someone is standing above me with their arms out. When I finally squint enough to see. . . *You have just got to be kidding me. Jesus? Now that is just*—"Goddammit," I mutter.

I cough when I say it and some of my blood comes out and runs down my cheek. And I drag my hand across my face to wipe it and when I look, it's . . . it's black. Okay, so this isn't the Protection torture dream—I'm still me. The Jump me, anyway, because I would've never survived this as. . . "Who am I?" I can barely whisper.

"Shh," I think I hear, but it could be one of them in my head. I got no idea.

And then things get fuzzy and the room spins and I open and close my eyes in slow motion, like a Protection agent raising his gun at an unarmed citizen. And then the nothingness comes—dark black.

* * *

I wake up this time to spikes of pain shooting through my stomach and I screech. Something's tugging at my guts. It's probably that little bastard, come to finish me off, because it's pretty bright and I squint. Not like before, but light enough, so I shut my eyes. Then the light goes away and I can feel him pecking and picking at my entrails and I groan. Bastard's eating my guts.

"I'm sorry," it's the voice of an old man.

I open my eyes a little more, because I can't believe. . . And I see an old man squatting over me. "Dammit," I mutter. All-powerful vengeance angel from Hell and a little old man angel kicks my ass and eats my guts for breakfast. So, I'm going out like Daniels. That is a bitch. Hell sucks ass. I gotta talk to someone about that.

"Quiet," he says. "You are going to need to save your energy. This is difficult enough without—"

"Fuck you," is all I can manage. I spit out some blood as I say it—slobber it more than shoot it in his direction. Maybe I can hit him with it. "Save it . . . for what?"

"If you are what I. . ." he says. He goes back to tugging at my belly, and then he mutters to himself, "I. . . This is just. . . An angel? . . . You will need your strength."

For an angel, he seems pretty surprised that I'm one. And I try to tilt my head up and look at him, and an acid feeling burns though my stomach. And the little guy's working on removing a big metal cross from my belly—same one from the roof. "Shit," I say, "ain't that a bitch."

Probably shouldn't be cussing so much, because I can tell by the collar on the little prick's shirt that he's a priest. In fact, for some reason, I think I know him.

The little gray-haired God-dog works on me for longer than I'd like, before he finally removes the cross from my stomach. I gotta say, there's no fire like a five-foot metal cross shoved through your guts.

When he finally cuts it free, he wipes his little knife on his shirt, closes it, and clips it back in the pocket of his black pants. I always wondered why the men of the cloth dressed in black all the time. It seemed to me that they should be in white. And if there was a Satan-worshipping church, they should be the men in black. Just the way my mind works, I guess. It's the little things—the illogical—I always wanted to understand. And that's one of them, floating around in the delirious dream I'm obviously having.

But it's no wonder my stomach is on fire, he was cutting on me with that knife! I roll my head to the side and watch him. He walks a few steps away and flops himself down on a church pew. Then he starts yammering.

He's gibbering and jabbering away, and apparently, I crashed through the roof while he was cleaning up some paperwork in the rectory. He came running down here and found me, just as a bright light flew out a huge hole in the roof of the church.

Bet if he told that story to the congregation they'd call the white-jackets to come and snatch him up. Guess it makes more sense for the 5150 crew to wear white.

Calm down, little nutcracker, I think. *Time for you to go to Heaven.* I cluck and chuckle a little at the thought and my guts burn acid to reward me.

My sick humor aside, the father is pretty shaken up, and he reaches into his shirt pocket and pulls out a leather-covered metal flask. His wrinkled fingers tremble as he unscrews the top, then he flips it up and takes a long swig. When he pulls it away from his mouth, a tiny deep-brown drop runs down his gray scruff. He reaches into his back pants pocket and pulls out a white cloth. Then he wipes the drip away.

I shake my head. *Old men and their handkerchiefs.* . . "You okay?" I ask him. I don't really care, but I'm not going anywhere—might as well shoot the shit. Scared shitless God-dog or not, he's not stabbing me with his knife, and that is . . . interesting.

I'll tell you one thing, I've never seen wider eyes on someone. But when he talks to me, he squints. And I don't know if the flask is because he has no idea what he's seeing, or if it's because he knows *exactly*, but from his yammering, it sounds like he has a better understanding of what's going on than I do. When he pauses, he takes another pull on his flask. He wipes his mouth with his shirt this time then he says, "You are an—"

"Easy, Father," I say. Then I open my eyes wide back at him. "You're gonna pop an eyeball. I think you need some glass—"

"You. . . The fu-fall. . ." now he's stuttering. And he takes another pull. The sauce always helps. Even the priests know that.

"Yeah," I say, "me fall from sky." Might as well start playing along. Doesn't look like the, "state the obvious" game is going away any time soon. "Take it easy. Find your glasses and stop sucking on that tit, because you're gonna have to patch me up."

Might as well get it right out in the open. I got the urge to slice his head off with my wing—something tells me that's what I should be doing—but I'm not going to be able to stitch myself back up. And I'm . . . woozy again.

"Your blood is . . . black," he says.

I get an annoyed look on my face, because what did I *just* say? "So what?" I say. Maybe I can give this guy some insight into his own faith. At least shock the shit out of him a little. "All angels have black blood."

He takes another quick swig. Then he says, "No, they do not."

I raise my eyebrows at him and look at his flask. He's not getting it or. . . *Oh, whatever.* "Yes, we do," I say. "I should know, I've. . ." But when I think about it, I realize that, despite the buckets of crimson I spilled on the roof and the street below it, not a drop of it came out of an angel. "What about the one that crashed in here with me? Pretty sure I got some blood outta him."

"The profanity," he says. "You cannot. . . I must ask you to. . ."

That's a pipe dream. At least he hasn't lost his faculties entirely. *Still useful.*

Then he looks around a little, like he's trying to figure out how to put his church, and his whole belief system, back together.

"Look, Father Ben, you—"

"You know my name?"

"I should," I say, "you married us." Because that's who this little guy is.

He squints at me again, and then he reaches into his shirt pocket. Booze must be kicking in, because he's less shaky now. And he pulls out a little pair of black-rimmed spectacles.

No wonder. No citizens wear those anymore. Little guy must be blind as a bat, because the lenses are glass-bottle thick. And he's kinda "weird uncle" funny looking, and I cluck and chuckle a little. It makes me wince.

Then he leans in as much as he dares, examining me like I'm a wounded cougar his wife is making him rescue. If they allowed him to have a wife, anyway. No wonder they're raping little boys.

"Jacob?" he says.

"In the—" And I cough out a little black blood. "In the flesh . . . and it's Jake." I feel a little weird. Like I'm running out of gas. "Used to be . . . anyway. Now . . . Father, all this chit-chit is. . . I'm tired. . ." My vision is blurry again. "So if you don't mind, I'm gonna. . ."

I wake up in another room. I'm still on my back and feeling pretty dizzy, but the sweet smell of molasses calms me down a little.

I stare up, and I guess my mind's still working—*dark wood ceiling and walls, a huge bookshelf along one wall, and a big stained-glass window*. No idea how the little guy got me in here. I must be twice his size. And my wings? I try to move them and fire shoots through the left one and I chirp out loud.

"Be still," a voice to my left says.

When I look toward it, the little guy is hunched over a large wooden desk, clear on the other side of the room. Got his head down, reading something. *Probably his Bible*, I think. Because if this shit doesn't send you to the owner's manual, I mean, what does?

And I can barely hear it, but the choir is singing out in the main church. Bet they shit themselves when they saw the hole in the roof. Wonder how he explained that? "Nice choir, Father. They're annoying as shit."

He stops reading and sits up a little, but he still doesn't turn toward me. "Yes, yes," he says. "It makes a particular sound, doesn't it. And you must stop cuss—"

"A shitty one," I say. I never did like sitting through the singing.

"Please," he says. "You must be familiar with it, given who you are. You know its sound."

And everyone from God to the Devil to the clergy themselves are speaking in riddles, pissing me off. "Know what sound? Put down that *Bible* and get that choir to shut up. They're killing my head."

"There is no choir," he says. Then he mutters, "Tuesday. . . I have no idea what I'm going to. . . The roof."

The choir keeps going and he keeps reading. I ask my body to move and I get more pain and a crackling sound for an answer. When I realize I'm lying on the floor on a tarp, I get more irritated. "Why the hell do you have me on the floor?" I try to roll over, but I'm still weak and all . . . sticky.

"I had to roll you in here on my car creeper," he says. "I could hardly. . . You are remarkably heavy. There was no sense even attempting to put you on the couch."

"You still got a guzzler? Benefits of the benevolent, huh?" I say. "Got you changing your own oil, though. So that's not totally legit." I look at the big brown leather couch next to me. "Leather couch grease-monkey," I chuckle softly and it hurts. And I try to sit up again, but the fire in my gut sends me back down.

"I told you not to do that," he says. "It says to keep you still."

"What says?" I ask. "Keep me still? I'm gonna kill that little fu—" And I wince at the pain. Dead man turned angel or not, pain is still a bitch.

He holds up a finger at me. "Profanity," he says. "And you are lucky that she did not kill you."

"She?"

"Yes," he says, "*he* is a she. You are—"

"That explains a lot," I say. Leave it to a woman to tear the living shit out of a man for no reason. "Mean little bitch."

"You have no idea," he says.

"If you haven't noticed there, Father Friendly," I say, "I'm the one on the floor with torn-up guts." I feel for my stomach. Angel, animal or asshole, you don't last long with no guts. But when I touch them, my belly is mostly healed back up. It's covered in sticky goo, though. "What the. . .? Why am I all sticky?"

"Molasses," he says it like he just explained why it's dark at night. "I had trouble finding enough. Only the black market carries pure. . ." And then he starts reading again. Not out loud, but I can just see his arm racing back and forth on his desk. And the choir fires up again.

"Dammit, I told you to shut them up."

"There is no way for me to read," he says. "If you want me to help you, you will have to endure the sounds. So be quiet and concentrate on healing. The molasses should help."

I sniff in a big whiff and smell the syrup. When I feel around, he's got me covered in it. I thought the smell was because *she* was lurking around. "What does molasses. . .?"

This time he looks up. "Wha—oh, yes," he says. "Think of it like blood. It's why yours is so dark. And the closest thing we have— molasses."

He's talking gibberish again, because pancake. . .? "You're kidding me, right? I'm made of pancake syrup? It says that in the *Bible*. Jesus, you guys are really pushing piss at the people now. How do you get anyone to believe that crap?"

"This isn't the *Bible*. This book . . . is the *Book of Blood*."

— XXXIII —

THE WHOLE THING comes racing back to my mind—every last stitch. *Book of Blood*, I think. And my eyes roll into the back of my head and the images hammer my vision like strobe lights. That little itch in the back of my head I wanna scratch, talking to God and the Devil—saying his name—all of it. What did they call—Life and Dal? *Makes sense*, I think. And now I know the dream's real.

"How did. . .?" I have no idea what to ask him first. "How do you know about that book? I never heard of it before. Not before I—" It's probably better if I don't tell him about meeting them. "Where did you get that?"

Now he turns his attention toward me. Then he pushes back from his desk and the chair squeals across the floor and the sound makes me wince. He stands up, walks around to the front of his desk, and slides the chair in front of it across the wood floor. The legs of the chair squeal across the floor as he pulls it next to me, and then he sits down and leans over to examine my stomach.

He sits back up and then looks around the room, like he's a dying bank-jacker who finally gets to tell someone where the credit-papers are buried. Someone that he knows won't rat him out.

He leans all the way down and whispers, like talking about it is a mortal sin, "Twenty years ago, I was in the basement."

And I bet I know what he was doing down there. "And he was threatening to tell his parents on you, so you had to—"

He stops whispering and says, "No, why does everyone assume. . .? You need to let go of your hatred and concentrate. This is no time to be rude for no reason."

"I wasn't the one who—"

"Not now," he says. "You want my help, you need to get serious. This isn't about little boys. We don't have time for you to indulge your arrogant ego."

Damn. . . He's right about two things. One, from what I remember, this guy. . . What was his full. . .? And I look at the name plaque on his desk. "Father Benito Octavio Benedetti" was one of the few God-dogs I respected. A straight-up, no-bullshit guy. He walked into Protection prisons and fifties to save souls, one murdering waste of blood at a time. He walked the talk—none of that preaching the Word from the pulpit piss. When he gave Kelly and me our pre-marriage counseling, he told us one thing: "Wake up in the morning and prop each other up all day, because the world is gonna do its best to knock the both of you on your ass." It was about as real as the church ever got for me. No way he's raping any kids.

The second. . .? I don't have time to lie around on the floor bleeding. I got a bitch to burn, maybe two. "Okay, you found it in the basement."

Now he eyes me like maybe he shouldn't say anything. After a couple of awkward seconds, I give him the eyebrows. I guess he comes to grips with it, because he says, "Under a great stone. It . . . it broke when I touched the writing on it . . . and then I knew. I understood."

"Knew what?"

He looks at me like I should get it. I don't. "Don't you see," he says. "The stone was a great seal. When it cracked open, I heard the voice."

He's off in Neverland now. God-dogs and hearing voices. Usually happens right before they look into the camera and ask you to call in with your hex-card number. And I chuckle a little.

"Yes, yes," he says.

He's getting that bug-eyed, wild look again. Or maybe he's been hitting the sauce harder since I been out cold. Hard to tell, because the stench-filled, piss smell of fear is doing its best to drown out the aroma of alcohol.

"I knew that's what would greet me when I came up from the basement," he says. "Ridicule . . . judgment."

I know I'm just encouraging him, but now I wanna know. "What did the voice say?" Mocking him? On another day, maybe, but it could help, ya never know.

He scrunches up his face and frowns.

I know the look, it's the same "Are you serious?" one I give people who ask me why I need a gun. *Gave* them, anyway. It feels like a long time ago, and if I remember, after a while, I realized it was no use talking safety and security with slaves.

It takes him about the same length of time to get that "Is this even worth my breath?" look off his face, too. Then he says, "It said, 'Come and see.' That's what all the beasts of the seals say. And I knew. I was sure I would be. . . I was no one, barely out of seminary. And I heard the voice of the beast of the Seventh, but there is no Seventh Seal." He opens his flask and takes a swig. He's trembling again. Then he screws the lid back on. "I would have been excommunicated at the very least. Maybe thrown in the sanatorium. So I hid it."

"Hid what?" On the floor, I can't see anything on his desk. "Show me what you're reading up there."

He turns to his desk, leans back, and slides a huge red book off it. The monstrous book drops heavily into his lap and he closes it and holds it up so I can read the cover—*The Book of Blood*. I can read it plainly this time. And now it's *my* eyes that are bugging out of *my* head. Not only can I read the writing, but now I know what's in it, too.

And he gets a satisfied look on his face. His frown turns to an eyebrow-high "told you so" look, and then he opens it and gets ready to read. "Mm-hmm," he says. He thumbs and flips the pages all the way to the back of the book. "You know this book, don't you? Listen to this. 'And I looked up and beheld a brighter angel than any in the heavens, ascend through the roof of the house of faith; and the rain went with her. And the blood of The Fallen had spilled at her hand as sweet nectar from the sap trees in the garden. And The Fallen laid in stillness in the house of faith. And judgment under my power was restored.' "

I wince as he speaks. *Ahh,* I think, *damn choir.*

He shuts the book and we stare at each other. Seems like a couple of minutes before either of us gets up the guts to speak.

I'm all guts today. "How long ago you find that?"

"Twenty years," he says. "As soon as I saw you lying there. . . I'm not crazy." He takes his flask back out, unscrews the top, and takes another swig.

"Jesus, Father, you're gonna suck the nipple right off that tit."

He ignores that one. "They would have. . . I knew they would have. If not for. . . Certainly for blasphemy."

He's gonna have to refill that thing pretty soon. Probably got a whole State liquor lounge in his big desk. Twenty years is a long time. Depending on how you pass the time, it can be a little too long. The father is going on about two years too many. I gotta get his mind on something else, keep him occupied. The killing was impulse before, blind rage on the rooftop. Now . . . I remember that I got a job to do. And if the stuff rolling around in my head—long ago flashes from the past—is true, he won't like it. "Read that to me again, will ya?"

He does, and the process seems to calm him down a little. The choir sounds still grind on my nerves, but if it stops him fidgeting, I'll suffer through them. When he's done, he rereads it in his head. Then he says, "That passage. . . I have never been able to . . . judgment under my. . .? Whose power?"

But by now it's obvious. "You should know, you wrote it."

It takes a couple minutes of protesting for him to calm down—denial is a powerful thing—and he's confused as shit now. "Voices in the basement," my ass. I point at his nameplate, but when he looks he still doesn't get it. I frown at him and say, "Benito Octavio Benedetti." And then I raise my eyebrows at him.

He's clueless—total alcohol-induced amnesia. "*Book of Blood*—B. O. B. " I can't believe it myself, but coincidence? Not likely. Still, there's no way he could have known any of the shit I've been through in the past couple of days. If that is how long it has been, because I'm losing track. "And that judgment part, that's my name."

"Your name is Jacob," he says. "And I didn't write this, I found it."

Twenty years. That's enough time to write a book that crazy. It would have to be an arrogant obsession. Something like that always is. It would leave even the strongest mind a little cracked. Especially if it all started coming true.

"My name is Jump," I tell him. "He gave it to me. And you can say you don't remember, but you wrote that book. I'd bet that on my last day in Vegas."

He's got a blank stare now. Confusion or denial, they still look the same. He shakes his head, probably hoping that will make what he's saying true. "I could not have. . .?"

And it all makes perfect sense to me. Seven days for her to build it. And now it's seven for me to burn it down. Time to get to the gutting.

— XXXIV —

IT TAKES ABOUT a half a day for me to feel well enough to sit up. After the father recovers from. . . Shit, he's not recovering, but at least now he's coherent.

He was a babbling mess for hours. When he finally calmed down, I sent him out for more syrup. Now that he's back, my body laps up the molasses like a dehydrated dog. Weird shit. I can't even pretend to understand it.

And he's back to reading his book—passing the time hunched over his woobie—scouring the text, trying to understand. Remember, maybe.

I'm going bat-shit and bored lying still during the constant choir crooning, so I sit up and flex my wing a little. *Better*, I think to myself. I'm starting to get a handle on my new best friends. Still no clue how I got my talons out, though. Gotta work on that for the little bitch.

He picks his head up from his book and straightens in his chair. Bug-eyes again. I'm getting used to that. And when I stand up and spread my wings all the way out, he slides one of the drawers on his desk open and reaches in.

I watch his hand disappear into the drawer. *Time to refill your little pacifier, huh*. I was wondering about that.

But booze isn't what shows up when he pulls his hand out of the drawer, and I'm staring down the barrel of a. . . I lean to the side a little to get a better look at the engraving on the barrel. Never stopped to think about it, but my eyesight is razor sharp and like . . . magnified if I want. I zoom in and read the writing on the side of the pistol:

King V99
K&T Arms

There's a little dirt left under his fingernails. "Dug it up while I was sleeping, huh." It's not a question. They inspect all the churches once a month—dogs and metal detectors, barking and beeping their way to the truth. Used to be one of the best places to stash them. Now . . . only way he has this thing is if he had it buried. Save it for a rainy day kinda thing. Guess I qualify.

Apart from staring at the father's pistol, there's something wrong. Takes me a couple seconds of looking at the little round opening at the end of his barrel to figure it out.

Not raining? I think, because when I slowly turn and look out the window, it's brighter than shit. The sun is breaking through the stained glass window in his office, casting rainbows on the walls. "Never figured you for a Gogo gun-guy, father."

When I look back, he's got both hands around it, and he's shaking worse than the gun. He glances at his book. "When you've seen what I have. . ."

And I push out all my feathers and I guess the scraping of steel and clanking metal sounds unnerve him, because—*Bam!*—he shoots me.

And the bullet bounces off and zings into a bookcase. It's an accident, I know, but he's shitting himself. "I'm sorry-I'm sorry!" *Bam!* And he does it again! "Oh my god—I didn't mean—"

And I screech and he drops the gun on his desk and grabs his ears and starts whimpering. Now I'm just annoyed. I fold my wings behind me—retract my feathers—even if I can be killed, I doubt it's going to come from the end of his little 9mm.

I look down at my lap. Gotta get some underwear, I think. Not that I give a shit, but I'm not sure if that would survive another one of the father's accidental discharges.

And now *I* drag the chair back over in front of his desk, scraping the floor like he did, slowly screeching his nerves on purpose. Torment is like a fine knife—depending on which end you get, it's either sugar-sweet or it feels like a bitch bee sting. And I slowly turn the chair backward, sit down, and then I lean in at him. I cross my arms on top of the backrest.

When he tentatively reaches his hand back toward his gun, I spread my wings a little, letting him know he shouldn't. Invincible or not, I don't like having a gun pointed at me, much less getting shot with it . . . twice. "So. . ." I say. "Father Ben. . ." And I raise my eyebrows and point to his big red book, open on his desk. "Where . . . in your little red manual there, does it say you are supposed to shoot me with a nine millie?"

"It . . ." And now he's reaching for the flask in his shirt again, shaking as he fumbles it out. "It doesn't." And he takes a good-sized pull.

"No *shit*," I say slowly.

"But you are—"

I watch him screw the lid back on his little pacifier. "Boozing and bullets," I say. "Tsh, tsh, tsh—you should know better."

I let him pick the gun up this time and he puts it back in his desk drawer, then slides the drawer shut. It's a good move for him, because I don't have time for this shit. It won't be long before that bright bitch is back. No idea why she left me leaking in the church instead of finishing the job. That was a mistake. And if this little boozehound did write this book, then I want some answers.

I reach over and touch the page that's open and a faint screech and cussing comes out when I run my finger over the parchment, "Rain. . ." it says.

And his eyes are wide when I ask him, "How do I kill her?"

It takes a few minutes for him to stop acting like a rabbit trapped in a cage with an eagle. Not sure if it's the five minutes or if it's his flask talking, but he finally settles down and makes peace with the understanding that he's helping me . . . and I'm not going to slice his head off with one of my wings.

I look out the window. "Okay," I say, "let's start simple." The sun is even brighter now. And from the angle of the "Jesus" rays, shining down into his office, filling the room with a foggy cone of light, I can tell it is afternoon. "Why is it sunny . . . in March?" At least I think it's March.

The father looks at the stained glass window above the big bookcase and he puts his hand on his forehead to shade his eyes. It's a common reaction on a winter day in the Northwest Quarter—seeing the sun is about like seeing God—it's hard to believe it exists behind all that gray.

And he mutters up at the window, from memory this time, "The rain went with her."

"That's pretty literal," I say to him. "I thought all this *Bible* and brimstone shit was an analogy or a metaphor, or whatever. That's what you preach, right?"

When he looks back down, I can see he's ready to get down to business. Self-preservation or not, it isn't every day that you get to live scripture. And he's excited now. "It's all interpretation," he says. "Some teach literally and others morph and meld the Word to their purposes. But faith"—he holds up an old finger and shakes it at me—"Faith is the key . . . and the testing of it. We all . . . every religion teaches this."

And he flips the book back to the end and "choirs" out the last few lines. I wince the whole time. Then he thumbs back a few pages and reads some more.

When he's finished rereading a book I'm sure he's read a thousand times, I say, "So, you wrote that . . . in blood, no less. Armageddon and God and the Devil? I still don't believe that shit. So tell me . . ." I really don't want to know the answer, because that means this old man has been off his State meds for a long, long time. "Where did ya get the blood?"

By now, he's coming to the realization that he is the author of this abomination. I'm sure it is confusing at best, especially given that he's sworn, or compelled by Christ, or some other horseshit, to only infect his congregation with the one "true" Word. But what he tells me next, neither of us knows how to react to it.

"It's . . . my own," he says. Then he holds up his hand. And I never noticed it before. . . For some reason I think I shoulda smelled it. He's got an ancient scar—crazy geezer had an IV line in a vein on the back of his hand.

— XXXV —

SO THERE IT is. The reality of it is simple enough. The believing? No wonder they call it faith. This crazy old priest wrote an unholy book in his own blood, and then the shit got real . . . and I'm living it. But how in the. . .? "Hey, Father . . . if you can still be called that." And I smile at him. "You're a sick bastard, you know that, right?"

He pauses at the statement, staring into space or judgment or some other daydream.

"Hey," I say a little louder, so I'm sure he snaps out of it, "how do you know how to. . .?" I point to the book. "What the hell language is that?"

He jerks his head a little and then stares past me. Through me really, because his face is glazed over—dumbstruck. "It's not only Hell," he says. "I did my graduate thesis on angelic script—the language of the faithful defenders of Heaven . . . and the fallen in Hell."

And that explains a lot. Spend enough time cramming your head full of these stories and pretty soon there's only one thing a guy like him wants—proof. And when you never get it. . . I guess it might be easier to conjure up a story of your own. So now we're all living inside his nightmare of a hallucination. And now he knows.

"I never thought it would. . ." he says. "It's just a book."

"So's the *Bible*," I say. "And look at all the shit that little fairytale has caused."

We both think about that for a couple seconds—him wondering

and me knowing. But wanting something to be true and believing it is doesn't prepare you for when it actually happens. I kinda wonder, if the real *Bible* started happening, would everyone *really* want it to be true? Throw a frog-plague down on the average citizen, today. . .? Yeah, not so eager to flip the switch on the blender when you're in it, I bet. "Well, you wrote this Armageddon son of a bitch, so how does it end?"

He thinks about it for a couple of seconds. Then he says, "First, don't call it that."

"What?" I ask. "Armageddon—end of humanity."

"It's not—"

"Why?" I ask. "Everyone knows the damn story. God sends angry angel down—that's me—wipe out the sinners. Badabing—reboot humanity. Judgment Day—simple shit. You should know that."

"It is simple," he says, "however. . ."

"However" again. I wish they would just start with the truth.

"We're already judged," he says. "And you," He looks at me with knowing eyes. He's a different little boozing bloodhound now, calmer, a little maniacal-looking, if you ask me. "You are the judgment, 'Jump.' Clever. He sent you to—"

"Who did?"

"God, of course," he says. "You are the wrath of God. Only in my book, there is no redemption, only vengeance. Because when I really thought about it—studied it and experienced man's true nature for myself—we are beyond redemption. And the picture that the true *Bible*—the original unaltered version—paints of God is not an understanding one. He is judgment and wrath."

Regret's an easy thing to smell when you are packing a ton of it yourself. But he's dead on. We've been at each other's throats so long. . . Our cages are so full of shit, I wouldn't wish that cleanup on the nastiest demon in hell. But I don't know how to break it to him—his foundation has been rocked quite a bit. Forget who I think actually sent me or not, probably both of them, but he's got to know. "About that," I say. "God is actually. . ." And there's just no way around it. "She's a woman."

That little tidbit is something the father never considered—who does, right? Not *even* women. But he takes the news in a different way than I think he should. And he whips open his book and turns to the first page. And he runs his finger and the choir sings—that's his translator. Screaming obscenities—I like mine better. By the nodding and grunting, it looks like he understands what he's reading, but he's not happy about it.

"That's not how I meant it," he says.

And I laugh out loud. What else can I do? "Lost in translation, huh. Go figure that shit. What's the matter, Father, someone misinterpret the Word?" And now I'm "bunny-earing" just like the Devil. I can see the appeal.

"Don't. . ." And he stands up and grabs a big, navy blue, hardbound book from his bookcase, and then he whips it open. "God is *not*. . ." He roughs up the crepe paper-thin pages until he crackles his way to what he's looking for. When he gets there, he pounds his scrawny finger on the page. "Right here."

Then he sits back down, turns the book toward my side of the desk, and taps his finger on the page a couple times. Underneath it is a symbol and a description written below the symbol in big bold letters:

186

***

BREAD OF LIFE

"Bread of life?" I ask. "Since when was. . .? I never heard God called that."

"John, six-thirty-five," he says it like he's saying his own name—not a thought to it. I guess you memorize the whole thing at God academy. But just to make sure, he's headed to his bookcase again and this time . . . it *is* the *Bible.* And he's obviously flipping to check and see if John was full of shit or not. "Here . . . right here."

And he hands the book to me and I read it to myself—run my finger along the words. The *Bible* doesn't screech:

And Jesus said unto them, I am the bread of life. . .

I frown and look at him out of the corner of my eye. "I don't mean to interrupt your delusion, but this says Jesus."

"There are those who believe that he *was* God."

"And you're one of 'em?"

"But he isn't a woman."

"Listen," I say, "before we turn this into a *Bible* lesson and that bitch comes back to finish me off, here's what happens: Jesus —'Bread of Life. . .' Why can't you just stick with one name? No, you gotta get all fancy, spouting 'shalls' and 'untos' and 'thous' all over the place . . . give everyone twelve different names to remember for one person . . . confuse the living shit out of anyone who bothers to read the whole story. Gets to the point that you are even confusing your-selves." And now I'm annoyed, because even I can figure out how this got broken. "Who gives the bread of life?"

I wait for him to say it, but he's not going to.

At this point, I'm beyond blasphemy, so I do his dirty work for him. "Bread of Life . . . breast of life—woman? So you go getting creative with your little angel scribbles and guess what, you got the same thing back—someone interpreted your little word in a way you never intended. *Shocker*, I know, but now . . . well, *now* there's a mother up there who gave birth to her precious little children of humanity and she's pretty pissed off that we didn't all turn out to be doctors and lawyers."

He's staring at me now—I'm telling him a story he doesn't want to hear.

"And you think the Devil is an evil son of a bitch? You have no idea."

And he slumps back in his chair, staring into the confusion of his broken-up faith, and then he reaches for his shirt pocket.

"Knock it off," I say, and I thrust my hand across faster than he can comprehend it, snatch the flask from him before either of us realizes I did it—I tear his shirt pocket in the process. And I unscrew the lid on his little "medicine cabinet" and pour it out on the floor. "There's nothing in here that's gonna help."

On another day, I might have disagreed with myself—emptied it down my own throat. I drank plenty after Amy. Anymore . . . it'll dull the pain, but the cut . . . booze just makes it bleed worse. And right now, not even sad to say it, I'm thirsting for that very thing—blood.

"It's not Armageddon," he mutters. At least his brain's still working. I can tell by the blank look on his face that he's wrapping it around the realization that he has penned us all into Purgatory.

"What is it, then?" I ask.

"Extinction."

FAILURE

— XXXVI —

WHILE THE FATHER sleeps off his morning booze and blasphemy binge, I finger my way through his book a few more times, ferreting in and out of the "dids" and "shalls," as I screech-curse my way to some semblance of understanding.

I'm slowly figuring out that the only thing worse than being a Protection lapdog for the State, is being God and the Devil's personal attack puppy. Cleansing humanity or not. . . I could really give a shit. From what I remember it's a tragic waste of blood anyway. But after damn near memorizing the father's unholy book, and figuring out what my new job is . . . well, let's just say I'm nobody's bitch.

"Father," I try to wake him up out of the cold stupor I let him slip into. Poor bastard fell asleep in his chair and now he's drooling all over himself. Boozin' and blasphemy, it'll wear you out. And he is out—not even a sleep jerk out of him. So I give him a loud screech to snap him back from whatever new blood book he's brewing up in there. "Wake up! We got work to do."

He's got a little bathroom off the side of his office—ah, the perks of power—and after he slowly trickles himself rid of whatever State swill he had in his little flask, he sways his way back and flops into his big leather chair.

I sit on the leather couch across from his desk. I can tell by the stiffness, there's one of those back-cracking, pullout beds inside it.

"Fine example you are."

He mumbles something back. Might be a curse. Right now, it's the least of my worries. Not that I'm afraid. I'm more worried that I won't get a chance to balance out the scales. But the father cursing?

"So I went through your—"

And he's snoring already, snorting in his sleep.

Shit. . . I brush at him with my healed wing. "Goddammit," I say, "pay attention." I'm a little too wild though, and my wing slices up his shirt and . . . shit, he's bleeding, I can smell the copper. Well, at least now he's awake, because he's squawking like a plucked pigeon.

But he was probably in the middle of some dream because he starts squawking nonsense, "Don't! You can't kill her. Take mine, but—"

Killing him's not even worth being disappointed over. "Get a grip. I'm not killing you. But you better get your ass sober or I might just cut you up so you can stay awake. And no more of your tin friend either. You really wanna sleep through your own story?"

"Doesn't matter," he says. "Humanity. . . We are all going to die."

"You're not dead yet," I tell him. "And trust me, you're gonna want to avoid it for as long as possible." Then I turn back to the book. "Boiling blood bastards," I mutter. Seven days. . . They want me to burn the garden in seven days. Then I get an idea.

Once the father stops whining, I patch *him* up this time. Using normal human supplies—couple a bandages, antibacterial ointment, and a good dose of rubbing alcohol I found in the church medicine kit. Nothing like some burning antiseptic in an open cut to wince you out of an alcoholic daze. Shoulda poured some molasses on the top of the little pancake pussy, too.

And I'm feeling a whole lot better now. Thinking more clearly, too. Sure the lust to get back to it is there, and the book says there's plenty more killing coming, but my little itch has returned—I feel like I'm forgetting a part of it. "You know, I noticed something," I say to him. Then I run my finger along a line and the cussing changes to cooing as I get to the part about tomorrow. "There's a point in here where you skip to the future. About right where we are now. What do you think —"

"May I see it?" he asks. And he winces a little as he reaches across his desk for the book. Then he spins it around toward him and starts reading it in his head from the beginning. He talks to me as he reads, "The *Bible* skips back and forth—past to present to future and back— sometimes in the same chapter. Part of the appeal of interpreting what it's truly trying to tell us. But this is. . . It is all in the. . ."

"What?" I ask. I can tell he's still got a little denial that he's the author.

"These things that happened are in the past," he says.

"Turn to now," I say.

He moves his finger along and finds the right point. As he does, his choir changes pitch and tempo and I grit my teeth a little.

He figures it out faster than I did. "This hasn't happened yet. And you. . . If you wanted to."

I smile at him—he may just be worth keeping alive. I give him my best Rural Zone accent, "Damn skippy, bubba," I say. "Time to get some shut-eye, 'cause in the morning . . . we goin' huntin'."

It's not long before we are both sleeping. And I got a stupid little rhyme jacking around in my head:

* * *

. . .some dreams we leave and some we don't
And some we can't . . . and some we won't. . .

And I know I'm dreaming. I swear, if they. . .

The sound of a little girl, screaming bloody murder, snaps me back into my nightmare. And then there's a woman crying with her. Not that I give a shit—there's going to be plenty of crying soon enough. But this . . . the feeling is different from the choir. Not only do I want it to stop—it's grinding my nerves like too much coffee—but I wanna find out who caused it and give them a little wing fillet. *Who. . .?*

The dream isn't coughing up the answer, so I try to push my way to it—brute force, that's the key. Well, mine, anyway. In another life, I would just torture it out of someone. But it's not torture floating through this vision—something a little more . . . eternal. And I'm reaching for the name, and I see a tall, pointed building and I'm almost to the top. . . *Gotcha!*

— XXXVII —

I WAKE BACK up to the sound of the choir singing again. And the father's still in his chair, reading away. Helluva alarm clock, I gotta tell ya. At least he's not sticking a gun in my face. No idea how long I was out, but I can tell by the drops running down the stained glass above his office, it's raining again. It's a nice, comfortable, dim gray out. Makes me feel better. Seattle without rain is like cake without frosting —just doesn't taste right.

He pauses when he realizes I'm awake. "Bad dreams?" he asks.

"Not as bad as some." The others were worse. In fact, that one was kinda sweet-tasting. At least now I got a direction to point the vengeance that's piling up. *Vengeance in the house of the Lord. . .* And I chuckle a little caw out at the thought.

I'm sure the cawing and cooing sounds take some getting used to. "Wh—what's so funny?" he asks.

"Isn't it all?"

"I . . . never considered. . ."

I smile at him. "Yes, ya did." And I point at his book. "That's a whole lotta considering in there."

Underneath all the crispy belief in his tightly-pressed black clothes, his bright-red blood flowed through a big question mark in his heart . . . and he transfused it into his book.

But as much as I'd love to piss around, licking my wounds in church, shooting the shit with the fallen father, it's back to the brim-

197

stone. *She smacked my ass down to a church of all places*, I think.

I'll get to that little shit, too. Right now, I got a plan to kill a couple annoying little birds . . . with the same angry stone. "Pack up your penance. We're going on a little trip."

I smell the piss of fear ramp back up. Coming to grips with his book or not, he's none too eager to go flying around in his own story, especially not with me. He says, "I—I have the church. And. . ."

But it's a funny thing about curiosity, and he has to have a pile of it by now. You don't write a book like that because you wanna sit in church, trying to convince people what you think is real. That book is about shoving it up the ass of authority. And in that, we both have serious questions for the powers that believe. And there's only one place I can think of to sink a talon into them both . . . maybe all three. Wouldn't that be nice?

"I can't—"

"You want answers?" I say to him. And then I flex my wings and scrape the steel against itself. They're strong—hardly a hint of the broken wing. "I know where to get 'em."

"Where are you going?"

"Purgatory," I tell him. And whether he likes it or not, "You're coming, too."

— XXXVIII —

THE TWO-STORY apartment perched atop the pinnacle of the Smith Tower in Seattle used to be some artist's little nest of inspiration. No citizen really knows who lives up here now. Powerful people, they like to hide in the sky, above all the messes they make. And even if you know where they are, it's almost impossible to drag them down to the street so they can clean it all up. But if you're searching for the buzzard that just shit down on the rotting carcass of your life . . . look up.

I know who's up here. Clawed my way through my dream to figure it out. It was easy to find the bastard after that. Hard to miss this assfucker's nest. Even the tip-top of the building looks like the head of a huge cock, pointed straight up at Heaven, as if to say, "You're next."

Nice fake fireplace, though. It's a huge, white-marbled monstrosity. I shake my head a little in disgust. The darkest creatures. . . Caves are always white. Everything is white in here, and he's got two snow-white, full-curl, Dall sheep heads, stuffed and hanging above the fireplace.

He's never been hunting in his life. And even if he had, Dall sheep? A long time ago—my father used to tell me about it—it was twenty grand apiece for a guided hunt in Canada. Twenty-five if you wanted to drag them off the top of a mountain in Alaska. Now, fifty thousand credits each . . . just for the heads. Only place to get them would be the black market. His wife probably "bravo mike'd" them because they looked chic in some old architecture magazine she read. Then again, she's probably on the board of "People for the Elite Treatment of Assholes," so who knows. And now I'm just working myself up, feeding my fire before I burn this place down.

The fireplace has a huge, six-inch-thick, marble mantel, too. Perched on it like an eagle—the ten talons on my toes, piercing into the soft rock. . . Yeah, I figured the talons out. Anyway, my wings tuck behind me nicely, right between the two sheep heads. And I reach out and stroke each of their necks—snowflake soft. It's a perfect place to perch, while I watch this guy and his wife sleep like baby seals. His daughter's room is in the loft on the second floor. For some reason, I can smell her up there. She'll be down soon enough.

I listen to him snore for a couple minutes. Bet he's not waking up to bloodcurdling screams from his daughter's headaches every night. No, he's smarter than that. And the first rule of drug dealer school is: Don't shoot up your daughter with your own dope. Yeah, I figured that out, too. And I'm having trouble holding in my amusement.

Look at him—Francis King, CEO of King and Tamonos Enterprises—monarch on the mountain.

This isn't the only mountain the good father and I are gonna visit today. I made him wait on the street. His part is down there. I don't think he has the stomach for what's coming up here.

I tilt my head and bob it up and down a little. There's a lot of annoying little angel-tics I have to get used to. And my talons scrape a trough in the marble as I grip down, and they squeak softly. Doesn't seem to matter, he is snoozing like a man without a care in the world. Up here—high above the cretins as they peck out lives from the scraps of the bones he sends over his railing— he can rain his benevolence down on citizens and consumers, like feeding ducks breadcrumbs at the State park pond.

I know it's nice—not a pigeon shit of a decision in his life that will ever come back to roost and rain down crap on his roof. King. . . He's the worst kind of ruler. Killer without a conscience.

Time for him to meet his match.

— XXXIX —

FATHER BENITO STOOD in the darkness and drizzle, in a doorway across the street from the entrance to the Smith Tower. He was so busy worrying about the instruction that his unholy creation, Jump, had given him, that he hadn't realized where they were going when they flew there. But he knew this building. It was the same place that she lived. He had to shake the thought. *One sin at a time, Benito,* he warned himself.

The rain leaked over the edge of the hood of his black rain jacket and a few drops dripped on his lips. He ran his tongue over them and licked in the moisture.

Dehydration was a constant problem and he always forgot to get enough water when he drank. He pulled out his little flask from the back pocket of his pants and sucked down a small pull of State liquor. He refilled it during his unholy creation's dream. A dream whose only details were that they were going to end every bad person's evil ways. Someone who preyed on children, Jump had told him.

Benito, he thought, *you have come a long way. Are you ready to meet your maker?* "I hope so," he muttered.

Jacob's. . . It was hard to think of the huge angel that way anymore. Unlike the gospel, Jump's orders weren't open to interpretation. The father only hoped he could carry them out, because the consequences were clear. "Do it or burn for eternity." Jump had seemed sure that he could arrange for that fate.

The father had never intended for any of this. But try as he might, he had never felt the warm touch of the grace of God or heard the heavenly voice of The Father sing in his ears.

After his seminary and graduate thesis were over, he felt certain that God would speak to him . . . in some way, at least. Something to help him reconcile the vileness of humanity and the pain and suffering he witnessed in the world—solidify his faith.

But the warm breath of the Word never whispered in his ears, so he took it upon himself to reach toward God. What came out ate at his soul and fogged his faith. But the words would not stop and he poured them out in blood across the pages of his book. When he finished, he realized how dangerous it was, so he hid the book away in the basement of his church and convinced himself that it did not exist. His flask helped. Now his unholy book had spawned an avenging archangel that had the answers he craved. The price—denying everything he had ever been taught. It was not the path he had planned.

Then again, he had already strayed from his faith . . . more than once or twice. *In another life, Benito*, he thought.

He motioned the sign of the Holy Trinity across his chest, and then he reached in his pocket and pulled out his Rosary. His lips trembled as he kissed the black and red beads, and then he began.

He spoke from memory, barely hearing his own words. The events in the church proved to him that his rituals might be just that. The glass sliver of faith he had left was shattered along with the stained glass in the roof, but old dogs . . . and old habits died hard. So he chanted . . . and prayed.

— XL —

I SQUAWK OUT a loud screech at Frank and his wife in my newly acquired tongue. If the two of them were awake and could understand, it probably would've translated as "Wake your evil asses up!" I'm not a hundred percent sure, I'm still learning the lingo. But right now . . . I'm in a mood.

And all the glass in the place shatters, and there's a helluva lot of it. The crystal chandelier explodes and the black market antique Chihuly glass art shatters everywhere. Oh yeah, no rules for the rich. The china, the dishes and the mirrors. . . Apparently, rich people like to look at themselves a lot. If I had to tally it all up, I'd say they got about seventy years bad luck, bursting and falling like raindrops of razors to the floor. Doesn't really matter, when this is all over, seventy years will feel like a five-minute wet dream.

And Frank jumps out of bed first—off and over to his side of the bed—away from his wife. So much for chivalry. And he's yelling at me. He hasn't had time to figure it out yet, so he's ranting at nothing, "What was. . .? Babs, what the hell's going on?"

"Babs". . . I assume that's his wife's name. When I look at her side of the bed, she seems a little more purposeful, and she reaches beside the bed and I see a flash of bright silver—holy shit, she's got a gun on her nightstand!

No burying them six feet underground for her, I guess. I don't know why I'm surprised by that, but before I can control myself I send a pinfeather at her shoulder and it zips through her back and right out her right silicone breast. The "pop" and ooze that follows confirms that.

Back when he bagged her, I bet she was as fine a trophy as the Dall sheep. Now, she's a hagged-out bloodsucker, looking like some bounty killer's bleach-blonde bitch. I send a couple of pinfeathers through her ass and hips—see if there's silicone in there, too. And she's spraying blood onto their nice white sheets and she starts screaming.

But somehow she makes it to the little pistol on her nightstand and she grabs it and spins around and—*Bam*!

And *holy shit*, blondie can shoot, or that was her last ounce of luck, because I feel the bullet sting as it slices across my face. And, not that I think it's any threat to me—I feel the wound heal up pretty fast—but I'm still not used to getting shot. Couple of my bigger steel feathers later. . . It's gonna take more than silicone to pump blonde-mommy's deflated chest back up.

And Frank's yelling, "Jesus Christ! Jesus Christ! Jesus Christ! . . ." Over and over again as if God is going to send her only son down to save him . . . personally. But that's just how they think.

I smile from the mantel. Maybe she just did the opposite.

He stops barking fast enough that I know that bone was probably getting expensive to keep gnawing on. An arrogant dog can buy another bitch to bury his bone in, but a little tree squirrel, worried about losing his nuts in a nasty divorce. . .? I just did him a favor.

"Goddammit! What the hell?" And he's jumping around in his little black silk boxers with his little Chinese symbol tattoo on his chest, and he's waving his arms at me. "Jesus Christ! Don't kill me. Don't kill me. I got—I got credits."

And there it is—credits. That's his real god—buy his way out of Hell. "Ass-ram rich," I think they call it. He hasn't got a good look at me yet, or I'm sure he'd be looking to negotiate with something else.

I don't even have time for the contempt, before his little spawn screams her way down from her loft on the second floor. Even in the dark, I can see the tan against her little wife-beater t-shirt and too-tight, pink hip-hugger panties. She's freshly back from Cancun, Mexico, or some other plump paradise, busting bills with her pussy-posse of Parisy wannabes.

And she's got her mother's genes—no way Frank's involved in the birth of this little supermodel-in-training. For some reason, I feel like I recognize her, but blonde-mommy was probably banging some State Revenue usage agent so he'd look the other way at all the contraband they got in here. Not even his own kid?

And she's yelling at her own parents to find out what all the commotion is about, and why she's getting woken up when she has to catch a flight in the morning. She's a furious little shit, I'll give her that.

And the whole flock of them are a walking, squawking cliche in the sky. I wish they weren't—it might make this a *little* tougher. No matter, when she sees her mother's blood-soaked corpse, she flips out and starts dancing and hopping and holding her mouth, and then she just vomits all over the place.

That's the drugs. I laugh out loud. I know, I know, but I just can't help it. "Hey," I say to her, "at least you won't have to go in the bathroom and stick your finger down your throat."

And I can feel them up in Heaven or down in Hell—wherever—

judging me for my cruelty and indifference. Judge me? I am judgment—God's judgment, her evil sidekick's, maybe even the father's, down on the street. But none of that is why I'm here. I'm here for my own. I would like to say I'm doing it for Amy . . . or Kelly, but that would be bullshit. This is about me.

"Shut up!" I yell at them both. It comes out as a deafening screech, and the glass doors to the deck of the penthouse blow out and so does the glass railing around it. And I laugh again and mutter to myself, "Glass houses. . ."

I think they get what I'm saying, because he shuts up. Her. . . She can't help it and she's sobbing and crying, grinding on my nerves.

"Just knock it off," I say to her. "You're hurting my head."

And then I spread my wings out as far as they will go—give them a good look at the nightmare they just woke up in. And I flap them just enough to hop down from the fireplace and onto the floor. When I do, they both back up, and they go gaping-mouth silent.

"Oh . . . my . . . God," he says.

Blondie-junior's hysteria turns to awe—it's not every day you see a winged man. "You!" she shouts it like she's pointing to a jacker that just stole her purse. And she's looking at me weird. "It was you." Then she looks at her mother. "You—you killed my mother!" she yells.

Guess it wasn't awe.

"Mercedes," Frank says to her, "don't."

I roll my eyes back. Of course. And I can't wait until these pretentious pricks start naming their kids "Tesla" and "Prius." And I fold my wings back in and pop out the talons on my left hand. That shuts her up.

And I walk to the woman's lifeless husk, squat down, and look it over while they watch. Nothing is coming out yet. I wonder how long it takes?

It'll be soon enough, so I grab hold of blonde-mommy's chest and ribcage, and I feel my talons sink in deep—pop the sack of silicone shit on her other breast. The slippery slime oozes out onto one of my talons. *Sticky. . .*

And they both gasp hard when I fling her body out the hole in the glass wall. They watch with their mouths open—blondie-junior, trying to feel more by whining, and her father, silent, glad as shit that it's not him. How do I know that? I can smell it on them both. And blonde-mommy and her oozing boobs arc and disappear over the railing.

Couple a seconds later, up comes that smacking, bone-splattering meat sound and "Mercedes" starts whining again.

"I told you to stop," I say. "He'll buy you a new one. You can probably share clothes. Win-win, if you ask me."

I need all three of them, of course. So no one's leaving the penthouse alive, but I'm not quite ready to let them know that. Something's still itching me about this girl, though. And my mind is getting flashes of some kinda shit. Some roof, but not the—shit, I don't have time for it. Cramming a year's worth of revenge into a few minutes is difficult, even for a vengeful bastard like me.

I turn and look at Frank. "You know who I am, Frank?" He should know.

Even now, he thinks he's important enough to banter. "Should I?"

"Don't get cute." And I start walking around the room slowly, hopping a little and tic-jerking my head from side to side, pacing my way back and forth.

I don't know why. Maybe it's because I've been lying on my back, busted up in a church. Maybe because this is like the "Christday" of revenge. Anyway, I'm antsy and I can almost taste the blood.

Blood's coming soon enough, but right now, I take in a big whiff of the putrid piss smell of fear.

"Okay," he says. "You're an—"

"You're a angel," little Mercedes says. Now she's pacing, too, biting her nails. "I told them that shit. I told them. I saw you. I saw her. I—I saw the other one, too. Angels, I fuckin' knew it."

And I stop and look at her. She's about as jittery as the father and his flask. But saw me?

"I knew it, I knew it," she says. "I *told* them I saw you. Bitches didn't believe me. *Doctor. . .* Therapy mother. . ."

And that's a little wrinkle in the parchment. I sniff in hard and then I smell it. The coke's easy to spot. Of course she's on coke—every rich brat and their mother can get the State's coke—but there's. . . Smells like . . . dove-angel piss . . . judgment or something. No idea how I know it, but it's like a dog marked a hydrant—a familiar smell? "When did you—"

"She tried to kill herself," Frank says. "We had to. . . The doctors brought her back and she was going on and on about angels. And—"

"I didn't try to kill myself," she says. Then she turns toward me. "I told him that." And then she turns back toward him. "I told you that. Psych *asshole.*"

Psych doctor. No one but a rich bastard can get access to one of them. Average citizen tells someone they saw an angel—one way ticket, 5150 hotel. But money buys a whole lotta crazy, so little Miss Mercedes. . . She'll be easy.

"It was an accident!" she yells at him. "I OD'd. I'm not some *loser* suicide." And now she's got her arms crossed tight, glaring at me. "Didn't believe me. There he is, right there . . . *daddy*. Now what are you gonna. . .? Ha, you are *so* dead."

And that last one is just—and I'm smack in the middle of an episode of "Beverly Bitches," listening to the two of them get ready to use me for therapy. Not happening.

"Stop!" I yell. Whatever glass is left breaks and falls. There isn't much, but it sounds like it keeps falling and the high-pitched sounds of shattering lasts too long. Then I realize it's not the glass.

I don't care that much about the sirens, but I can hear the faint sounds of dove-angel screeching. And now, I got no time for this shit.

And there's no sense trying to carry *her* up—she's marked already— some other angel's cab credits. I move toward her.

She backs up a little. "No-no-no," she says, "you said I could—"

But I grab her and out the window little Mercedes goes, screaming her way down, cussing at me all the way until she smacks and explodes meat on the street. Hers will be the guide.

"Holy shit! Holy shit!" he yells. And he can see it coming—powerless in his own ending. "I'm sorry. Jesus Christ, whatever I did, I'm sorry. Please-please-please! If I would've—"

And that's how it is for everyone, I bet. I look at him and mock-wave my hands as I talk, "Oh, if I'd only known, I would've done it differently. I would've been nicer, I wouldn't have forced your daughter to get those shots."

And now he knows why, and he starts crying and begging. It's pathetic, really. Jesus Christ, if you're gonna play chicken with God— stick a dildo up her children's asses your whole life—don't be a pussy and turn the wheel at the last minute. You gotta plow head-on through the fence around her garden and do a couple of donuts in her daisies. Let her know what you really think about her "rules of the road."

I tear him up just enough—make sure he's still conscious for the flight down. *I owe the father that much*, I think.

And that is just a—no idea where that thought came from.

I got no time, those souls are coming out any minute. I look at him —any more and it might take a bucket to get his body down to the street. It's not enough, not by a long shot. It'll have to do. Today, I got bigger bitches to boil.

— XLI —

I GRAB FRANK by one of his flapping arms and I get a moan and then a scream back. Then I fling him out the broken windows, send him into his own final fall. And I hop to the ledge and jump, follow his whining body down in a wings-back power dive. I almost slam the pavement with him, trying to make sure that I don't miss them, but I pull up at the last minute and his sack of meat cracks wide open like guppy guts. Brains and bile burst out the sides of him and splatter across the street.

And I open my wings wide—slam the brakes—pull up and flap over and then I hover, waiting off to the side of the street in the shadows of an ally. And then blonde-mommy's husk—shit, her body is unrecognizable—starts moaning and her soul wriggles its way out of her titless, gutless pile of bile. And right on time, a dark-colored dove-angel—express driver to Hell—shows up, and apparently they got both flavors down there, because this dark girl angel is pulling and tugging at blonde-mommy's soul. But it doesn't look like the writhing little maggot is quite ready.

Who is, really? To tell you the truth, I was kinda counting on them not wanting to go. I'm counting on something else, too. We'll see.

And there he is, just like I told him—lucky for him—and the father rushes from the dark doorway where he was hiding and, quicker than the little boozed-up priest should be able to, he slings his

Rosary beads over the dark angel's head, around her neck. Then he's on her back and she takes off with both of them. And she's squawking and screeching at him, trying to shake him off. But if he's done what I told him to, he's been chanting in that doorway for long enough.

I send a couple of sharp squawks and screeches at her, "He's coming with you." And quicker than that, she stops squawking and starts flapping slowly and the three of them are headed up. And I'm sure the father's shitting himself, and I cluck out a chuckle and a little caw. Some things just work.

When little Mercedes' maggoty butterfly claws its way out, a bright white angel screeches his way down through the fog and snatches her up.

The white angel hesitates a little—drops her to the street and picks her up a couple times—before he looks around and then looks up in the sky.

Whatever he's waiting for doesn't happen, and he flaps and starts flying up.

Apparently, blondie-junior didn't try to commit suicide after all. *Even after all the other shit?* I think. And then I remember where we're going. I don't think it matters much which color "cabbie" picks you up. I think the point is where you are headed. Because, dark or light, these angels are all flapping in the same direction. And that's what I was counting on the most. *Homing pigeons.*

And then I hear Frank's husk howling like a shot dog, and it's my turn. I hope this works or the father is gonna have some explaining to do when he gets where they are going.

Then I hear it. Screeching and squawking down through the fog like it's going to miss the last chopper out of Baghdad. And as soon as the sound breaks through the mist, *it* is a she. Tough luck, sister.

This one is gray, and she spins and darts in a beautiful display of flying that would make a hummingbird hang up her wings. This ain't her first rodeo—the little chickie has mad flying skills. Too bad. . . No idea why I care, but. . .

When she swoops in on Frank, his soul is fighting her hard. And she's flapping and squawking and beating her wings on him, but Frank is a fighter. He distracts her just enough.

When I slam into the back of the little gray angel, she's caught completely off guard. I mean, who attacks an angel coming to pick up a soul? That's probably the look on her face, but I can't see it, because I sucker-punched her from behind. And she drops Frank's soul and tries to screech at me, but I've got both sets of hand talons around her throat and my feet talons are buried ten spikes deep, through her back and into her chest. The sound comes out as muffled chirping. But no matter what language it is, it's not hard to recognize the word, "No. . ."

I rough her up quite a bit before I drop her. I don't want to kill her, but I can't have her following me either. Regardless, I can't be distracted if that bright bitch shows back up. I hover a little and watch as gray-girl flutters and limps her wings off into the fog.

Before all the judgment starts, angels are tough, chick or not. I got a cross through the gut that proved it, remember? So don't go giving me any of that "beating up on women" shit, because I got my ass kicked by one of them. Regardless, the father was right—angel blood is red.

* * *

I head down to snatch up Frank. Well, his rotten soul, anyway. I leave his wasted husk of a life where it should be, splattered on the street, washing away with the cleansing truth of the relentless rain.

And I clamp my talons down on Frank's maggoty moth and fly up after the others.

"Sorry, sweetie," I squawk it toward where I last saw the little gray dove. It's the least I can say, I took her ticket back.

— XLII —

WHEN I CATCH up to the dove-angels transporting the souls I just served up, the father is holding on for dear life, probably scared shitless about where I told him we are headed.

Yeah, I told him. He didn't believe me. But like I said, believing and seeing for yourself. . .

And the one carrying Mercedes. . . He's in the lead and flying toward a huge bright hole in the star-studded black of space.

I hang back a little. Despite the saddled-up father, they don't seem to notice that anything is wrong, but I'm not taking any chances. I zoom in and scan the bright hole ahead for any sign of that aggressive little angel, bursting out of there. But she doesn't show herself and the other two angels cruise along like this is just a routine flight from Seattle to salvation. They've done it a million times.

The one in front doesn't look back. He's focused. The dark one packing the father glances back at me a couple times, but whether she's afraid of me, or the father's Rosary "bit and bridle" are working like I figured, she stays in formation.

And Frank's soul is squirming around down there in my talons. He knows what's coming. I squeeze tighter. I could say it's so I don't drop him, but that's bullshit. Whatever vengeance I missed on him when he was alive, I figure I can get in a couple licks before I tuck him safely in at the hotel Hell.

* * *

It seems like it only takes a few minutes. Might be more, the whole time thing is messing me up. But there's no time to wonder, because the leader is through the bright light and his wings are cupped up like a duck landing on his favorite pond, and then the other one cups her wings too—sets up to land beside him.

They circle together and I cup hard to catch up. I can feel the crisp cut of the snowflakes as my wing feathers slice through the falling white. And there's the mountain and the roof of the huge temple on top of it rotates open slowly, and the leader dives down and so does his wing-woman. Then I set my wings and drop in hard beside them.

Get ready for the show, I think, because, "Surprise, mom, I'm home," seems a little bit too risky. So until I figure out exactly what I'm going to do next, I tuck in behind the tail feathers of the other two and flutter to a soft landing behind them.

I didn't notice them when we landed, but the grandstands in the shadows of the huge arena are packed. Only these fans are all clucking and screeching, and squawking and cawing like . . . well, like tens of thousands of angels. Millions is probably a better guess, because the place is stuffed like a turkey. Light, white, black, dingy gray, and when I look, there's even some golden angels perched on rows of railing that encircle the entire stadium.

I can barely look at the golden ones, because they are so bright. But every one of them is flapping their steel wings, cawing like they are prepping for . . . war.

And as fast as the roof opened it closes, and the whole place goes black. Then a huge cone of light blasts the entire arena and I see her float out to the center.

There you are. I look over at the father and he's hugged so tightly to the back of his ride that you can barely tell he's there. In fact, with his black clothes and jacket on, he kinda blends right in with her dark back feathers.

He looks at me and I smile and wink back at him. Then I lean over and whisper, "Careful what you wish for."

And he squeezes his eyes shut, preparing for the worst. Freshly landed in the middle of the Hallowed Hall of the Word . . . safely tucked atop the Great Mountain of the Eternities . . . on the back of an angel in the Arena of Reckoning—I memorized all that shit— I bet he's probably second-guessing how badly he wanted to know.

And I recite the passage in my head: *And high on the Great Mountain of the Eternities, in the Hallowed Hall of the Word: the Destiny of Souls, the Bread of Life and the Dark Angel of Light did know of their loins.*

I must have read it ten times while Father Benito slept, before I figured it out.

I guess I got it right, because here we are, right at the beginning of his little red book, slipped in the back door to Heaven with the words he wrote. Well, not quite Heaven, but Purgatory is close enough.

As fast as I finish patting myself on the back, six golden angels scream from the sides of the hall and snatch the three souls at our feet and head back to the edge of the arena, into the shadows. I barely catch a glimpse of them as two golden angels each—one for each arm —shuttle the souls out little holes at the bottoms of each one of the grandstands. This place is like a huge football stadium—tunnels out to . . . somewhere.

And God—I know Life when I see her now—shines the cone of light in the center of the big arena—brighter than before. She's definitely running the show. And she holds up both of her hands toward the crowd and then she speaks, "And I saw the dead, great and small, standing before the throne, and books were opened. Then another book was opened, which is the *Book of Life*. And the dead were judged by what was written in the books, according to what they had done."

It's easy to recognize scripture—incoherent babble—but the father is better at interpreting this crap than I am. I lean over toward him, as nonchalantly as I can. I really don't care, though, because I've been here before. Or at least I dreamed I was here. Regardless, I whisper at him, "Father, open your eyes and get off that thing."

I pry his trembling hands off his dove-angel steed, and then I tuck him and his beads under one of my wings. I need him close—that's why he is here. Because if you are going to send a snag-and-bag team on an overseas mission, somehow I know you gotta have a linguist. More shit I gotta reconcile later.

I tilt my head down a little and whisper under my wing, "What's she saying?"

He's too terrified to talk or he doesn't know. It takes a couple seconds before he whispers back—I can barely hear him, "Revelation, twenty-twelve—judgment."

And when I look back up, two golden angels have dragged blonde-mommy's soul back out from the tunnel, and they are holding her by the armpits and she's wriggling and writhing, standing tall in front of "the man" . . . or woman, as the case may be. And I smile at her. *Sucks for you.*

Then. . . I have no idea what to call her now. There's a million names to choose from. While I'm finding one I like—

"No whoremonger. . ." she says. Then she hovers toward blonde-mommy.

And a murmur of clucking starts slowly building in the hall. They know what's coming. Who doesn't?

Life slowly continues, ". . .hath an inheritance in the kingdom of the Word."

Now I find a name that makes me smile and seems pretty pertinent. I whisper under my wing to the father, "Then the Queen of Hearts said, 'Off with her head.' "

I can feel him freaking out under there and an urgent whisper comes back from under my wing, "Stop doing that," he says. "We are in deep—that's Ephesians, five-five, adultery."

"Then what are *you* worried about?"

He could be right, but if they're dinging us all for adultery, half of humanity is screwed. So to speak.

And then there he is. The long-licker himself—the Dark Angel of Light—comes to the center of the arena, and then he growls at blonde-mommy's soul.

She struggles in the two golden angels' arms, but it is mouse against the mighty and she might as well settle in, because it's going to be a long hard ride for her.

Then the Dark Angel says, "By the law of the Word, we of the second Heaven claim this soul for the kingdom of The Lion."

And, if I didn't see it myself I would call myself a liar, but blonde-mommy sprouts deep rusted-orange colored wings. They rip apart her back and she's screaming and moaning and the crowd goes apeshit. And a roar of cawing and clucking rumbles the arena grandstands until it feels like it shakes the whole mountain. Then raw, rusty, steel feathers sprout from everywhere but her face. And quicker than she can get used to her new bondage outfit, a third golden angel flies in from the side of the arena with a— "Holy shit," I try to whisper it under my wing to the father, but it comes out a little louder than I wanted.

And blonde-mommy's soul screeches out a hideous cry, so loud that everyone in the grandstands gasps out a huge coo.

Now the father is like a prisoner with a hood over his head, more afraid because he has no clue what's going on out here. "Wh—what was that?"

"They just branded the living shit out of her," I tell him.

I watch molten steel feathers fall away from blonde-mommy's lower back, and she's got a new glowing-red, demonic tramp stamp. And in a flash, the two golden angels that were holding her up, flap her limp body away. I watch her glowing back and flopping wings as far as I can, then the three of them disappear into the dark shadows of the other end of the arena. And she's gone—out the exit—probably prepping for a little fun with her two new pimps.

And I can't help thinking to myself, if they just put this stuff on the PIN, we'd probably all stand up straight and start spouting the party line. It's damn sure beating back the flames of my overblown thirst for revenge.

And I'm involuntarily bobbing my head, waiting for Frank's turn. But little Mercedes is next and they drag her to center arena. The gold-winged jailers—doesn't take much to recognize the lapdogs of authority—tug at her arms as she squirms, waiting for her judgment. And, judging by the clucks and caws coming from the flocks on both sides of the grandstands, it feels like it could go either way for her.

I can't help thinking that at this pace, the place could never keep up with the flow of dead souls being flown in from the garden. It's like a meatpacking plant with only one butcher. And then I remember my own experience, my own fall. In and out of time—speeding up, slowing down, and back and forth from dream to reality. Time is relative. Gotta be, only way they could keep up.

"For if you forgive others," the "Queen" says to the crowd, "your heavenly mother will also forgive you."

And a murmur of cooing in agreement grumbles forth from both sides of the grandstands, before it dies back down to low clucking, and then to silence. They all know that chapter and verse.

And I hear a whisper from under my wing. No idea what the father says. When I don't reply, he says it louder, "It's heavenly *Father*. Book of Matthew. They can't just change—"

"Don't lose your head," I whisper back to him, "our turn's coming."

He never even thought of that. And now he's dead silent. I hope he can keep it together for the main event. *I'm gonna have to reread the Bible*, I think, *so I can figure this shit out myself.*

Trouble with bringing along a linguist, when the shooting starts, there's not much use for them.

When two of the golden guardian angels. . . They give a whole new meaning to that one—guess we interpreted that shit wrong, too.

The gold-feathered jailers drag Frank's soul out in front of her, I can tell what Mercedes has to do to save herself. But forgiveness must be a tough order, because she gets enraged when she sees him and starts thrashing and fighting the two guardians that are holding her up. And I wonder. I mean, it's a little too much protesting over an asshole dad. It has to be something else. And sure, the guy is evil, and I'm more than ready to watch him burn. . .

And the whole stadium can smell it on him and the cawing and screeching starts like a wave through the gallery. The cawing is the loudest and I figure out that most of that is coming from the dark angels, maybe some of the gray ones, too. The screeching is the white and gray angels, screaming for judgment.

And the Queen of Hearts' hands come up and the roaring caws and screeches die down and then they stop, and a low scraping and squeaking sound of metal feathers bristling, replaces it.

The father peeks his head out from under my wing . . . ever so gently. Probably curious about what caused the silence. I don't think he can see anything, though, because I'm a couple of feet taller as an angel and there's a crowd in front of us.

I can smell the fear on him—the smell of piss wafts into my nostrils. And I notice that a couple of other angels start jerking their heads around and putting their noses to the air. They smell him, too.

Too early. Oh, what the hell, I could go at any time, but I wanna watch Frank's face when they judge him.

Throwing a bastard's bimbo out a window—pretty good. Sending her little coke-head brat after her—better. Watching the look on your daughter's tormentor when he realizes he can't buy his way out of Hell —priceless.

And I smile toward the center of the arena—at him and her. However I came to be what I am, right now, I'm pretty proud of myself. And I can't help chuckling—hell, I don't want to—this shit is just fun. Like I said, savor the small moments.

Then the Queen of Hearts speaks again, "None of you shall approach to any that is near of kin to him . . . to uncover their nakedness."

And there it is. *His own daughter?* Guess I had that father thing figured wrong, but the trouble with ultimate power and wealth, you get bored with everything. Pretty soon, they "do" anything . . . and anyone for entertainment. And I'm giddy thinking of what they are going to do to him now, because if that doesn't buy some blood, I don't know what does.

And the father mutters, "Hypocrite."

This is no time for *Bible* camp, but it's hard to ignore that one. "Whoa, calm down," I whisper down to him. "What are you talking about? That's incest, he's toast."

As far as I know, the rules are pretty clear on that. Then again, what exactly do I know, and I remember her reaction to me questioning her authority.

"There is so much incest in the Bible," the father says. "How do you think he. . ." And then he looks up above the center of the arena, gazes at Life. He shakes his head. "There's ten billion of us. She went from two to ten-*billion?* You have to suspend the rules in order to do that."

And there's that angry little demon, buried inside him, popping its head out. He's got an axe of his own to grind and swing.

* * *

By now, the gallery is going wild, cawing and clucking, and cooing and screeching in a roar of disapproval that shakes the whole hall. And the mountain trembles beneath the hall so hard that I look up to make sure the roof's not coming down. And I never noticed it, but the roof is transparent from the inside, and I can see the dark night of space, sprinkled with bright stars.

When I look back, little Mercedes's soul is busy going nuts, like someone's pit bull trying to clamp its jaws on a poodle at the State's dog dump. And she's fighting against the two guardians, holding her back. And she's yelling and screaming and spitting at her father's soul like a rabid dog. She should probably be careful about that, because this isn't just about him.

And Frank's soul has just had its world turned upside down. Couple a days ago, depending on how long his fall was, he was probably out on his yacht in the San Juan Islands, banging a couple of his secretaries. Now, writhing in pain as the two guardian angels sink their foot talons into his back and buttocks, I can't help thinking, *Not so funny when it's your own ass, is it?*

And the Queen of Hearts pauses, and she hovers in the center of the light. Her transparent wings are fluttering and flapping gently, and I'm so excited to see Frank judged that I forget to look at her tits. Okay, I glanced.

Then she waves her hands in circles toward each section in the gallery grandstands. It reminds me of an executioner whipping up the crowd, letting the accused feel what's coming, before he lops off someone's head.

If it was torture I might know where that thought came from, but I have no idea where the images of beheadings are coming from.

Yet this spectacle seems to be serving double duty, because now she's got the crowd hushed down to feather-fall silence in anticipation. She's a showman, no doubt about that. Come to think of it, they both are. And this is—son of a bitch, it's no different!

Since the dawn of time, the rich and powerful have known, that if you want to distract the masses so you can get away with some nefarious shit, bread and circuses, baby—nothing better. Bleeding, branding, and brutalizing souls is no different—great entertainment for the feathered followers.

So what in Heaven or Hell do "mommy" and "daddy" have up their sleeves?

— XLIII —

I GOT NO more time to figure it out, because it looks like it is time for the Dark Angel of Light to take over center stage in the arena. "Dal"—acronyming the Devil?

And he moves right up to the edge of the big cone of light, circling and snapping at Frank's writhing soul. But now, the angry Dal is a true dark angel. His huge red feathers spike from his wings like jagged machetes and they glisten black oil that drips down onto his body feathers. And when he flaps his wings, the scraping metal sends sparks flying and his wings ignite and spit flames up in the air above him. And there's no horns or tails or red scales on him, just the deep, seductive fire of Heaven's blackest heart.

And everyone knows Frank is fucked. It's just a matter of how bad it's going to be, because he looks to be the main event. By the way she's snarling and screaming, they could probably let Mercedes tear his soul apart and call it justice. Somehow I don't think that's gonna happen, though. Probably have to earn your talons before you get to go ripping souls apart in the arena. In fact, the way she's yelling at Frank. . . She doesn't forgive and forget pretty soon and she'll have a molten tramp stamp like her mommy, faster than she can say, "Who brought the lube?"

And here he goes—the Dark Angel of Light, working the crowd into a bloodthirsty rage with the Word. And he is growling pretty loudly when he starts his speech, "Defile not ye yourselves in any of these things! . . . For in all these the nations are defiled which were cast out before you! . . . And their land is defiled." And he points down at Frank. "And behold, their defiled land does vomit out her children!"

And the whole message is coming out like one big fire-and-brimstone browbeating. "Stay in line, shut your mouth, and do what you're told."

Intimidation or elimination. Unbridled authority. It's the same everywhere.

I look down at the top of Father Benito's head, still peeking out from under my wing. Bet he wishes I let him keep his flask. Trying to get a good look at the literal interpretation of the Word, he's shaking like a leaf. Guess I might as well educate myself while Dal is putting the fear in everyone's feathers. "And where's that from?" I ask the father.

He shakes his head. "He's paraphrasing, but that . . . It's Leviticus . . . eighteen, I think. But he's not supposed to be reading it."

And the crowd is really whipped into a flock of blood-boiling birds. And I'm staring and the father is gawking, because it looks like this thing could go all "Hitchcock" any second. And I wonder what a kamikaze stampede of crazed angels would look like.

Three white, black and gray feather-sparkling dove-angels spring from their perches and they start circling, flying around the edge of the huge hall in perfect "V" formation. And the crowd goes wild for it. Nothing like a flyover at half-time.

And then the doves twist and turn and dart and flare their way around the edge of the arena in a crazy display of flying skills that reminds me of the little gray-girl I had to beat up to get up here.

And the Dark Angel of Light is just fueling the fire. He's got one arm stretched way above his head, and his long index finger is extended straight up, and his wings are on fire and he's got them spread out wide. He keeps the tempo up, yelling at the crowd, "And ye shall not commit any of these *abominations! Within your own nation!* "

And the whole thing is just an awesome sight—total Supersport spectacle. I'm actually screeching right along with the crowd in the gallery.

And the Dark Angel is smiling, and here comes the big finale. "Nor with any *stranger that sojourneth among yooouuuuu!*"

And then light explodes from everywhere like fireworks. And I squint my eyes shut and when I open them back up, I'm still clucking a little chuckle, but when I scan the great hall, the flying angels are nowhere to be found. And everything is silent . . . and a million fallen and faithful angels are staring at the Dark Angel of Light. And I look and he is stone-still in the center of the big jeweled arena, with his long finger pointed . . . right at me.

— XLIV —

I LOOK RIGHT into Dal's eyes and he smiles. "Shit. . ." I mutter. Because really, what else is there to say?

Then I look up, and about a hundred feet above the center of the arena is the brightest, whitest ball of piercing light that I've ever seen. And the light it casts looks like a giant disco ball at an angel-rave, glistening and shining mirrors of illumination into every crevice of the huge Hallowed Hall. And if Father Benito's got his own book figured right . . . I know who it is.

I raise my head at her and screech out a war cry. And my feathers tighten over my entire body and all of my talons pop out. I shove the father away from me, and then I spread my wings wide and scrape my wing feathers together in a loud squeal of steel, and I yell at the little ball of bright bitch, "Rain!" She's who I came for. *Hounding me through the end, my ass.*

I jump up and leave the father rolling on the ground in a circle of confused and back-fluttering angels—the six just landed dove-angels that were flying around the arena. I'm pretty sure they were supposed to snatch me up and haul me up front. Not happening.

It only takes a couple of flaps before I'm up to full speed, pumping hard, headed right at Rain. I can feel my rage boiling for blood and without even thinking, I tuck my wings and spin as I'm flying and I shoot pinfeathers at her. No idea how many, but it's a lot. I'll give her the big quills later. I don't wanna kill her just yet. Right now, I'm more interested in giving Rain some pain.

But she flits like a hummingbird and "fairies" herself out of the way. Then a bunch of urgent screeching yells come from the grandstands. Cries spike from behind her, as my feathers fly past and find their way through angels in the crowd. No telling which kind they pierce. And judgment night at the arena has just become an audience participation, contact sport. Because . . . doves and ravens, if you're gonna gawk at the hawks, better watch out for a rogue feather or five.

And I bank a tight turn, trying to catch up with Rain. As I do, out of the corner of my eye, I catch a glimpse of several angels fluttering and flapping like I've seen wounded ducks flail for altitude after they've been shot. And the harder they flap, the slower they fall. But fall they do, splashing down hard on the diamond and ruby-studded floor of the arena.

Death doesn't look like the movies, especially when its angels caw and cluck and screech, and pour blood on the gem-studded floor. And I don't need my boozing *Bible* translator to know what they're yelling. Every last one of them is calling for their great mother—the Chosen One—to save them.

But self-preservation goes all the way to the top, probably stronger all the way up there, because when I glance back over my shoulder, the Dark Angel of Light and the Queen of Hearts—the Chosen One, herself—are both high-tailing their tail-feathers toward the exit at the side of the arena . . . together. And they got half a dozen golden bodyguard angels around them by the time they disappear out some kind of twisting door. It looks more like a portal, because it seals up behind them all by itself.

When the faithful see that, the hall erupts and the entire gallery of angels takes flight. And they are cawing and clawing for altitude in a big tornado of talons and feathers, headed straight up. Apparently the roof is the followers' exit, because it opens up a huge hole to the deep dark of the star-studded space. Then a million faithful and faithless angels stampede from the Arena of Reckoning and the Hallowed Hall of the Word. They leave the Great Mountain of the Eternities behind.

When I look back for the father, he's running toward the center of the arena, at Mercedes and Frank. No idea what he thinks he's gonna do for them, because Mercedes is loose now, already transformed into a deep gray angel with dark armored feathers. And she's busy ripping the living shit out of her father's soul and chunks of it fly from her talons, and the chunks are writhing in agony.

Revenge or forgiveness—burger or salad? Sometimes it's just better to eat what you want and deal with the consequences of the calories later. Frank's not resurrecting from that mess. Not today, not tomorrow, not as anything a man will recognize anyway, because for some reason, I don't think souls die. That would just be too easy.

Anyway, no matter how many chunks Mercedes rips him into, they all keep moving, trying to get back to each other. And when they do, they catch fire and melt and mold back together, then they go wiggling for another chunk. Trust me, it's just nasty.

And I would love to join her down there—my thirst for revenge on that bastard is bone-dry again—but like I said, choices. "Rain, I'm gonna gut you!" I screech up at her.

When I finally catch up to the shining little whelp, Rain is as bright as ever. I can barely look at her. If this angel is a her, because I haven't actually gotten a good look at the bitch. I'm blinded and sunburned every time I get close.

Whatever it is—she, he, or a he-she, hermaphrodite bitchboy—I don't give a shit. I slam into her. At least I think it's her, but as it happens—a split second before I was gonna sink my foot talons knee-deep in her ass—I crash into a huge pillar, and chunks of granite and gemstone fly off of it. And then I'm spinning out of control.

When I come out of the spin, I shake my head, flare my wings, and bank hard to follow the little shit and—sure the light's blinding, but it's nothing compared to the flash of stars in my head when Rain rams into me going at. . . The Chosen One herself only knows how fast this little bitch can burn through the atmosphere. Because now we're through the roof of the great hall. And she is screeching at me and her wings are hammering me, and her talons are deep in my side and back.

I'm pissed, but the rage doesn't seem to be helping me fight her off. I screech back at her, "I'm gonna tear your wings off! Get off me, bitch."

It's the truth, if I could just get a hold of her. And I may be blinded, but I still got my wings and I flap them hard, fighting against her and we both spin and flap, and flail and screech at each other, and I can tell that we are both falling . . . again. And I'm getting tired of this shit. Another fall? I swear if she breaks my wing this time. . .

For some reason I don't think she's trying to kill me. That's not good news for her, because as soon as I get the chance, I'm—

Then she screeches something at me that catches me a little off guard, "You have to go back!"

"Go back?" I screech back at her. "Sure, as soon as I kill you!" And I fight hard to break free, but she's determined. I'll give her that.

We keep at it for a few more seconds and then I feel it—we fall back down the same hole I snuck up here through. And she's sending me back down, plummeting toward the planet. Back to Earth, back to the garden, back to the destiny I was sent down to fulfill . . . back to the rain drizzling, foggy reality of the end of humanity.

— XLV —

AND I'M IN another bad dream. Aren't they all? I don't seem to have the ones with the puppies and perfume. In fact, the reality of life itself seems to be just some angry angel's nightmare.

I can smell the molasses pretty thick though, and I'm waiting for her to appear again—chastise the shit out of me for breaking up their little bloodsport game in the Arena of Reckoning.

I hope she does show up, because now I'm the angry angel, and from here on out, this is gonna be my nightmare. I've past pissed and I'm ready to rain down punishment. I really don't care who gets wet.

They didn't want me in life, they don't want me up in Heaven. The two of them want me to—"You want me to burn it down?" I yell up into the nothingness. "Okay, I'll do your dirty work, ya lazy—" And I spread my wings to full width, checking. Little bright bitch didn't break them this time. And I remember the two of them, running out the exit in the arena. "Keep running, because when I'm through. . ."

And I know I'm talking to myself more than anyone . . . or any-thing else. I'm threatening the dark inside the dream to make myself feel better. But I got nowhere else for the rage to roost.

Father. . . I think that's my inner voice. I have no idea why, but it seems like the right thing to say. "And if I find one fucked-up feather on him, I swear to you. . . Because I'm coming to collect him . . . and I'm bringing fire and fury with me!"

"Father. . ."

And there's that critical little voice in my head—been gone for a long time—reminding me that I left the only guy that's helped me to fend for himself in the fray. Not like that was my plan.

The fact is, I didn't have a plan after we got up there. Bust down the door, crack beaks, next. Seemed like as good a plan as any. To tell you the truth, I was surprised we got that far.

"Father. . ."

And I get it. Annoying. "Yeah, Father," I mutter. I'm talking to myself, because there is no one else here. "I got it."

It feels like I'm back in my own fall, because the light is getting brighter. *If it's her, I'm—*

I wake up to the brightest, whitest angel I've seen so far, and she's shining and standing over me and—"Son of a bitch!" I grab her by the throat and my talons pop out before I know it. And I'm just about to slice her face off with my other set of claws, because I don't care which one of the two of them this is, one of these bright bitches must pay! And she's choking and—

"Father," the bright little shit manages to gasp out a coo in a voice I . . . I recognize.

"Jake, don't!" and it's another voice I can't quite place, but know I should be able to, and my confusion is just getting worse. I want . . . no, I *need* to sink my sins into someone and draw blood for what I've been through, but—

"Jump, stop!" I recognize that voice, but that's just impossible. I left him back in the arena.

"Father?" I say. And I stand up fast, trying to get my bearings and I frown and screech loudly, because my side and chest are on fire and dripping with . . . molasses again. And this is just another cruel dream. I turn and try to figure it out before this one boils me. And there's the father, and the church, and the hole in the roof and. . . Who is struggling in my grip? And I look at my fist and it's—it's too bright. And I know it's that little bitch, Rain, but it's not.

I can barely see her through the flickering bright light, and it's . . . it's—"Amy?" I say.

Nothing in me wants to let go of her, but I have to drop her and her light flickers a little, but then turns back to bright and I close my eyes and I can hear her squawking softly on the floor, and then she's clucking and coughing, trying to stand up.

I can barely see, but she has pure white wings and white feathers all over her and they are like . . . plastic coated scales—smooth and hard. And a little gray angel limps over to help her get to her feet and I recognize this one right away.

"Holy shit," I say. "Kelly?" And now I know I'm dreaming because that's just impossible.

The little gray angel is hurt bad. Doesn't take an angel medic to call that one. She's limping and holding her chest with one arm, but instinctively helping her chick up with what little she's got left. And my mind races to figure out what this new dream is trying to tell me.

"Leave her alone," Kelly says. "What's *wrong* with you? You could have killed her!"

And the rage is hard to beat back. "Killed *her*?" I say. "That little—" And I look down at my chest, oozing black molasses like a sap tree. "She almost killed me . . . twice!"

And it's gotta be some messed-up trick, but there they are, my angel and my sweet salvation—Amy and Kelly-girl. And I look at Father Benito and he's just finishing a pull on his flask. And I give him a look.

"I realize," he says. "I'm still trying to. . ." And he takes another pull.

"I thought I took that from you," I say.

He shrugs. "All that. . ." he says, "I don't think I would have made it out without—"

"Just how *did* you get out of there?" I ask him.

And then there's a voice from above me, "I'll tell you how that miserable cocksucker got here."

As shot as my nerves are at this point, before I know it, I jump into the air. And I flap through the pain from the holes in my side and back, and I'm airborne. I fly into the heavy wooden beams, high above the pews in the church.

And a little deep-gray angel hops from beam to beam, trying to get away from me. I crash into a couple of the beams, swiping my talons at her, but she finds a tight little spot where the big timbers meet the steep angle of the roof. And she's jammed in there—perched and cawing—laughing at me.

Then I try to swing my wings at her but they just gouge the already damaged roof. Once I slow down, I realize who it is. "Mercedes?" I say. Because that's who I left in the arena, cawing and slashing at her father's soul with her talons. But this cackling, cawing, devious little angel isn't—she's more like a copy or something. It still looks like Mercedes—rage-red hair and a little skinny from all the drugs and partying.

"That's *not* my name," she says. "You—"

"What is it now, then?" I say. And I cluck out a little laugh. "Tesla?"

"Hey, fuck you . . . *Jump*," the little gray angel says. "You killed me —you're an asshole."

"Really? Still?" I say to her. "After what he—"

"I named her," and Father Benito has found his benevolent big-boy voice. I can smell the difference. "On the ride back, I named her Fury. Her name is Fury. Now, let her alone. We have real work to do."

And the father sounds like a referee. I guess he's got the colors for it. So that's how he got out. I must have had that figured right. Only angels are allowed in and out of Purgatory. And if you aren't one, you better be on one.

"Cocksucker and his beads," the aptly named Fury says. "I shoulda tore you in half. You wait until I get these off, old man."

"Yes, you could have," the father says to her. "I'm grateful you didn't." Then he raises his flask at her. "Blessed art thou amongst women."

And when I look closer at her, I can see the father's black and red Rosary beads and silver crucifix, hanging around little Miss Fury's fine feathered neck. And I caw out a laugh at her. Then I look back at the father and wink. "Look at you, Father, all blaspheming and bronc busting."

He smiles a little back at me. And the father has finally found his faith. Might not be the one he set out to, but faith it is. I can smell that on him, too. His spine seems a lot stronger for the revelation.

"Fuck the both of you," Fury says. "Like, I wouldn't even be here, if it wasn't for you."

I flap down and land with a thud in the middle of the center aisle to the pulpit at the front of the big church. I'm still groggy from the dream. "That must have been some ride," I say to the father.

"She's . . . spirited," he says. And he takes another little pull from his flask. Only now there's no trembling at all. And he looks at the other side of the church, toward Amy and Kelly. "But we have others to tend."

And now the father has a newfound faith and a fresh flock to fret over. And isn't that just the very definition of a priest? He's had a big day. Hell, we all have. And I gotta get on this, because I'm about to take an ass-whipping. "Kelly?" I say, as I walk toward the both of them. She's got her back to me and I look at her wounds. *How did she get so. . .?*

Then I figure it out. "I'm . . . I'm sorry."

"For what," she spins around and screeches at me, "almost killing our daughter? Jesus, what is wrong with you? You could have. . ." And she turns back to Amy or Rain or whoever that is.

I think about protesting, before I figure that's probably not the best move. But I don't think I was any closer to killing that bright little angel than Rain was to letting me.

It's the least of my worries now, because despite sucking angel shit at defending myself against my little baby—the brightest, and apparently baddest, angel in Heaven—I can see by the deep punctures and scratches beneath her mother's back and leg feathers, that I put a serious hurt on Kelly. She's the gray angel I maimed so I could forge my way into Purgatory.

It might not be the best time for a family counseling session, because Amy . . . Rain . . . is confused, like she just snapped out of a coma and everyone is telling her she's a god.

That's what the father tells me he made her in his book. But right now, she's back to being a thirteen-year-old kid, trying to figure out why her father was choking her. *Dammit. . .* The shit I gotta repent for is piling up.

Only, she's a thirteen-year-old kid who just happens to be the brightest, whitest, most powerful angel from Heaven. She's also back to shining sunstar bright.

And I'm squinting, trying to get a look at Kelly's wounds. Because however intoxicated on revenge and vengeance I was when I gave them to her, now I'm like a dumb drunk, waking up after his first blackout, realizing he beat the shit out of his wife. *I'm an asshole.*

It's a strange feeling—according to the father's book, I'm just a little love child of wrath and evil. And I'm supposed to be hip-deep in the guts of humanity by now.

I'm squinting too much to worry about that, though. The bright sun off of Rain is just blinding. "Jesus, Rain," I say. For better or badder, that's her new name now. But she's just so . . . bright. "I just wanted to—"

"Leave her alone," Kelly says. "Haven't you done enough? Always about what you want, isn't it? Never even consider what anyone else needs, do you?"

And Kelly isn't doing so well or else that tongue lashing would've lasted longer. She kinda peters out before she really gets it going.

I look back at Rain. "Jesus, what did they do to you?" There's gotta be some reason she would attack her own father.

"Jesus is right," Fury caws down at us. She's still content to watch from the rafters. "She's like, burning my eyes. I need some sunglasses."

And the words barely leave her lips before the father and I are staring at each other like a couple of cavemen who touched the flame and realized, fire—hot. "Ain't that a bitch," I say.

He looks at me and then at Kelly and Rain and he squints. To Seattle citizens, used to living in half dark most of the year, using sunglasses is about as obvious as . . . well, healing an angel with molasses.

"Shit," I mutter.

And little miss "Cancun," perched in the rafters, is pleased with herself. "Yeah, who knew, right," Fury says, "not you two dumbshits."

She's a malcontent after my own heart. I get the rage. Considering the blood on the street below her molesting daddy's penthouse is probably still wet, she's being rather civilized. Because looking at Rain and feeling my guilt grow while the father walks over and tries to figure out how to patch up my handiwork on Kelly. . . If it was me, I'd swoop down from the top of the church and claw the living shit out of the lot of us . . . on principle alone.

Principle? Who am I kidding? Whatever upside-down code of conduct I might have had before I died, flew out the attic with Kelly and Amy's souls. But now that they are back. . . Did they ever leave? Doesn't matter, because it feels like I got a little good trying to claw its way back into my life.

Hope I survive that.

Father Benito's serious voice cuts my soul-searching short, "She needs blood."

He's right, because Kelly has slumped down hard next to Rain on the floor. Her armored feathers have lost their shining gray tone and they are going limp. Impending death doesn't look any better on an angel. Dying as an angel? *How many levels of Hell are there?* I think.

And despite this reunion, nothing is getting any better. I killed my baby in life and I'm gonna be responsible for killing Kelly after, because she's got ten leaking holes and we are running out of time.

I hang my head a little. This is my Hell. "How long?" I ask.

The father is busy dabbing Kelly's wounds with towels, but he knows what I'm saying. "A day and a half . . . maybe two," he replies.

"Shit," I say.

Two days to finish off humanity or it is Purgatory for everyone . . . forever. But whatever tiny amount of time the zoo animals have left to enjoy the smell of their own shit, Kelly has less.

"Angel blood," I mumble, because we won't be replacing Kelly's bright, rosy-red liquid with molasses. That would be too simple, now, wouldn't it? "Where the hell. . .?" My first thought is Rain.

"Good luck finding that," says Fury. "I hope she *dies*. Then you'll know how it feels."

The father and I look up at her and—we don't really smile, but it's like figuring out the answer to a tough crossword—the "ah-ha" must be written all over our faces.

God-dog or not, the father's got the same self-satisfied look on his face as I do. Not that I have much luck with it, but sometimes it's just better to keep your mouth shut.

"Oh, no," Fury says. "No way! I just got my wings. The blood— that shit kills, and I'm not . . . what makes you think . . . and my mother. You can suck each other's dicks on that."

The father and I scrunch up our faces at the thought. I tore up the kid's mom, threw *her* out a window, then put her through Purgatory. She's probably still angry about getting revenge on her father. But with Kelly bleeding out on the floor of the church, I couldn't care less about the little spoiled-spoon's losses. She's giving up the blood if I have to gut her to get it.

But something Fury said doesn't sit too well with the father, because he's staring at me funny. A kinda maniacal mad-funny.

Five minutes, off to the side of the pews, listening to the father whisper-yell at me for killing Mercedes' mother, and I'm confused as shit.

"I realize she was one of your church-goers, Father," I say. "But she lies with the devil, she better expect to die right beside him. As far as I'm concerned, all the credits she cracked came from her husband selling the shit that killed Rain—Amy. Just as responsible as him."

"She was a . . . a good woman," he says. "You didn't have to—"

"She shot me," I say to him. "What was I supposed to do?"

I never see her ease up behind me, but Kelly joins in. "Always someone else's fault, isn't it," she says. I turn toward her, but she limps over to the father's side of the argument and gives me some more. "You killed that poor girl's mother?"

"She's not poor," I say. It's a defense. Granted, not a good one, but it's what I got. "They got rich off of—"

"If you think you can justify it with that," she says. "Look at you— you aren't even sorry, just looking for a way out of it. Still a little boy, aren't you, playing like a man."

"What the. . .?" I say. Then I look at the father. "Help me out here."

He frowns and kinda laughs, but not really. "I'm on her side."

But a couple more minutes into Kelly word-whipping me, and her eyes roll back in her head and she almost falls to the floor before we both catch her.

Then the father motions toward Fury—Mercedes. "Go ask her," he says. "Do it nicely, or heaven help me. . ."

I look at Kelly. She's passed out and we need the blood now. "All right already," I say, "but if she says no, I'm taking it. I—*we* don't have time for this shit."

I play as nice as I can, but I think the father's beads have more magic in them since his own fall, because Fury grudgingly flutters down from the rafters without much coaxing. Or maybe she can see the look in my eyes, that I don't need her alive to get the blood.

Okay, okay, I wasn't going to do it. Kelly would've kicked my ass anyway.

Fixing Kelly is a little simpler than a full-on transfusion, because when the father cuts Fury's arm with his little pocket knife and pours her blood over Kelly's wounds, they start sucking it in like little vampires. She gets better fast, faster than a human, anyway. Then again, I figured that.

However "mortal" angels have turned out to be, we flap back from an ass whooping a lot faster than a man. Or maybe it's because she's a woman—the whole "I will make your pains in childbearing very severe" thing, and she can take more pain than a man.

Whatever it is, I smile down at Kelly and stroke her head feathers with my hand. I think it's funny that we've shit-canned the "Your husband will rule over you" part. Because if I'm sure of anything . . . we make it past the bloodbath chapter in the father's little story—survive my new vengeance-filled duties. . . When Kelly is back to full strength and she screams "Jump!" at me, I'm probably just going to shit myself and say, "How high?"

"Rain. . ." Kelly manages to say. "I'll be okay. . ." But she needs the rest more than she knows, and she slumps over from exhaustion more than anything else. Then she's out cold.

I look at the father and he nods his head in understanding and gives me a "she'll be fine" look. He better hope so. She dies because of me this time, no amount of blood is going to fill up that bucket of guilt.

The socked-in fog has got everything outside a deep gray and inside it would be just plain dark. The hole in the roof let the rain in and it shorted out the lighting in the whole church.

Rain watches us hover over Kelly like any thirteen-year-old would —scared for her mother, and a little curious, too. It was the father's idea to put her up in the rafters after we coaxed Fury down. Rain is better light than the green cast of the fluorescent stuff, anyway.

I can tell Rain doesn't really know what to say about me choking her. For some reason, I don't even think she remembers trying to kill me. "Is she going to. . .?" she asks.

"I'm sorry . . . About. . ." I look up at my darling baby. "She's not dying."

"I hope she dies," Fury says. "You killed my whole family."

I'll give her a little rope, because she's right. Not too much, though, she's starting to grind my mind with her bitching. "Give it a rest. Probably did you a fav—"

"Daddy?" Rain says. Her eyes say it all. "Why did you. . .?"

And for some reason, I feel like I need to justify it to her. "Her dad was the guy who pumped those—he made your head hurt, honey. Probably a whole lotta other kids, too. So I—"

And before I can finish, Rain turns to Fury and says, "I'm sorry."

And that shuts me up for the first time in as long as I can remember. Kid went through more physical pain than I have in my life and she's still. . . She's her mother's daughter, that's for sure. She sure as hell didn't get the "forgive and let live" from me.

And it looks like Fury is going to give Rain both barrels of her wicked whip of a tongue, but instead, she flaps down from the rafters and perches on the back of one of the pews. Then she folds her wings around her entire body in an egg-shaped cone of "leave me alone." And she starts cooing, probably brooding over the cut on her arm . . . and her semi-voluntary donation of blood, among other things. I hope she's getting good and angry under there, because tomorrow I'm going to give her a place to point all that pissed-off . . . fury.

While everyone comes to grips with the fact that, somehow, we all ended up together in this church—as angels, no less—we listen to the sirens race through the city. *Homing pigeons,* I think.

And drone strike warnings vibrate the thick layer of fog over the city. Citizen stompers, letting everyone know they are going to blow the shit out of something. And about every five minutes or so, a drone screams by, rumbling the rooftops of the scrapers outside. Then a few seconds later, a huge explosion lights up the fog and shakes thunder through the ground. I guess the powers decided that the appearance of a flying man, killing their lapdogs, warranted a little martial law misery for their minions. Because anyone I left alive out in that dragnet of death is gonna wish I ripped them apart on the street.

And we listen and brood in silence and confusion about what in the hell all this shit means. Because if you've ever had one of those dreams where you get everything you think you want and then someone wakes you up and says, "Surprise, you're still in your shitty life." I can only speak for myself when I say, I just wanna go back to sleep, because this whole nightmare just sucks.

However. . . Now they got me doing it. It's nothing compared to the brick wall that humanity will hit in two days. The father says our little joyride to the arena in Purgatory put us one day closer to the ultimate judgment day. And I sort of wish there was, but the father doesn't think there is any way to avoid it. He says the two of them are sure to plug up our little security breach. We won't be sneaking in the back door to that party again.

The bitch of it is, there's only one way he knows to get an invitation.

— XLVI —

ONCE THE FATHER and I finally get our flock of angels semi-patched up and put to sleep, cooing and cheeping themselves through whatever real dreams a fallen archangel has . . . I'm not really sure what we should do next. But after we both agree what has to happen in less than one day, the father has backed off on being so pissed about Mercedes' mother.

I know one thing, they need the rest before their big day starts in the morning. And I don't know if Kelly will be up for it. . . Come to think of it, I hope she forgives me when she wakes up, because I don't think I can get the job done with just me and Fury.

So now it's me and the father, watching over the flock like shepherds. And he is sitting sideways in a long pew at the front of the church, and I'm perched on the back of it, a few feet away, talons digging into the deep brown wood. More shit he'll have to repair if he ever gets to the roof. And we listen to the rain dripping through the big hole in his church and the soft sounds of his new flock cooing, dreaming the dream.

And when Rain sleeps, she looks like a bright candle, flickering in the dark. And the whole inside of the church has turned to a cave-like cavern illuminated by flames. The shadows jump and flit around like ghosts. In another life, I would have said it was eerie, but I feel pretty safe and comfortable in this one.

And Fury is sleep-jerking and softly cawing on her pew, like she's dreaming herself through her father's guts again.

"What was her name?" I ask the father. "He called her—"

"Babette," the father says. "Her name was Babette . . . and she was good people."

"Sorry," I say. I don't know if I am or not, but Kelly would want me to say it. *Kelly*, I think. "Yeah . . . hey?"

"Yes," the father says.

I look at Kelly, resting and recuperating like the angel that she is. Bet she's not boiling in blood, or having psychotic dreams in her sleep. "What did you name Kelly?" I ask.

He smiles at me. "It wasn't too difficult," he says. Then he chuckles a little. "She has always been your only salvation."

And I cluck out a little laugh, because that's exactly what Kelly is to me. "There you go again, all literal."

"The very best parts of the *Bible*," he says, "and my book, can be interpreted in many different ways. For our purposes, literal will have to do."

"Leads to trouble," I say. And I look around the church at our flock. "Just look at them, walking, squawking, misinterpretations of the Word. Me too. I think it's just messed up, the way everyone pretends to know what the *Bible*—"

"I don't think so."

"Really?" I say. "Exactly what did you change in there, anyway?"

"Just enough to get the point across," he says, "maybe a little more."

"You sure that's the only way?" I ask. "I mean, it seems wrong, especially you being a priest."

And now the father looks older for some reason, like he's been here too long. "As opposed to what," he says, "letting us continue down the same path we're on? We will never avoid the crash. In fact, we may already be in it."

And I know he's right—we are the back-stabbingest, pettiest, most oppressive ghouls that ever crawled on our bellies through the bile of reality shows on the PIN. Humanity died a long time ago. Only thing left to clean up are the humans. "It's too bad."

"Bad?" he says. "Bad is perspective. Is it too bad for a starving baby if it was never born, or is it too bad that it was, only to suffer and die in the agony of hunger and disease? Honestly, I never understood it. How can he—"

"I never understood it either, Father," I say. "I mean, you got billion-dollar yachts with assholes in the galley, eating contraband sushi off some chick's naked tits, and then you got a starving mother with five kids and she can't feed a one of 'em. What kinda species are we?"

"That's not what I was saying," he says, "but I see your point."

Things have to get pretty messed up for a priest to start agreeing with me. And I don't think either of us knows what to say about that, because we sit there in silence for a few seconds, saying nothing.

By now, you know I can only handle a few seconds of not hearing my own voice, but it's the father who breaks the silence first, "What I do not understand is why he wanted to keep knowledge from us in the first place. And then he punished us once we got it." And he turns his head and looks at me with pained eyes. "If you had knowledge and understanding, wouldn't you want to give it to your children? But he punished us for it." He turns back to staring straight forward, probably at Jesus staked to the cross in the front of the church. "However, I agree with you, he does seem to be indifferent to us punishing each other. Did you know that to some, the serpent in the garden was the hero?"

"How the—" I pause when he cocks his head to the side and frowns at me. "I'm trying . . . Jesus."

"Try harder," he says. Then he continues his story. "The snake gave us what he would not—knowledge."

And I know he's seen it with his own eyes, but he still can't bring himself to admit it. "*She*," I say.

"Yes, yes," he says, frowning at me. "That . . . it simply makes no sense. The *Bible* is rife with the oppression and domination of women, and yet if it weren't *for* women, the church would have died long ago, starved and withered on the vine for want of money and followers."

"Ouch," I smile when I say it. "Your flask has got your filter way off. Better be careful with that. Trust me, no one wants to hear the truth. And next time, she might rain down wrath on you."

"I'm sure that is coming."

I glance around the inside of the father's own sanctuary, trying to find topics to keep us awake. And with all the statues of saints and angels, and the ornate stained glass, not to mention the building itself . . . and the land it's on. . . "How much does a place like this cost, anyway?" I ask him. "I mean, it doesn't look like you're hurting?" And then I can't resist. I may not be as angry as I was yesterday, but wife and Amy back with me or not, I got a mad streak like the stripe on a skunk, and you can pour as much Purgatory on Pepé Le Pew as you want, it will never change the smell. "And then there's the kiddie dungeon downstairs—"

"Jacob."

And I cluck out a chuckle and say, "Sorry." I'm not, but like I said, that's what I'm supposed to say, right? I pause a little . . . letting the air clear from the poor taste of my joke. But as soon as the smell wafts away, I'm back at it. "Okay, but seriously, how much?"

The father laughs at me now. Then he says, "You don't want to know."

I shake my head and look at the pulpit. "Buying their way in to Heaven," I say. "Shame on you, Father. Letting them think they can —"

"Oh, no," he says. And I can tell by the look on his face that he knows exactly what I'm saying. "My job is simply to remind them to be generous."

"Uh-huh. . ." I say. Then I smile and check on Kelly again. She's still snoozing, breathing a little better now. I whisper anyway, "Father, you know what the difference between a whorehouse and a titty-bar is?"

"For Heaven's sake. . . . Please, it's still a. . ."

I can tell he has to think about it for a few seconds. Despite his whole life, there's a hole right through his faith, as big as the hole in the roof of his church. Authoring the book that will end all humanity, bluffing his way into Purgatory, not to mention his shattered beliefs. . . I'm guessing it's getting tougher and tougher to keep up the charade.

I ignore him, because for me it's about seeing the look on someone's face when I do something you aren't supposed to . . . cram it in authority's ass . . . and break it off. "Well . . . *Father* . . . a whorehouse is a place you pay for pussy because you know you're gonna get it. . ."

"Mother of Mercy, you are just . . . unredeemable."

". . .and a titty-bar is a place you pay for pussy, knowing you're not."

I can tell he kinda wants to laugh, but he just can't allow himself to. So he makes the sign of the cross over his chest, kisses his thumb or some other cult shit, and then he looks up at the statue of crucified Jesus behind the pulpit. "Forgive him." Old habits. . . Then he turns back to me with a look of disgust on his face. "And your point?"

He knows the point, but he's doing the same thing I am—shooting the shit, passing the time, trying to keep his mind off the fact that I'm gonna kill everyone on the planet tomorrow. One thing's for sure, neither one of us wants to sleep.

"No point. Just"—I look around the church, for effect—"once you get inside and see all that glory . . . tough to remember which one you're at."

A couple hours and too many jokes in poor taste later, and we are deep in the calm before the storm. We alternate trading barbs and sleep-jerking for about an hour, before I finally let the father nod off a few times. And when he does, I can smell that he is holding something back. Some little shred of insanity that he just won't let go of.

I catch myself sleep-jerking a few times, too. And in between my visions of the Dark Angel and the Queen of Hearts, entering the exit tunnel together, I hear the father whimper out, "I won't let you do it again."

So I wake him all the way up with a little jab from my wing. Still don't know my own strength, though, because I poke him a little too hard and send him flying into the aisle, flopping and flailing like a fallen angel. "Wha—what? Who did. . .?"

"That's the question," I say, "isn't it?"

I watch him drag his confusion back onto its place on the pew and his mind back to its new understanding of reality.

"*What* aren't you going to let *who* do?" I ask. "You better spit out the last piece of it, or tomorrow—just as easy to spark up the fire with you."

"I don't know—"

"Oh, you know, all right," I say. And I sniff in deeply and I can smell the piss of fear, but the burning pepper of frustration and anger, too. "You're just not telling. So cough it up, or I'll choke it out of you."

By now, he knows my temper can go either way. And whether it's that knowledge or the fact that a guy can only carry so much guilt all by himself, he starts spilling his guts. Once he does . . . it's the first time that I would have rather remained blissfully ignorant of just how badly power can break things. Because whatever blasphemy he's been boiling up in his book so far, this shit is worse. I'm surprised he's not bursting into flames right in front of me.

When he finally spins down his story—I can handle the first part, but the second. . .? I say, "You've got to be kidding?"

"If only I. . ." he says. And he pulls out his flask.

At this point, I'm not busting his balls over the booze, because after this new shit, I might need a swig or six myself.

"I wish I were." And then he takes a long pull, trembling a little again.

"No wonder you're sucking on that thing like a tit," I say. "That's just—you're burning with me for those, father."

"I didn't write it that way," he says. "It's just what happened—that's their interpretation of it. But when I saw them running from the arena, and then when I got to Fury, I could . . . feel it. Like a vision or a smell. It was simply there, all around me. The truth . . . and what they were going to do."

It takes a couple of minutes of silence for this new poison to infect its way into my understanding of reality. It's hard to swallow, even for me. "Just what did you *think* 'loins' meant, anyway?" I ask.

"It's figurative," he says. "I never meant for it—"

"Tell that to Matthew and John and whoever," I say. "Jesus, why can't anyone just write a book that makes sense?" And before I know it, I've found a subject in my head that I can rant all day about. This will surely keep us awake. "That's the same thing those idiots did with the old Constitution. 'A well regulated militia. . .' It's the goddamn *people's* right. They *were* the militia. And now everyone wants to interpret the living shit out of it. Why can't someone just say, 'Keep your ignorant, uneducated hands off my guns and I'll let you spout all the stupid shit you want to on the news.' Because I gotta tell ya, they killed more of us with the First Amendment than anyone had guns to keep up."

And I can tell I've lost him, because that's what happens. In fact, that's what *did* happen. The PIN spewed and spouted so hard and long at the public, and the citizens spit so hard back, that I think everyone in the middle just finally tuned out. And once the big fat middle class stops giving a shit. . .

And that's what happens to me. "Ah, hell with it all, Father."

"Huh—wha. . .?" he blurts, before he nods off again. And he's fallen asleep.

And what did I just say? I nudge him awake. "Ya see?" I mutter at him.

"See what?" he says.

"Doesn't matter *now*, does it?"

"I guess you're right," he says. "I still can't believe that—"

"Yeah," I say, "and I can't believe a priest—"

"Jacob. . ."

Disbelief—the whole reason no one lifts a trigger-finger until it's too late. But despite all this shitty news—old and new—I feel worse for him than me. Poor miserable son of a bitch had to fight his way all the way into Purgatory to find the truth of the Word that he's been waiting for, and when he gets it—it's lost love and false faith—more bad news.

But which part is the worst? That God and the Devil are in the whole thing together? That they've run this charade over and over again, back and forth since eternity? Or is it that I'm their bastard love child?

I know my vote. "Misinterpreting morons," I say. "We should kill them all."

When I say it, we both look up at the cross behind the pulpit—Jesus splayed out in sacrifice. We gnaw and think and grind the gears in our ever-dizzying heads for . . . minutes, at least. Both of us hoping we are dreaming and neither of us wanting to say anything that will wake us up so it has to be real.

Once I wrap my wings around it, I'm back to flaming pissed. "You sure there's only one way to get back up there?" I ask.

"Pretty sure," he says, "but . . . what do I know?" He's staring into himself now. "I'm a priest of the Word, enforcing the laws of despots."

I look at him and he's still zoning out. I frown at him, but he doesn't notice. "Well, that's pretty clear," I say. "Only question is, what are ya willing to do about it? Because I'll tell you what"—I look back up at the cross—"I'm not going out like him."

"Huh?" Now he's snapping out of it.

"Look what they did to him," I say. "Killed him just for trying. That is *not* me."

Now I go off into my own mind, because I've had enough of the authority, and the torture, and the manipulation by the powerful. In this world or the next . . . or, if the father is right, the next one after that.

"I understand," he says, "but that is not what they want."

And I know what they do want. "They want an ocean of blood and sacrifice for their little reincarnation arena?" I say to him. "I'll drown them in it."

It's a bold statement, but one that by now we both know I'm capable of. One thing they might not know up in Heaven—you go keeping a pit bull around as a pet, it's only a matter of time before he gets pissed off and mauls you.

The father talks to me for a while after that, but I'm off in a conspiracy rant in my head.

Once I snap out of it, the first sentence I can comprehend is, "You have until the end of the seventh day."

"And we're on the sixth," I say. "I got that. Cute, he—" Shit, now he's got me doing it. "*She* builds it in seven and that's how long I have to knock it down."

But there's still something on him. A little tidbit I can taste.

Then the father gives me the death blow. "Once we are all gone. . . If and when we come back. . . Nothing changes after that, no one will remember their past life, and we will all just do this over as someone or something else. With both of them as our masters . . . again."

"Oh, now goddammit," I say. "What kind of Hindu cow-shit is that? You don't. . . Catholics don't believe in that reincarnation crap."

He cocks his head at me, looks me in the eyes, and raises his eyebrows. Then he points to the cross—crucified Jesus behind the pulpit. "He did."

FURY

— XLVII —

WHATEVER DNA LIFE and that devil, Dal, gave me from their unholy "loins," the father says I have a seriously overdeveloped sense of revenge and vengeance. Because when I finally figure out what I'm gonna do about all this, he thinks it's pretty rotten, even for me. But if I had to put it in my own words . . . I'm just a sore loser.

Whatever it is, I make him spend the rest of the night rewriting what's left of the "shalls" in his book—all the stuff that hasn't "come to pass," as he puts it. And I pass the time re-familiarizing myself with the other book—their *Bible*. Because if there's one thing that is constant throughout the world, the universe, and eternity, it's that the people who write the rules . . . never follow them.

It's still pretty dark out when the father and I wake them all up. And they squawk and caw in protest as they pull themselves out of whatever cozy feelings they could claw from their dreams.

Kelly—sorry, "Salvation"—looks a whole lot better after a night of rest and, for better or worse for me, she's downright chipper. We'll see how she is after I give her the glorious news.

And Fury is Fury. "You're such an asshole," she says, "can't we just sleep?" Then she stretches her wings out to full width.

I didn't notice it before, but the little angel's gray spiked span is wider than mine. That'll either make her fast as hell or give her more feathers to fire. Whatever the wings do, it's sure to be useful today.

She flaps and flutters her way back into the beams above the pews. Then she hops around a little until she finds a perch she likes.

When Fury finally roosts, I look up at her and frown. "Are you done, Paris?"

"What?" she says. "I like it up here. Go fuck yourself."

The perching thing is probably left over from living in the loft above her parents' penthouse, but her last statement reminds me that it's been a while. And I instinctively look at Salvation. *Not the right time*, I think. Though, it's always the right time, isn't it? And I stick a little pinfeather in the idea—tuck that little prick away for after. If there is an after.

When Rain wakes up, her flicker turns back to blasting bright white light throughout the entire church. And we all recoil and caw and squint and look away from the wood timbers she's perched on. I'm sure from the outside that the hole in the roof looks like a spotlight to Heaven. Or a super-duper shopping beacon at midnight on Dark Friday, beckoning the blasphemers to mow through more plastic from Chinasia. And I smile. I'll need that judgmental, ranting anger later . . . today, of all days.

"I'm sorry," Rain says. "I can't help it."

And from her it's all honesty. The girl doesn't know anything else. She is sorry, and I'm sure she would turn it off if she could.

Fury puts a wing over her face. "Like I said—sunglasses!"

"Quit your bitching," I say. And then I show them all the little gifts I got to commemorate the dawn of a new day. Sounds too poetic for me, but it's kinda sarcastic, too, so I like it. Decadent, like opening your gifts before Christday. Or the twelve days of Hanukkah, or whatever shit the mindless crack credits to celebrate.

And, yes, I realize they are bad thoughts, and they are blasphemous, and they make me damn near unlovable, but trust me, it won't be the worst thing I do today . . . them either.

"I slipped out after the father fell asleep on his book, and I—"

"Where did you get sunglasses?" Salvation asks me.

And in the grand scheme, it doesn't seem all that big a deal to me, but I know what she's asking. "Uh. . ." I say, readying for the ass-whooping. "Ten talon tribute?" And I cluck out a little chuckle before I have to cover my mouth.

Salvation just looks at me in disgust. I remember that one, all too well. "You didn't. . ."

"Oh, please," says Fury. "He jacked them. Gimme mine. She's killing my eyes."

And before I let the trouble train leave the station—because today we just need to get to it—I throw up a pair of deep gray, dark-black-mirrored sunglasses, complete with adjustable neoprene strap. Fury snatches them in midair and inspects them with a caw of approval. And she puts them on, adjusts the strap, and looks right at Rain, testing them.

They must pass, because she says, "Suh-weet." And Fury is smiling and bobbing her head and she caws. "You look *good*, girlfriend," she says to Rain. And just when I think she and I might be able to come to some sort of middle ground, she looks back down at me through her new sunglasses and says, "You—still a asshole."

Whatever sunglasses do for the appearance of a human, on a dark gray, onyx-shining, anger-filled angel. . . Fury looks scary as shit. Her eye sockets look like the Queen of Hearts' big black orbs. And today, little Fury is gonna be fine.

I give Salvation hers—deep gray with a bright red logo. Then the father gets a pair—black with white, of course. And finally I toss a pair up to Rain and put my own blood-red ones on.

It's the first time I've seen my little girl smile since they rolled her into the ER on the rainy night she died. And she's still bright as light gets, but at least I can see the dimples in her little cheeks. And however old she was when she thrashed and threw her own father out of Purgatory, this young lady is one brilliant ball of bright. The pure white sunglasses with sunshine orange mirrored lenses make her look even more benevolent.

And Fury is the first one to comment. No surprise there. "They all match?" she says. "Shit, her logo's even gold. What are you, gay?"

"Hardly," I say. And I got nothing beyond that, because *Bible* or not, I'm not even going there.

Kelly-Salvation isn't one to get glazed over with gifts. "Can you just tell us all what's going on, please? Because, I know you—you don't hand out presents for nothing."

And I get a guilty look on my face, and the next thing she says makes me speechless. It's hard to do.

"Yeah, I see you there," Salvation says. "We'll get to you clawing me half to death and choking your daughter later. Right now, spill it, soldier, because I'm in no mood for one of your little wild-hair adventures."

And spill it I do, gallons and gallons of blood red, bad news. . . . Depending on how you look at it, I guess.

Despite the clucking and cawing, I can tell that they all fundamentally understand what I'm saying. But understanding doesn't make the doing any easier. Never has, never will. As a matter of fact, the hard part's always in the doing. That's why everyone talks about how shitty things are, instead of picking up a shovel and digging through the crap.

Then the father finally speaks up. Until now, he's been content to watch and wonder about the finality of his own fate. At least, I figure that's what has to be on his mind. But then he says, "It is far easier to talk of righteousness. . ."

And we all stop and look at him, waiting for some profound wisdom to help us through it.

What he delivers is short and sweet, but it doesn't make anyone feel any better. ". . .than to walk its prickly path."

Now I'm staring at him—melting down whatever mercy might have crept back in the door with Amy and Kelly—because I know what he has to do. And I think his statement is more to psych himself up than it is to help any of us come to grips with the task.

"That is . . . beautiful," Rain says.

She has no clue. Innocence. Wish I could get mine back.

"What book is that in?" I ask him.

"Book of Benedetti," he says.

Salvation laughs a little. She remembers how he used to be, and that little tidbit is classic Father Ben. Way back when he knew how to interpret the Word for the good of his flock. Now, he's trying to laugh his way back to his broken faith.

He chuckles and says, "But I will give you something a little more pertinent to the current cross you must all bear. Ephesians, six-twelve."

"Afeesa what the. . .?" Fury says. "Can we just get on with it?"

I don't think tourette-girl has ever seen the inside of a church. At least I can. . . Yeah, I'm full of shit.

"All in time," Rain says to her. "Let the father speak."

And whatever is going on up there in the rafters—I don't have a clue—but my little Rain is getting a handle on how to calm the fury inside of . . . well, Fury.

And when Salvation and I close our mouths, the father continues, "For though we walk in the flesh, we are not waging war according to the flesh. For we do not wrestle against flesh and blood, but against the rulers, against the authorities, against the cosmic powers over this present darkness, against the spiritual forces of evil in the heavenly places."

And I'm thinking he's full of shit again, because that is just way too. . . And I warned him about the literal already. I lean over and whisper in Salvation's ear, "That shit's not in the *Bible*, is it?"

"It's Father Ben, Jake," she starts to say. And then she raises her eyebrows at me, like I'm talking during the sermon in church. I guess that's pretty much what I'm doing. "Shh . . . *Jump*."

The father hears me and, I mean, I told him we needed to turn the tables on them, but this is some Revelations shit, right here. "Holy shit, Fath—"

"Or maybe you prefer some Corinthians," he says. "Chapter ten . . . three through five, if I remember."

And now he is just in the *zone*. I can hardly reconcile this version with the flask-sucking boozer I had to pop off his little tin tit. But he doesn't care about my disbelief, or judgment, because his is crystal clear. He says, "For the weapons of our warfare are not of the flesh. . ."

And now I know why he wrote the book. I also know that he's ready for it.

". . .but they have divine power to destroy strongholds."

And I raise up my left wing and—

— XLVIII —

THE LOUD CAW and then the screech shakes the father's entire church. And then the words, "I'm sorry." But it's not my voice speaking, and Fury swoops down from her perch and cuts the father's head off with one lightning fast thrust of her wing.

And blood spurts from his neck and his head rolls across the floor. And then his body slams down in the middle of the aisle to the pulpit and blood continues to pump out his neck, while the rest of him jerks and his nerves kick his legs and feet—his last earthly protests as a man.

Rain and Salvation screech in surprise, and then Rain shines brighter, if that's even possible. And Kelly screams and tries to look away. But I make my angel, Salvation, look back, because today . . . this is as good as it gets.

Salvation hits me in the chest with a fist. Then she looks back down at the father's body and she says, "Why did you. . .?"

And Rain stares at the body, like she's never seen death before. Maybe she hasn't. I don't know much about what she's done since she's been an angel. But then she's looking at Fury and me, and she realizes that I knew it was going to happen. Well, I knew, but it was supposed to be me that did it.

"Why, is right," I say to Fury.

And it almost looks like Fury feels . . . bad. She shakes the blood off of her wing, and then she mutters at his body, "Miserable old cock-sucker." And she looks back at me and she's wild with anger. "Don't you even *start!* I knew that was coming. I'm surprised they didn't. I could smell that on him like, before he started spouting from the *Bible.* Believer bullshit. You knew he couldn't go with us."

Then Salvation gets it—the sacrifice. "Unless he—"

"Unless he is an angel," Rain says. And she understands, too. And there goes her innocence, fluttering out the hole in the roof.

There really was no way around it. By the end of this day, the father's severed head will seem like a paper cut.

And I know Fury is just trying to reconcile who she is now and what she has to do, because this is the same kind of blind rage she had toward her father. It's not her, it's that little helpless feeling inside her —knowing the truth, hating it, and living with it anyway. "Fuck it," she says. "Anyways, he was *your* friend." She flutters up into the rafters with Rain. Then she hops to her perch. "Like, I did you a favor. Now, are you telling her the rest, or do I have to do all the work?"

Fury—she was probably listening to us all night, pretending to sleep under her wing cocoon. In any case, she is dead on. Maybe not for the reason she thinks, but she is right. And I look up at Rain and say, "You have to take the father's soul up—"

"You're sending her up there?" Salvation says. "I don't think I'm—"

And before this goes all "Reality Rerun," I need to nip it in the bud. "She's the only one who can get in and bring him back. And we're gonna need him."

"You are so full of shit," Fury says. "You don't want her to have to see you—"

"Enough!" I screech it out pretty loudly. Louder than I wanted, and all the stained glass in the church erupts and showers down to the floor in a rainbow of razor blades, shattering what's left of the denial in the room. "She's going up, and we are going to work. I told you what we have to do. Time to do it!"

The debate and protesting that follows from Salvation finally gets interrupted when the low moaning sound mixed in with church choir music starts emanating from the father's decapitated husk. And I can see his soul squiggling and squirming its way out of his lifeless cocoon. And now we got no time left.

"Rain," I say it in my father voice. If I even have one left. Probably comes out like more of a mean teacher, because I get a wing to the ribcage from Salvation. So I dial it back a couple of feathers and say, "Take the father's soul up to the arena, get him his wings, and bring him back here. That's the exercise. Nothing else, nothing extra . . . just get it done."

And with no protest at all and not another sound out of her, my little bright ball of light is down from the rafters. She clutches up the father's moaning and writhing soul and heads out the hole in the roof. And then she's gone.

And I shouldn't be—I'm still not sure if our job is worse than hers —but I'm happy that she's going up there, because now . . . we gotta gut the garden.

— XLIX —

THE GOOD NEWS, I tell Salvation and Fury, if the father and I have it figured right, a "day" of creation, or judgment for that matter, is not necessarily twenty-four hours. It's more like, as long as you need to get the job done.

In the *Bible* and the *Book of Blood*, time is relative. "How else do you think she built it in 'seven days?' " the father told me. *Remember that*, I tell myself.

But the bad news—the other thing the father is right about—none of it is permanent. For some of them it's too bad. I wish it was longer. But eternity looks to be an everlasting assfuck by the same souls on the next round. That is, unless we can kill the powerful people that are responsible for all this. Then maybe, just maybe, humanity's got a chance at redemption.

It's a strange thing—archangels killing for the Word. The first ones in the street and on the roof were instinct, like a little baby learning to crawl. But this. . . Once I figure it out—get good at it—the whole thing actually gets harder. Practice makes perfect sense in most things. Not this.

It's not the mercy, mind you. There are so many people on the planet that need killing. . . Probably why we never got around to fixing anything. I mean, where do you put the piss, shit, and disposed plastic from ten billion citizens, moaning and crying for more? I guess you could build a shit-rocket—send the whole mess into the deep depths of space. But then who are you, really? The Rural Zone guy in the trailer park next door, throwing his beer cans and bottles over the fence so his neighbor has to pick it all up?

I like the ranting. Always have. For some reason I think it's funny to state the obvious to people, and then watch them squirm as they try to deny it. Ten billion people. . . Jesus Christ!

The magnitude of the task gnaws at me the most. I mean, how do you free ten billion souls in one day? Not to mention clean up afterward? Never mind all the animals, plants and fish, too. Though, come to think of it, we got a good jump start on the animal extinction issue, so hey, things are looking up.

Because this is not a Noah repeat, and it's not Jesus giving man one last chance, and it's not the second coming or any of that rapture crap either. This here . . . this is the end of the inhabitants of the earth, all of them. The garden is rotten. Time to clean up all the decay, plow it under, and plant new seeds.

The bloodsuckers—the State politicians, the bankers, and the revenue agents—they go easy. There's a lot of begging and bargaining —rich and powerful people confuse those two with bulletproof. It's a common mistake, but nothing a few feathers to the guts doesn't fix. And I can hardly manage any mercy for people who make a living lying and cheating and stealing. In fact, I try and make it as painful and prolonged as possible.

Watching a vengeful angel rip out your guts on your boardroom conference table has got to rank right up there with losing all your credits. But no amount of money is buying them out of this game.

Then there's the Protection traffic agents. . . And I know it's petty, and I'm sure there's people who deserve it more, but I hate those bastards. "Do you realize you were traveling faster than the posted speed statute?" Of course I realize, you condescending prick, I was driving the damn guzzler, wasn't I?

And that's talons to the testicles for the lot of them. I even rip one of the sons a bitches right off his motorcycle—swoop in and tear his head off, then watch his headless body ride the two-wheeled guzzler down the freeway, until it finally loses control and splatters in front of some citizens.

Secretly, they laugh from the safety of their guzzler seats, because they have all licked the tip of a traffic agent's dick while he pisses in their face, doling out his condescendingly obvious advice on life.

Of course the motorists, they're toast too, so the laughter is short-lived.

Yeah, revenue agents and traffic enforcers—nobody likes those bitches.

When I stop to think about it, I realize that mommy and daddy have turned me into the exact thing I despise. They've sent me to collect their debts. Break the rules, pay the tax. Only this fine is final —imprisonment in eternity. And I think about what Dal said the "J" stands for again—judgment, justice . . . jail. What's the difference?

I send Fury after the pedophiles and molesters, and the rapists and the child traffickers. Seems like the right thing to do. I watch her first few, making sure she's got the hang of it. Judging by the number of severed pimps and screaming sociopaths she leaves in her wake, Fury is fine on her own.

And Salvation is wounded, or at least I'm still feeling guilty about it, because I shadow her for her first few, too. But whatever damage she had after I blindsided her is pretty well healed up, because there's a smoking hole where the data-farm in Utah used to be—Salvation likes her privacy.

I get a good chuckle at the sight. And she's fine too, so I send her after all the militaries on the planet. That's her little treat. Not that you can blame the guard dogs for biting who their masters tell them to, but everyone is everyone, so—she's always kinda been on the fence about war, anyway.

I guess she's funny that way, because the rest of us. . . Well, not anymore, but back in the dream called life, and judging by how many different conflicts we created so Protection defense contractors could stuff their jowls with more. . . War, we *love* that shit!

I guess normally I would've done it differently—gobble up the peas and piss before we got to dessert—do the hard stuff first. But sooner or later this job is gonna start to suck ass, so I figure it is better if I work them up to it.

I would like to say that I paused and wondered if we were doing the right thing—carrying out the will of the Word for the creators of humanity. I would like to say that I had a lot of guilt, while I was tearing limbs and ripping guts and cutting out the lying tongues of the filth of the earth. And I would like to say that we *all* had a change of heart and just *couldn't* go through with it. And I would love to say that we stopped at the teenagers, or the women, or the girls . . . or the babies. . .

Oh . . . I bet you didn't know that archangels had to kill babies, did you? Neither did I, but like I said, everyone is everyone, so the little squealing, future assfuckers of the earth go, too. Not like we weren't setting up assembly lines to abort them. I know that sounds a little hypocritical, given, but despite the understanding that we should feel some kind of mercy or remorse, none of the three of us can manage one ounce of pity. We're avenging archangels, for God's sake—by the time we show up, it's too late for all that redemption shit. Not my department.

And I have to cluck out a chuckle when I say it to one of the begging little bitch "Prime Officer of the Board of Directors" I stomp. I always wanted to say that to one of them.

The trouble is, you can only ever complain to the credits-checker about the long line at the mart, and he has as much control over fixing it as fleas have on where a dog shits. And bitching to him is just about as effective as. . .

And I just have to shake all the shitty thoughts, because though mangling metaphors to amuse myself is fun, it's not getting me any closer to getting this job done.

Back to business.

After a couple thousand, ten thousand at the most, I get numb to it. And then it gets tedious, and then it gets common—no different from a couple old guys on a park bench, reading the front page of the Protection daily while they feed the pigeons. "Another rich asshole got his heart ripped out by an angel last night, Phillip. Oh heavens, what's the world coming to, Edward?"

So I settle into a little groove of gutting and it's talons-tits-testicles, talons-tits-testicles—the whole process gets downright average. And if there's anything I hate more than gun-grabbing, revenue-ripping politicians, it's the assholes of the average. So I invent ways to kill in order to entertain myself—keep myself awake.

I come up with funny names too—amusing to me, anyway—just to keep it interesting. There's "Politician Pie," for those annoying little citizen council meetings where wannabes go to boot camp to learn how to pretend that you have a say in how things are run; there's the "Weathergirl Wail," but that one goes a different way than I expect, because when they finally realize they don't have to suck any more cock, trying to get themselves to the "Mornings with Morons" show on the PIN, they get a peaceful, accepting look on their faces and just bleed out in silence; and my personal, all-time favorite "The Gun-grabber Gut-pile," reserved for ignorant and uneducated people who truly believe that once the governments of the world have all the guns, it will be all cupcakes and cream cheese anytime they have a disagreement with their citizens.

And I fire up the worst and the longest and the most ludicrous conspiracy rants in my head that I can in order to keep my rage up and my adrenaline pumping for the task at hand.

Ever try to wipe out a planet? There's a few points where I could use an energy drink. *Maybe Fury has some extra coke?* I smile at the thought.

And I could pretend that I cried over the loss of the shopping sprees, and the reality reruns on the PIN, and the trillion meaningless holidays Protection invented to keep poor people poorer as they crack credits they don't have on more plastic shit they don't need. . . I could pretend that I understand how a multimillionaire cinewave actor could get on the PIN and guilt a bunch of citizens, scraping by a week at a time, to donate credits to save the starving African babies or some other futile crap. Especially when the little cry-baby could just whip out his hex-card and come up with the whole amount out of his therapy money. But that's never the point, is it? Not with the rich and powerful—they feed off *your* guilt and *your* money, not their own.

And I could delude myself into believing that if people would just stop listening to the same lies over and over and over again, because they were so drunk on faith in their leaders that they couldn't see the wrathful truth if it was an archangel ripping off their nuts. But, pushing stupid prick and pussy to Purgatory isn't about pretending.

And I know in your head you want to ask the question, so yeah . . . sure—some of them *are* good people and some of the bad ones *do* try and repent—tell me all the good they've done, and that they don't deserve it, and how cruel I am, and how unfair. But I just laugh right in their faces. They just don't get it. This whole thing—life, death, reincarnation, eternity—the Protection motto actually got it right, go figure. They screwed up the true meaning, though. Go figure that, too. "Ensuring peace and prosperity . . . for all."

I think everyone realizes it, but no one slows down enough to do anything about it. Hard to slow down when you're clawing the aisles for more cheap crap from Chinasia. But make no mistake, humanity is a team sport, and on this round . . . we lost.

And *son of a bitch*, I have to stop in mid-gut on some poor repentant bastard and check myself, because I'm monologuing in my mind. Jesus Christ, I *hate* that shit!

— L —

FURY, SALVATION AND I planned to regroup at around three billion, because, figuring out the time-zone thing when we are racing all over the globe, lopping off heads. . . Synchronize watches, while the relativity of time decided how fast it was going to play out. . .? I don't think so. Any Vegas blackjack dealer will tell you—it's easier to keep track of the count.

So we meet on the top of Mount Everest—my idea. Closest place to Heaven on Earth, I figured. Trouble is, it's so cold, we last about ten seconds before Fury is bitching to go to Mexico.

When we get there. . . I don't know what Mexico she's been tripping to, snorting coke, getting high on her own judgment, tanning on the beach with her daddy's hex-card, but the real Mexico—the one the Mexicans live in—is a sludge-filled, shitpile of slime.

Trick question—how hard is it to just round up all the drug lords, murderers, and teen-tit traffickers in Mexico and slice out their souls over breakfast? The answer is, it's not. The trick . . . start with the Protection agents.

— LI —

ALL OF THE angels perched in the Hallowed Hall atop the great mountain, watching the cleansing of the garden. They knew they had seen it before—over and over for all time. But something was different.

It was a treacherous game to play—each of them planning for the other's demise. But the lust for power tugged at them both, so Dal and Life each plotted and calculated their next move while the other did the same.

Dal stood in the center of the arena. He said to Life, "Look at him, he is making great pace. I told you he would—"

"It is far from complete," said Life. "He still has time to figure it out. We must—"

"Why do you worry so?" asked Dal. "It has been this way forever. My reign shall be no different, I am afraid."

"I shudder to imagine it."

And shudder you will, Dal thought. "These are your rules, not mine. Try to follow them this time."

"Whatever do you mean?"

"Whatever you are thinking," Dal said, "it will not work. I will rule, you will serve. It is written."

"I realize this," she said. "I helped write it."

"Shall we send the gatherers?"

"Not just yet," said Life. "I want to see some more."

Dal knew she would get drunk on the misery during a Judgment Day. She did every time. It would give him just enough of an edge. "Ah, there you are, my lady," he said. "A few more then? Enjoy. I'll go prepare the first flight."

— LII —

I HOPE THEY are watching up in Heaven . . . or Hell or wherever, because I don't know how many angels "The Queen" and her "Dark Asshole" have at their disposal. There were a million at least, flocking out the arena up there. But down here, the world is turning into a moaning, wriggling, writhing toilet full of floating souls, wailing and waiting to be flushed down the drain. It's starting to get messy. I hope they send the soul patrol down here pretty quick, because the noise is grinding on me.

But as it turns out, they *are* watching and soon enough I hear the distant cooing and cawing, and the wind rushing under what sounds like millions. . . When I spot them, it looks like billions, as the winged warriors of the Word show up. And they twist and turn, and spin and dive, swooping down onto souls like eagles fishing for trout.

If you've ever seen a tornado of ducks and geese twist down and descend upon a freshly cut cornfield, and then strip it clean of every last spilled kernel, that's what it reminds me of. And I know I have a job to do and I know that time itself is running down, but I just have to pause the pain for a while and watch. And I remember hunting ducks with my dad and I smile. I remind myself to savor the spectacular, as well.

My dad. . . Is that a memory or was that real life? The difference is foggy in my mind. The father was certain he was right. "*Book of Blood*," I mutter.

I don't have long to ponder the thought before this flight of faithful and fallen ascend back to the heavens with the whole point of this exercise tucked tightly in their talons. And then it's back to the brimstone, because three billion isn't even halftime.

By five billion, Fury is just warming up. There's a lot of pent-up rage in there, and she doesn't look to be running out of fire to fry people any time soon. So I send her on her way to clean up Europe. She's a spoiled, international jet-set brat—I figure she's the best one to send to police the pompous. Besides, I sure as hell don't want to have to deal with France.

Regardless, my little Salvation and I have some . . . unfinished business to attend to.

Uh-huh. . .

Huh? . . . What? I don't know if it's my inner voice, or them talking to me? "Oh," I mutter, "that's just wrong."

Because this is The End. The time for fornicating is over. I mean, look where it all led. Anyway, I don't even know how it would work on an angel. I guess I could figure it out, and once I did . . . well, then yeah, sure . . . of course.

— LIII —

I FORGET ABOUT the . . . distractions, and Salvation and I have a little chat instead. At first, she doesn't really want to talk about it, but when I tell her that I had to watch, helpless during the whole thing, she's madder than if I had never even known. Can't blame her, really. But it seems a long time in the past for some reason.

Doesn't really matter, because the both of us remember it the same way. And if there is ever going to be something good that comes out of this horrible and better off long-forgotten day, it's going to be this next part. Because love and lust and the ludicrousness of this life might be a long-lost memory in the next one, but this . . . this next part is about hate . . . and hate never forgets.

I bet you thought I forgot, didn't you. Not likely, but the hardest part about being responsible for The End is that you still have to tie up all of the loose ends you left back at the beginning of your own life. Create too many of them, and it can be a mess. Being an angel doesn't exempt me from that.

When Salvation and I catch up to them, they are busy doing what rats do, looking for a way off the sinking ship.

Because a hundred and twenty meters under a sandstone mountain, behind six-foot concrete walls and huge concrete and steel doors, just outside the village of Svalbard on Spitsbergen. . . Hell, I can't pronounce the shit either, but I know what's really under the mountain on this island in Norway, and it's not what the Protection says it is.

The permafrost and low earthquake likelihood are nice, and the whole thing is far enough above sea level that even if the polar icecaps melted, everything would stay dry. And all of that makes it a great place to house the world's global seed supply should the earth, say . . . be burned to a cinder of ash and need to be replanted, or some other angel-fairytale shit like that, for instance.

But the hardest part about storing seeds isn't protecting them from the heat and the moisture, or any other environmental hazard from above. Because if you kick over the global food supply, what you are gonna find underneath it . . . is rats.

— LIV —

IT'S FREEZING IN Norway—I feel damned near as cold as Mount Everest. It could be colder. And the whole landscape is covered in snow. Reminds me of the Great Mountain of the Eternities. But there are no angels inside this sandstone, snow-covered lair of liars. By the smell of the fear and panic, the inside of this molehill is filthy with rats.

Most of them only have one job—protect their powerful leaders from The End, even if they have to cough up their own souls to do it.

And I think to myself that it's ironic—all the resources that are put into saving the very assholes that ruined the whole planet in the first place. They build elaborate, highly secure, underground cities for themselves, because they know that after the shit cools down—after whoever is left swims to the surface through the sea of shit they got thrown overboard into—the people they drowned are coming to drown them. And it won't be any nice slow lube session either.

No, those people know that their only hope. . . Their only salvation will be to hide until it's all over, and then come out at the end of it, pretending that someone else made the mess and they are humanity's last hope of cleaning up that "other" guy's mistakes.

Today, my sweet Salvation and I are here for two little raping and murdering souls, in particular. It'll be a bonus if they're holed up with their PAIC boss—the bastard from the roof where I jumpstarted this whole messed-up journey.

* * *

It's a little-known fact—at least outside Norway—that *in* Norway, expensive State-funded construction projects have to include some kind of work of art. . . . I shit you not. "State" funded. . . They say it like it's some kinda separate entity that allows the rest of the population to enjoy the fruits of its labor and generosity. The reality—God or government—you work for it, they take it, tell you to be grateful when they give it to someone else.

And as we stand outside the door, marveling at the roof and vault entrance—the hole down to this rat trap is filled with highly reflective stainless steel, mirrors and prisms. They all act as a beacon, reflecting polar light and shining a network of two hundred fiber-optic cables that gives the place an eerie blue and green glow. And I shake my head at the whole gaudy waste of citizen-slave blood, sweat and tears.

Salvation can tell I'm grinding up a rant in my head. You don't live with someone that long without being able to read their revenge-filled queues.

"Jacob. . ." Shit, that's her reprimand voice. "You need to stay under control. Amy is still up there with them."

And she's right. Brightest angel or not, we both know who Rain's dealing with.

"What?" I say, "I'm just gonna let 'em know we're here. And it's Jump."

She knows that's bullshit and she plugs her ears and pushes out all of her armored feathers. And I spread my wings as wide as they'll go—right in front of the security feed by the entrance—and I screech a scream out that is louder than anything I've yelled since this day of judgment started.

And Salvation is blown backward, and all the mirrors and all the prisms explode into a fine glass mist, completely obliterating the beautiful benevolence of the State government of Norway.

When the first six scurry out, I let Salvation cut them to pieces with her pinfeathers and quills. They barely get off any shots, before they are bloodstains and brains. Then we step over the steaming puddles of rat bile and the severed limbs and heads, and walk to the big concrete door.

And Salvation knows they're inside—she says she can smell them. I wonder how, but I'm not asking the question, because all I can smell is my own vengeance, bubbling like acid from my stomach and burning the back of my parched thirst for payback.

If the big door did make them feel safer before, it doesn't after Salvation rips it open like a tiny sardine can. And then there's running, and gunfire and smoke, and yelling and shouting and screaming. And when we both spin and send hundreds of ballistic fire-feathers into the fray, limbs and blood and guts and brains splatter the inside of the big vault. It's like shoving rats in a blender, and I can only hope that the ones we're after are still living, because this fate is just too good for them.

But when we slice and cut our talons through the ones left alive, Salvation stops over two of the chopped-apart bodies and stares. And then she starts to cry.

By the time I calm her down, I'm more pissed than when we poked our way into this nest. Women and crying just makes me want to kill whoever caused it.

"That's them," she says.

It's all she has to say. Five billion souls in, we both know that revenge is bittersweet at best. It leaves an ice cold, empty pit in the middle of our stomachs that begs us to keep trying to fill it with boiling hot blood. The only problem, every time we do . . . it just gets colder.

We never do find the two raping, murdering interrogators' boss. Sometimes the eagle gets the rat, and sometimes the rat slinks away.

Does Salvation feel any better having quenched her thirst for vengeance with blood? Does judgment feel worse that we didn't find the bastard? Well, if you're asking if I think it was worth it—did we get what we came for?

When Salvation's done thinking whatever she has to, she sniffs a little and wipes her face. Then she says, "Does any of this matter?"

I look around the bloodstained, concrete graveyard of limbs, and then I breathe in a great big whiff of gunsmoke and guts. "Not to them."

— LV —

FROM MY PERSPECTIVE, six and seven billion souls go out kinda like they came in—one minute there were five billion souls on the earth, begging the State to feed, clothe and protect them, and in the blink of an eye . . . there were seven. And eight, nine and ten aren't a whole helluva lot different.

Then, before the three of us know it, the journey to judgment and justice for the earth's ten billion souls is almost complete. I say almost, because before we started I was crystal-clear on where we would end the day.

I gotta tell ya, for three angels from the rain-drenched streets of Seattle, talon-tuckered at the end of a tough day of delivering God's will of the Word, there is no place quite like the sun-soaked sands of the Middle East.

And perched at the pinnacle of the Burj Khalifa—the highest man-made structure on Earth—it feels like the breeze is the breath of angels, warming and fluttering our feathers with gusts of hot air from the desert below.

The Burj makes the scrapers in Seattle look like scrub brush under a towering pine tree. It was built by over seven thousand skilled workers trucked, flown, or billy-club-kidnapped in from South Asia. They were paid around six credits a day. The back-busted laborers got about half that much. Yes, the world has come a long way from the slaves at the pyramids on the great Giza Plateau.

"Makes you wonder," I say.

"Wonder what?" Salvation asks.

And for a girl that spent most of her mortal life sucking on her mommy's silicone tits, living in a dream world bought with her daddy's raped and pillaged credits, this sight is as real as it gets for Fury. She gives me a look and says, "Don't go fucking this up. Come on, look at this shit, it's awesome."

And I have to admit that the view is incredible—no wonder birds like to sit on top of buildings. But I know this place is just filled with more rats. I can smell them inside, waiting for their credits to save them, because by now there is no doubt that this day is their last.

"Just. . ." Fury says. "Look, I'm wiped. Can we just enjoy the view for a minute? South America sucked. And Africa? Why did that have to be me? Just don't fuck up Dubai for me, okay? I always wanted to go here with my—"

And then I think she gets it. For richer or rougher, this is her new family. And revenge-filled, angry heart or not, we're the only ones who care what happens to her now. We might be the only ones who ever did. She stares at the sun setting across the ocean—crimson and red— the colors of the day. "Fucking Dubai. . ." she mumbles.

Dubai. Where the wealthy and wonderful go to get away from it all. All the lawsuits, all the molestation charges, all the taxes, all of the rest of us cretins of civilization. Highest building on Earth? Not anymore. We level the whole place—send it back to the sand as the sun dips below the sea and the world turns to darkness. The whole thing would have crumbled anyway, crushed beneath the weight of the wealthy's thirst for more.

— LVI —

MILLIONS OF FAITHFUL and fallen angels rested and wondered about the Word of the two heavens, rustling their feathers and watching in anticipation from the grandstands of the arena. Seventh days were always long, but as seventh days went, this had been longer than most.

Building it or breaking it apart—it really didn't matter—a tough day transporting souls in or out of the garden was exhausting work. But this time had been different, there was the smell of revolution in the air—an unholy discontent, worming its way from the husk of the eternal sameness of the faithful and faithless snowflakes. And a tremor rumbled through their beliefs as they watched the darkness—the great black nothing—descend upon the garden.

Their Dark Angel of Light stood at the center of the huge arena. Only he and Life truly knew what was coming. He watched the black nothing descend, just as it had before.

The Protectors had played this godly game since time was created, and he longed for it to be his turn atop The Great Mountain of the Eternities. A lion to replace the lamb and then the lamb to replace the lion. Back and forth, upside down to downside up—such was the Word.

But somewhere along the way, the Protectors had all become drunk on their own thirst for power. The dark more than the light, but the call to stay on top of the mountain had touched them all. He felt that when they joined. So Dal looked for an edge—something he could use to tip the scales of judgment in evil's favor. Something to anchor him at the peak . . . and then allow him to stay there for all the eternities to come. Then one day—another boring, soul-sucking day —a priest lost his faith . . . and then wrote a book. And Dal knew when the next Fallen appeared, it was his chance.

Men had written books about their experiences with *her* since she had taken her throne back at the dawn of this eternity. But none had written a book that spoke to him. So this priest's unholy word against humanity and its destruction caught his eye, and he summoned its word and took it in for his own. And their own seed, Jump, became his pathway to dominating and enslaving Life for all eternity. She would be his queen. Not that she wasn't already, but now she would be his slave.

— LVII —

AS LIFE ENTERED and fluttered to the center of the great hall, the cooing and clucking wasn't as loud as it had been. As the faithful grew nervous, she paused to find the words that would calm her children.

The road had been long on this current eternity. The sands slipped slowly through the hourglass, but now her time—her reign—drew near to a close.

To a being of the light and a deity of the first truth, the Word had been all that she had to maintain control. But the faithful and the fallen began to question that word. They searched for meaning in it and fell into disbelief.

When it started, she had little concern. It had happened before and she had dealt with it harshly, swiftly, with fear and punishment. But whipping a slave was only effective so long as the slave minded being whipped. So when the misery of daily life in the garden surpassed the punishments she sent, the power she drew from the faithful slipped into decline.

Now she could feel him, hot and hateful, impatiently waiting for his time. Her Dark Angel—she could scarcely think of Dal that way any longer—would soon rule over her with the flaming fist of a master, once slave. It was the ordained order of all the eternities, that the Protectors should trade role for role, but she had grown to believe it an unacceptable fate.

She had sent word to her children, over and over again, commanding them to worship her words, and condemning them for the mere thought of his. It had not been enough. Try as they might, the children of the garden had not been able to rid her of his impending rule. And now, in the final hour of her reign, she grew more desperate. He would not know her as she had allowed before.

It was directly from the Word, specifically to this purpose, and of him that she spoke to the gallery, "My children. . ."

The roar of feathers, ruffling steel wings, cut her speech. She waited impatiently for the clucking and the cawing of the angels in the gallery to settle. Once it did, she continued, ". . .as my time draws to an end, be sober-minded—be watchful. For your new ruler prowls like a roaring lion, seeking only to devour. For even he disguises himself in darkness as an angel of light."

She kept him in the corner of her eye as she spoke. If he came at her, she would unleash her wrath, but it would be far better for him to fall back into his pit at the hands of his own followers . . . and hers. Cast down at the hands of his faithless would be worse than when she did it herself. She smiled.

Another term—remain in power. It was all a ruler ever wanted.

— LVIII —

DAL COULD SEE that Life was coming at him sideways, but that was *his* way, not hers. Slithering through the garden on his belly was a trick he had mastered. He had done it time and time again, sneaking in and out of humanity's dream, convincing them that he did not exist, and better, that she did not either.

But the author of the book was his hole card, his ace of faith. The dark, blasphemous *Book of Blood* sealed that one's fate, and the father became one of the Dark Angel's faithless flock. Not even the Chosen One's champion of light could change that. She had tried and failed to ferry his soul in and out of the great hall unnoticed, but once the father got his wings, she was captured.

"Bring out our Faith!" Dal yelled to his followers. "Bring me the priest."

And two golden angels flew from the side of the arena. Each held an arm of the newly minted angel of the Dark Word of the *Book of Blood*—Faith, bonded and chained around the neck. They dropped Father Faith at the feet of their master and pinned him to the ground with their talons.

Dal would give them the show first—let them see his power over the Dark Word's author. Then he would kill the only one that could alter his future. It was a simple plan.

He slithered next to Faith, knelt beside him, and snarled. His wings spit fire and his tongue lashed at Faith's face. "Speak, priest," he said.

Then he looked at the Chosen One. "Tell us our fates."

The father coughed and yelled and squinted at the pain in his back and arms—talons pierced his newly grown plumage as his captors' claws squeezed past his steel feathers into his flesh and bones. But he spoke from his own faith, not hers or his. He said, "The judgment of my world is now the judgment of this world . . . and the rulers of this world will be cast out from it."

And a roar went through the gallery—the faithless and the faithful cawed and clucked loudly.

And Dal roared at Faith and cawed violently. And flames flew from his wings and rage filled his eyes. He could kill their Faith if he had to, but it would be better for his followers, and hers, to choose to follow. "It is *she* who shall be cast from the shadow of the great mountain, and I shall put claim on your soul for the next! None can save you, or her, from this fate, for such is the power of the Two Words."

Faith looked up at the grandstands. The awesome sight of a million angels and what he was about to do made him smile. They were not the only ones who could bend and twist the Word to suit their own purposes. But all his life he had waited to feel the Word—see Heaven. Now that he had arrived, they had both lost their luster.

Faith spoke calmly, loudly, so all could hear. "My brothers and sisters of the Words of the two heavens, you have been deceived . . . but not by this dark angel alone. For I know your tribulation and your poverty . . . and the slander of those who say that they are gods and are not, but are truly deities of arrogance and jealousy."

And Dal raised his wing, preparing to end Faith's speech—splay out the guts of the father of the book, the new law. The law that was soon to be hers, as well.

Life would be his slave of the flesh and he would know her again and again. And he smiled and he swung at Faith—

— LIX —

RAIN COULD NOT remember her own judgment in the arena, but the judgment of the father seemed to last forever. The Dark Angel, Dal, tormented and tortured his soul, for hours it seemed, before giving him his wings. Then they took him from her and imprisoned him beneath the arena—put him in the Dungeon of the Damned, where the Chosen One and the Dark Angel kept the darkest *and* the brightest souls. Holding them until they forced them to fight for the sport of the crowd.

Rain knew that, she had been imprisoned there herself—caged behind iron bars covered with Rosary beads and crosses, unable to break free despite her newly bestowed power.

She could barely remember her own soul now—an archangel forced to fight others in the arena. But none had defeated her—none had come close. She cowered in her cage between matches, wondering and wishing that she could remember. But when she finally did, she was deep in the fall with her own father.

It was tougher for angels—they were not programmed like man—but she finally found her own free will and removed the yoke from her neck. Yet once she challenged authority, questioned Life, she was sent to the dungeons and chained for annihilation—the only way to destroy an angel.

Rain looked down at the Rosary beads and cross around her neck. It seemed like a privilege when they put them on her the first time—

Life had told her it was a medal. That's the last thing she remembered before the fall with her father. But when she brought the priest's soul to get his wings in the arena, two golden angels had attacked her and put the Rosary yoke back on.

Yet after the church, Rain wasn't the same innocent soul turned angel of bright. She would not be put under the spell again. She would not sleep through The End.

Rain waited in her sweltering dark cage as the golden guardian angel jailers stood watch just outside. She listened to the lust of the crowd in the arena, and then to the dark angel's speech. Then she heard the father—Faith—give his own.

Rain's light flickered despair in her cell, for she had failed the only thing that her father had entrusted to her—the safe return of Faith to the garden. It didn't seem right—punishing the father like she had been punished with headaches in her life. After all, the dark angel himself had told the crowd—her brothers and sisters of light and darkness—that the priest was the author of the new Word. Would he kill the author? How could he?

She was afraid of Dal, but now she was afraid of Life more. When they dragged her from the arena, she could hear him, snarling and barking like a vicious dog at the father. The priest was laid low in the center of the field of diamonds and rubies. She knew now that they both intimidated all into following their rule. Dark angel or Life. . . They would kill Faith? Kill the father? She would not let them.

— LX —

I LOOK AT Salvation and Fury. I don't think they understand, but I know what's coming now. Hell, the father and I planned it. I couldn't tell Salvation—she would have never let Rain go up there.

I didn't tell either of them, but I knew neither the father nor Rain were coming back. Those two wouldn't let them come back. Arrogant, oppressive and angry doesn't mean stupid. Them or me, though, is a toss-up.

And by now, the father's soul is an angel and the only thing that the dark bastard could do to him. . . I try not to think about it.

I hope this all works, because if it doesn't. . . Let's hope it does, because otherwise, ten billion souls. . . The father? What a waste.

And Salvation says to me, "She's not coming back, is she."

She's not asking. It's more like, "You better know what you are doing, because if my baby. . ." Or some scary shit like that.

"She'll be okay," I say. "She's not our little girl anymore." And I rub all of the healed holes that the bright angel of light—Rain—punched into me during the last few days. "Trust me, she can take care of herself."

"For your sake," Salvation says, "you better hope you're right."

— LXI —

WHEN LIFE LET her loose back in the Arena of Reckoning, Rain knew what her master wanted. It was hard for her to resist with the beads around her neck. She blasted Dal with her brightest light yet, before he had a chance to behead the father.

She watched him recoil from the truth of her light. Though he was fire itself—spat from the dark pit of the burning lake of oil—her light burned at his feathers and beat down their flames. And he took flight away to the shadows of the hall and landed on the other side of the arena.

The Chosen One watched, standing next to Rain, hands on her shoulders, grinning as her finest fighter yet sent Dal flying for cover. She smiled and then addressed the gallery, "Oh, how you are fallen from Heaven, my Day Star, my sweet son of Dawn! How you are cut down to the ground. . . . You who laid the nations low! You said in your heart, 'I will ascend to Heaven; above the stars of God I will set my throne on high; I will sit on the mount of assembly in the far reaches of the North; I will ascend above the heights of the clouds; I will make myself like the Most High.' But you are brought down to the far reaches of the pit by *my* light and *my* truth."

Dal snarled at her. Life's bright champion of light was becoming a nuisance. He had known the warmth of the Chosen One's grace and favor before. It was fleeting and always ended the same way—cast from her side to rule in the bottomless pit of desperation and death. He knew Rain—her newest lapdog—would suffer the same fate. But for now, she needed to wait her turn.

Dal flew and the great flapping sound of his flaming wings burned through the air above the arena. He swooped at them both and spat a huge stream of fire. The two bright angels split and flew in different directions. Dal followed Rain, shooting fire and trailing black smoke.

With each blast, Rain flitted to avoid it, but Dal flapped his great wings to fan the orange flames and he shot another and another, chasing her around the arena, flying behind her bright shining light.

When she turned and slammed into him, Dal went crashing to the floor in a huge ball of orange fire and black smoke. When the black cloud of soot cleared, he sprang up and flew at her and shot fire from his wings and it engulfed her, and he fired all the feathers he could and Rain crashed to the floor of the arena, losing feathers and blood. And then she was back up and Dal flew at her again.

The Chosen One motioned toward the dungeons—she would not lose her champion this easily. Though she had never been bested since she arrived, Dal might be too much for Life's unseasoned archangel. She would get more practice.

As quickly as Rain entered, two of the golden guardian angels from the dungeon snatched her from the floor of the arena and dragged her flickering body back through the tunnel, flying her to her cell below.

— LXII —

FATHER BENITO WATCHED helplessly as Rain was forced to fight with Dal. But weakened by a Rosary, she was unable to mount much of an attack. He knew now why Fury had hated them around her neck.

He had already surrendered hope when they took Rain during his judgment. Now Faith had to trust in his comrades. They were all he had left.

But if it was to be his last day in eternity, he would not go out like a lamb . . . or a lion. He spoke to the crowd as if they were his final words. Short and sweet—that was how he had always delivered bad news, "The dark angel has no claim on my soul."

And Faith shook the talons of his two captors out of his side and off of his arms. And he spun and shot feathers at them both, piercing them and sending the two golden guardians, flailing and flapping toward the sides of the arena, squawking and screeching from the sting of his steel.

Then he stood and looked at the gallery. He could see Dal flying back—a huge ball of flame, preparing to silence him with fire. He flapped his newly minted wings and then hovered twenty feet above the center of the arena, so all could see and hear him. He said, "I will no longer talk much with you, for the new ruler of this world is coming."

And then he recited the ageless prayer. The rest was up to them.

And just like he told Jump, he altered it just enough to get his point across, "For light is his Mother, and darkness his Father, and he is their Son, and he is judgment, as my own judgment and yours was in the beginning, under my power for eternity, in this, our world without end. Amen."

Neither of them could deny *that* word.

And then Dal's flame melted Faith's feathers and burned his flesh and boiled his blood. And Faith felt the agony and the darkness of wrath. But if his brothers and sisters could have seen his face through the flames, they would have noticed his smile—Jump was coming—right before he went to the black nothing before the next eternity.

And Dal's flame fell down to a flicker. And he stood over Faith and growled to himself, "And now you are mine. You and your *book*."

— LXIII —

IF YOU'VE EVER been deep in the forest at night, you would know the kind of darkness that descends over the three of us . . . and the planet. A thick blanket of black and the only light is the stars. A million. . . Billions of tiny points of bright pricking through the black of eternity, flickering like the truth in a dark sea of lies.

You can't see the truth from the city. You have to go to the deepest, darkest woods of your soul. Because the city is full of its own light, an artificial brightness that masquerades as the truth of time. Lost in the forest, that's where the light is the brightest. Because in the depths of your soul, shines the light.

"Are you joking me?" That was what I said to the father when he told me that philosophical shit. But the guy was dead serious and now I know he was right. Because once we crumble the last lying, greedy, conniving flicker of the artificial light of humanity. . . Once Dubai falls, it's a hell of a lot easier to see the truth in the darkness.

And there it is, shining like it was always there. A huge trail of bright stars in the sky—the pathway to Heaven.

I stare up at the twinkling trail of tiny lights. "You ready?" I ask Salvation and Fury.

They both know they are going.

"Like, where the fuck else we gonna go," Fury says, "Vegas?"

Salvation laughs a little. "Not anymore."

They both cluck and coo, obviously remembering what they did in Sin City. They told me about it, but maybe there's something more.

When I quit chuckling with them, I say, "I still can't believe you—"

"Whoa-whoa," Salvation says.

"Oh my God," Fury chimes in, "don't you know anything?"

Then Salvation clucks out a little giggle. Apparently the girls had more fun leveling that place than they told, because she looks at Fury and says, "What happens in Vegas. . ."

Fury smiles an evil little grin. Kinda gives me the shivers. "Dies in Vegas," she says.

Then the two of them start flapping slowly toward the bright trail of stars in the dark night sky. And I can hear them above me, clucking and chirping at each other, lazily fluttering their words and their wings, pretending they aren't shitting themselves at what's ahead.

When I catch up to them, I say, "All right, ladies, foreplay's over. Time to start fucking the faithful."

I smile to myself and fly ahead. Then I listen behind me—I hate secrets.

"Fuck," Fury says, "is he always like that?"

"Little girl," says Salvation, "you have no idea."

I smile in front of them and think, *We might just make it.*

— LXIV —

THE TRAIL OF stars doesn't work like the hole to bring souls does. It grabs the three of us like the jet stream currents, and Salvation, Fury and I rocket faster than any of us can fly on our own. Then the stars blur to streaks of bright light and then we are just . . . there.

When we appear at the entrance of an access tunnel on the edge of the arena, I can see that the dark bastard is deep into a rabble-rousing speech—he's busy whipping the crowd of angels into a frenzy against Life. And something is lying at his feet.

Dal's voice booms, "This two-thousand-year reign comes to an end, my brothers and sisters, and the light turns to darkness, and evil to righteousness."

I can see a black angel coming down from the roof of the great hall. A huge iron key dangles from a great chain in his hand.

Dal points to Life. "And with this key," he says, "I seize the dragon's tail and bind her, and throw her into the pit, and shut it and seal it over her, so that she might not deceive you any longer, until this next two-thousand-year eternity ends."

And it's working pretty damn well, because the clanging of wings and the loud screeching of steel feathers fills the arena with the frenzy of the faithful and faithless, clamoring for blood, clucking and cawing for change. I don't think they have long to wait.

And I've seen all this shit before—two sides of the same coin—bad and worse—State politicians on the left and the right, each telling the masses that the other is the greatest threat to their freedom and faith, turning man against brother and daughter against mother, twisting words and telling lies to keep the people at each other's throats. Then they laugh and pillage, and rape and plunder the whole time they are in power.

It's complete bullshit—mind control at its finest. Because one of them beats the people with his left hand until everyone begs him to let the other one beat them with her right. And the only truth in the whole mess. . . The only shred of reality in between the lies and the manipulation and the fear and the desperation is, that they are both just gonna beat the living shit out of you . . . every last day of your life.

And when I think that the rant in my head has just about got my black blood boiling enough, I realize that the thing in the middle of the arena—in the middle of the arena next to the Dark Angel—is the father's charred, angel-winged body.

It is him, isn't it—Faith? I mean, who else could it be? And then I think, *Oh, you mother. . .* That better not be Rain, because I don't see her anywhere. Knowing is not seeing it for yourself, though. "Mother-fucker!" I yell at Dal.

Technically, I guess it's true, but it's not the time. And I race at him, leaving Salvation and Fury to gawk and get their bearings at the edge of the jewel-studded field of the Arena of Reckoning. It's a fitting name for the place, because that's what I'm bringing.

It only takes a couple of steps for me to flap and take flight. And I pump and push on the air in the hall and I can hear my wings swooshing loudly. And then the clucking and cawing of the crowd in the grandstands turns to a roar and then screeching confusion, but the gallery isn't flying away this time, because tonight—Faith or Fury, Lion or Lamb—none of them cares—they came to witness judgment. They are here to see blood spill for the Word—they want to see the gladiators fight.

When Dal sees me, he roars and bursts into flames. And huge plumes of black smoke and orange flame boil from his great steel feathers. But it's too late and I ram into him as hard as I can and a huge plume of smoke and fire blasts heat toward the roof. The fireball is so intense that the whole gallery gasps as the entire hall flashes orange from the flame.

And we are rolling and tumbling in a ball of spitting and snarling and growling, and lashing teeth and tongues, and clawing talons. And then the whooping and the hooting starts.

I know I should feel the gouges in my side—he's pierced me at least twice—but the only thing I can taste is sweet rage and vengeance. Burning smoke and acid coat my nostrils with the hot smell of flaming oil. And I should be on fire, but for some reason I'm not, and even he is confused by that, because he pauses for a split second. But his anger is an unquenchable fire—trust me, I know the look—and he is hell-bent on shooting it up my ass.

"Not today!" I yell at him and throw him off me in a rolling ball of sparks and flames.

And when he recovers, he springs onto all four sets of talons like a cat. In a flash of flame, he's airborne and flying in a tight circle, headed toward the roof.

I doubt that he's running. Shit, I wouldn't run either. But an attack from above is dangerous—high ground is an advantage—so when he banks and his trail of fire heads back down toward me, I jump up and flap hard to meet him.

At about fifty yards between us, the both of us are blasted by the most powerful bright light I've seen. And we both spin out of control, flapping and flying backward to escape it. And I cover my eyes. I'm sure he is doing the same, because the light is so hot that the feathers around the edges of my face burn a little.

Then a voice shakes the entire mountain and the hall shivers and shakes. "Enough!"

— LXV —

AND SHINING AS bright as she ever has, is my little Amy—Rain—in the middle of the arena. And I can barely see her, even with my sunglasses on, but when I do I can tell she is scared.

Standing next to her, with her arm stretched out and gripping Rain on the shoulder is the Queen of Hearts—the Chosen One. She says, "Who among you challenges that vengeance is mine?"

And the both of us—the bastard and I—flap and then flutter to the gem-studded floor of the arena. I have no idea why, but I'm listening instead of ripping the guts out of them both.

"I will choose how to repay," says the Queen. "That is my right."

And a roar of agreement caws through the great hall, as the faithful get ready for what she has in store—her judgment.

"And I will execute them all with my wrath," she says. "So you will all know that I am the Chosen One, when I lay my vengeance upon them."

And she's holding Rain and I hear Salvation screech from the edge of the arena for her chick. I hold my hand up behind me, letting her and Fury both know they should wait. Because I can see the death and destruction behind Life's glowing black orbs. She is ready to burn it all down to survive.

Nothing worse than a lame duck leader. They got nothing to lose and that makes them totally dangerous. And isn't that just the true definition of a God. "Bitch. . ." I mutter.

And the dark angel beside me grunts his agreement. I'll get to his guts soon enough.

"Their end will correspond to their deeds," the Queen says.

And the crowd goes nuts, flapping and cawing and screeching like rabid soccer fans. When it looks like the gallery isn't going to settle down without some intervention—

"Calm yourselves, my brothers and sisters," and yes, that's my real voice, booming above hers. Because while the father was busy rewriting his *Book of Blood*, I was busy boning up on the bile of the benevolent in the *Bible*. "Did not you serve the Lord your God with joyfulness and gladness of heart, for the abundance of all things? And therefore shall you not serve your enemies whom she has sent against you?"

And that little bit throws a serious wrench in the Queen of Hearts' little plan to start lopping off heads. And I can see that she is pretty pissed off now, because no ones like their own words shoved down their throats.

But if there's anything I can tell you about what I learned from old archived fight waves—the faithful fans are some fickle fuckers when the fighting starts. In the beginning, they tend to swing toward whoever gives them the best show, and then—once the blood starts spilling—it's back to who they think will win. They switch teams like a bisexual bitch in heat.

I can see she is angry, but this next part infuriates her. "For I have seen her wrath and I have delivered it in kind," I say. And I look toward the side of the arena at Fury and Salvation.

And my sweet Salvation is just awestruck—her mouth is slightly open and I've made her speechless. It's hard to do. And I smile at her. She knows I'm an angry son of a bitch, but this shit. . . I rarely calm down long enough to debate with someone.

"And I rained Fury and Salvation down on those you were all sworn to protect. We left them as she commanded!" And I raise up my arms at the gallery, and start to turn slowly. "In the end, they wallowed in hunger and thirst, in nakedness and blood, lacking everything. And I watched them all perish at her command. Trust me, brothers and sisters, she is a heartless, unappeasable, slanderous, without self-control, brutal and unloving ruler. And she will put that same yoke of iron faith around your neck . . . until she has destroyed you all."

And the gallery goes absolutely wild. Because there are some camp-fire stories that are true. No matter how beautiful and benevolent someone seems on the outside, there is someone, somewhere who is sick and tired of her shit. Judging from the cawing and hooting and howling coming from the grandstands, a whole lotta someones.

Now, the Chosen One totally panics. Because the only thing a big, bad, benevolent angel fears more than losing her power, is getting tarred and feathered by her flock afterward.

And she points at the dark angel next to me . . . and then she starts making mistakes. "I am Life—the Lord your God," she says, "who brought you out of the dark angel's house of slavery. And he shall *not* be your god before me. You shall *not* bow down to him or serve him, for I—the Lord your God—am a jealous God. And I will visit your iniquity on your children to the third and the fourth generation of those of you who dare defy me!"

Apparently angels can. . . I think. *Not the time.*

Then the mistakes get bigger, and a bolt of white hot lightning flashes from her pointing finger and pierces into Dal and he pretty much explodes in a fiery flash of moaning souls and crying babies.

And a huge ball of orange flame rolls slowly toward the ceiling above the arena. And the great mountain shakes so hard that chunks of the pillars holding up the roof fall away and crash to the floor, sending white and red jewels flying, like bits of broken promises—crimson chunks of lies spray across the arena.

And the gallery is "screechless"—half of them staring at their master and the other half wondering where the finger is going to point next.

Then she says, "And when the two thousand years are ended, the dark angel will be released from this prison where I have sent him. And so I have released him from his present one."

Release. . . *I guess that's one way to interpret it,* I think. And if I was going to feel some sort of kinship with who the father said was mine, it should be now. But I got nothing except more empty vengeance in my heart—she just took more blood away from my parched thirst for revenge.

Then she looks at me, and I have no idea what's next, because if a few talons can pump black blood from me, what is a lightning bolt from this bitch gonna do? But then I feel something from him. His exploded chunks of a corpse, anyway.

A low moaning of souls builds and builds until everyone in the gallery can hear it too. I can't see the faces of all the angels perched in the grandstands, but I am sure they are pigeon-shitting themselves at the sound—at least half of them, for sure. Because she just killed their master and now whatever power he had, is smoking and steaming out of the chunks of him on the floor of the great hall. And when it does, the steam wafts around, circling in an orange fog of confusion for a little bit, before it pauses and races, and before I can do shit, rams itself right down my throat.

And I can feel the bile and the hopelessness, and the misery and the pain of billions of misspent souls—fallen angels roosting their faithlessness right inside my heart. I can feel the father's soul, too, mixed in among them. And that shit right there . . . was *not* in the plan. Though I'm starting to see that the plan is breaking apart at the seams.

Then she says to me, "You are of your father, and your will is to do your father's desires. He was a murderer from the beginning, and has no kinship with the truth, because there is no truth in him. When he lies, he speaks out of his own character, for he is a liar and the father of lies."

And that's a whole lotta lying from a woman who knows how to tell them. But whatever I was before and whatever I am now, I'm no bitch, hiding behind lies.

— LXVI —

THE GALLERY OF angels doesn't stay hushed for long. At least half of them can see that the tide is rising against them. Which half is anyone's guess, though, and the clucking and cawing starts. Then the screeching and screaming comes, like a billion drunk football fans, threatening and spitting beer at the other team. And once the kickoff starts. . . There are no "Angel Arena Security" to call when the enraged followers in Heaven start to brawl.

And I give Rain the signal to fly. . . . Then again. And I zoom in on her face. She was too bright before, but there's something around her —"Rosary. . ." I mutter. And that's how they got her to turn on her own father.

But I'm guessing by this point, even the Chosen One has no idea who she's dealing with. And I jump up and fly—faster than even I think I can. And before I know it myself, I'm holding the Rosary beads that were around Rain's neck and I land back where I started. Because no matter what happens to me, Rain doesn't need to defile herself with what's coming next.

And as soon as she realizes it's gone, Rain bursts light so bright that every angel in the arena clamps their eyes shut at the sting. And then she shoots straight up like a comet, leaving a trail of white sparks and shooting stars behind her. And the roof opens and she's out. And the last ounce of innocence and hope in this hall flies out with her.

And *that* is how you turn the tide against a titan.

I'm hardly through. I boom out my voice—more lion sounding now—and try to hush the gallery, "There are six things that I hate!"

And that calms the place down a little, because they all know the chapter and verse of that. But, fair warning, because I look right in her face . . . and bastardize the shit out of it on purpose. "Nasty, black, haughty eyes . . . a bitch with a lying tongue and a heart that devises wicked plans . . . lust-filled feet that make haste to run to evil's bed"— I pause for a second and look to the grandstands. They're eating it up. Then I look back at her—"a false god who breathes out against the truth . . . a hand that compels others to shed innocent blood!"

And now the crowd has joined together and the screeching and cawing has turned against her. And she's waiting and I can see the glow in her black orbs growing.

And I smile and continue, "And any Devil-fucker who sows discord among my brothers and sisters!"

And what did I say about fickle fans? But before I can wallow in the self-satisfied sarcasm of my own bastardized words, a bolt of lightning hits me square in the chest and sends sparks and fire flying up in the air above me and I'm hurtling backward, wings useless to stop me from slamming into a pillar at the edge of the great arena. And everything goes dark.

— LXVII —

WHEN I WAKE up from the consequences of my self-righteous rant, Salvation and Fury are hovered over me like a couple of State Med-mart nurses, wondering if they are wheeling me to recovery or tagging my toe for the morgue.

It's the first time I've seen Kelly—Salvation—worried about me since this mess started. "We—we thought you were—"

"That was brutal," Fury says. "She fucked you two *up*."

I flap and struggle my way to my feet. "Thanks for the support," I say. "I notice that you didn't rush right out to rescue me."

Fury says, "We didn't know what to like—shut up, you're fine."

When I look, the lines are pretty much drawn right down the middle. I don't think any of the fallen or the faithful know quite what to do. The Dark Angel of Light is dead or gone from eternity or whatever, so the black ones are without a leader. They are lined up along my—our side of the field. For black or blacker, it's my side now, I guess. The pure white angels are largely on Life's side of the hall. I'm sure a few of them are questioning her judgment right now, but self-preservation is pretty powerful and fear goes a long way toward buying loyalty for that. The gray angels? When I look at our side of the stadium. . . "What's with all of the gray geese?"

Salvation says, "I—"

"You should have *fucking* seen it, Jump," Fury jumps in. "Remember the father's speech right before—in the church? Salvation like,

321

hammered her with it. And then, all of those gray ones just flapped their way over here and landed without saying shit."

Apparently, while I was out, Salvation gave a little speech of her own.

"Impressive," I say to her.

She smiles at me as she holds my arm to see if I'm steady. "I find my tongue when I have to."

And isn't that the truth. Because, though Salvation is content to let me do most of the blathering and bitching, every once in a while. . . I'm just sad I missed one of her famous "brimstone blowouts."

"Okay, catch me up," I say, because this looks to be a pretty big fight.

And Fury is drunk on the adrenaline and whatever else she might have found to snort, because bug-eyed and blazing fast, she launches into an explanation, "Okay, so we got here and the father was toast, so you were like, smacking fire with the Devil, and then *she* smoked his ass with lightning, then Rain flew straight up out the roof, and then you were talking shit at everyone, and then she lightning-bolted you, and then you were trashed, and we thought you were dead and Salvation was like, 'Prickly path of righteousness, and oppression and evil in Heaven, and shit.' It was *awesome*. Then you woke up."

And I slowly turn toward Salvation, my eyes wide enough that I bet she wonders if they'll fall out of the sockets. "What . . . the fuck?"

"I'm aware," she says. Then she shakes her head as we both look across the arena at the white angel army of the first Hell in Heaven. "I hope Rain never grows up."

Fury looks, too. Salvation and I see them at about the same time that she does.

Then Fury says, "Oh . . . shit."

It's the right response.

"Motherfuckers," I mutter. Because on each side of the Chosen One are Fury's—Mercedes' parents—Frank and his tramp-stamped, bounty hunter, angel bitch.

But they are seriously . . . nasty. The only thing uglier than the greedy, gluttonous, vain bastards in life are what they turn into in Purgatory.

"Do you like my new pets?" Life yells across the arena at us. "You will join them shortly."

And now she's sounding a little less like a "lopping off heads" chick and a little more like a "boil a bunny on your steps" lady.

But as scary as *she* is. . . Whatever Frank did in life has warranted him packing the most hideous face I have seen. Warts and pustules ooze black bile down his cheeks, and his wings seem deformed for some reason. When I zoom closer, they are malformed and tiny— doesn't look like he could fly with them.

But the worst thing on him is a huge, hulking—he looks like a rabid dog in heat. It's hard to shake the image. "Be careful that filthy dog doesn't hump your leg with that thing," I yell back at her.

And now her true colors are coming out, because she points to Fury, and then she says, "He tells me he's going to fuck your little friend there with it."

And I look at Salvation and raise my eyebrows. "Did she really just say that?"

And I can tell that Fury doesn't remember most of what happened to her back in life. And that's good for her—just the way we hoped it would go. "Hah!" she says. "He touches me with—I'll tear that thing off!"

And Salvation scrunches up her face in disgust. "Oh my God," she says. "That is gross. Can you get on with this, please? Don't let her talk again."

Now, children, before you start squawking and screeching, asking me why we don't all just fire our feathers to mess each other up, there are rules to the game . . . and besides, what fun is fighting if you can't taunt the other team first?

Now . . . as bad as Frank looks, blonde-mommy is worse. Her light locks have turned to twisting, albino snakes and her tits are oozing. . . Who the hell knows what the electric-yellow stuff is. And the both of them look tiny next to Life, but then I realize that they are down on all fours like . . . well, like dogs in heat. And then they race at each other and—all three of us wince and recoil at the sight.

"Ew!" Salvation says. "That is just—I think I'm gonna—"

And I don't know what took this long, because ten billion souls and one bounty killer's dog-bitch later . . . Salvation finally pukes.

Nerves. . .

But it's probably more scarring for Fury to see, though I can't imagine it looked any better when she walked in on them in life.

"Goddammit," she says, "they were *always* doing that shit. And if it wasn't him, it was—sick old. . ." Then she cocks her head and shakes it at me. She's angry, more than usual. Can't say I blame her. "When we win this thing, I want a law in the book that says no sex after you are like . . . thirty."

I smile at her, but before I can say something sarcastic back—

"That's just not happening," says Salvation.

We all kinda smile at each other over that, but it is short-lived, because from across the arena, Life's voice laughs back in a maniacal cackle like a thousand crows just lifted off a dead horse carcass.

When I look across at her. . . Trading taunt time should be over, but I can't resist just one more, so I yell across the field, "Looks like the bitch is in heat."

"Which one?" Salvation mutters. And she is airborne before I can say something sarcastic back.

"Son of a bitch," I mutter. And I'm up and flying behind her.

— LXVIII —

FURY ROCKETS PAST me, flying faster than I'm going to be able to catch up, and then Salvation shoots by, too. With those wide, sleek wings, Fury is just insanely fast. And she's a hundred yards ahead of us both when she slices into Frank the freak, and for the second time in I think as many days, she's slicing and tearing at the little pit bull from hell. And he's yelping and howling and biting at her. And Fury is clawing and cawing back.

"Yow!" I wince and yell to Salvation, as Fury gets her proper revenge on him. "That has to hurt."

"Pay attention," Salvation yells back, and then she slams into the first line of white angels, her wings stretched to full width, slicing through snowflakes.

"I a—" I try to say.

But Life hammers into me and she's screaming and screeching and *Jesus*, she is strong, because I'm flying backward again. Only this time she's clawing and cawing at me and I'm just getting beat to shit in the face by her near-invisible wings. And I can feel my black blood flowing down my cheeks and the rage is in me, but I'm not getting anywhere with it.

She drops me and I plummet, flipping and flapping toward the floor of the arena, and somehow I manage to pull myself out of the spin—ten billion kills later, I'm a little better at this now—and I bank hard and head right at her. I twist wildly and spin like never before, and I loose pin feathers and flight quills in a streaming torrent of slicing steel rage.

And the whole arena slows down and I look at her face and she's wild-eyed—intoxicated on the power of her own wrath. And I look around the arena and angels fire feathers and claw and caw at each other below, as white and gray and black hounds of the two Heavens run red with the blood of their brothers and sisters. And snowflake plumage turns pink and wings sever and limbs and talons fall to the red and white jeweled floor of the arena. Everything turns to a bathed-in crimson death match of damnation and fire.

And I can feel my rage growing—the pointlessness and waste of it infuriates me. A civil war? For what? So someone can stay on top—stay in control? And I feel my wings turn to jagged sharp swords and fire shoots above me as I follow the feathers I fired.

She flies straight through my blanket of fiery quills and several of them slice right through her, leaving small specks of blood forming on her shining transparent white feathers. Not that it matters, because seconds later she slams into me full force.

But this time I catch her by one wing with a talon and I shoot fire at her, but she hammers me with a bolt of lightning that blinds the shit out of me . . . but it doesn't kill me.

Whatever DNA she donated with "daddy," that lightning trick doesn't work quite like it did on him. In fact, it kinda supercharges me, and I throw her off and she goes spinning.

When she regains control, she hovers and looks at me, confused. *Didn't know I could do that, did you?* I think. But when I look down, I'm losing some "molasses" of my own.

Then two gray angels slam into her at a speed so fast I can barely see that they are women. And she goes spinning out of control, but then flies up above, finds them—shooting away—and she sends bolts of lightning at them and they crash, smoking and burning and leaking blood on the floor of the arena.

And I spin again and let loose hundreds of feathers at her. They streak across the arena like orange tracer rounds in a firefight. She sees them coming, but there are just too many and the tip—a foot or so, maybe—slices off of her right wing and it goes spinning down like a helicopter crash to the floor.

But she's back and racing at me, with noticeably less flight control than she had before. As she flies, I can see blood spraying from her severed wingtip and the patches on her chest feathers are getting bigger. And even if it is black molasses, blood is blood—losing it is bad. You don't last long doing that.

When she crashes into me this time, it's a pretty even match. The wrath of God versus my red-hot, rant-filled rage. That's a draw in any world but the real one, so we stalemate and beat each other senseless in midair. And before we know it we are both flopping and flapping on the floor of the great Arena of Reckoning, turned to a river of blood.

"When I'm done," she screeches at me, "I'll give your wife to the whoremongers and feed Rain to my dogs."

And that is just not gonna happen. "When you're done," I yell at her, "you are gonna wish you never fucked the Devil to have me."

It's probably the wrong thing to say, because she flaps up and hovers and lightning bolts fly from all of her fingers, every direction at once. And I fly backward when one hits me, but I'm up pretty fast. Five angels of varying colors aren't so lucky. Neither is Salvation, and I watch her fall from the sky—wings folded and flapping aimlessly—then she bounces on the ground in a whump, and she's down, smoking and motionless on the floor of the arena.

And now the only thing this benevolent bitch hasn't taken from me is my little girl. And my stomach acid turns to liquid hot rage and I feel every feather on my body as it catches fire and shoots flames above my head. And I jump up and race at her, flapping hard, leaving a trail of black smoke. I feel a couple of stings on my way—lightning bolts, or maybe feather she fired—hit me. At this point, who knows? I really don't care. And when I get to her, I engulf us both in a huge ball of orange fire and black smoke. And flames shoot all around us as we fall back to the floor.

If the queen isn't dead, she's damn close, because now she's rolling, trying to put out the flames on her wings. And I jump on her back and sink my talons deep and she lets out a loud caw and screech and she's—*Son of a bitch,* I think, *she's yelling for help.*

No sooner do I translate it, than a bunch of white angels grab me in their talons and lift me off her back. Half my size at most, it's difficult for them to pull one wrath-filled archangel off another. And I jerk and screech at them and blast flames in every direction at once, burning every one of them down to black, smoking feathers and squawking beaks.

And as soon as they let go, I fold my wings and drop in a dive right at her. But she's up, too and sending bolts of lightning at me and this time they are brighter and hotter. I must have done something to piss her off. When they hit me, I spin to the ground and land in a crash and a few of my flight feathers rip out and embed in the floor of the arena, sticking almost straight up. Then more white angels are on me, pecking at me, trying to carry me off, but I flap my wings and set them on fire, too.

I fly to the tip top of the arena, ascending until I'm almost at the domed roof. And I know she's behind me, chasing me and screaming in rage. So I slow down and let her grab on and then . . . I spin around and grab onto her with every talon I've got. And I've got both her wings in a vice grip as we stop flying and start falling. And she's screeching at me and I'm cawing at her . . . and that's exactly what I want.

When we slam into the floor of the arena, I feel a big wind come out of her—millions of souls—babies and women, crying—and then a steel spike feels like it jabs into my chest and I look into her black eyes. She seems stunned or something, and then I smell vanilla and molasses everywhere. And I'm lying on top of her and we are both impaled on the wing feathers I lost when I crashed. Smells like my blood is—yep, I'm bleeding down onto her chest and my blood is burning her like acid. And the smoke comes up and when it hits my nostrils it smells like burned chocolate chip cookies. I shit you not. *No wonder she can get away with so much crap*, I think.

Let me tell you a little secret, you wanna win a fight, don't go getting all merciful and complacent when you think the other guy, or crazy demigod, is down. Give them everything you got until there is nothing left of them. And I'm on top of her with all twenty of my talons. And I'm pecking and tearing and clawing until I see guts. Because the only way this fight ends is with her insides . . . out. Only way to be sure.

And then it's done—simple as that. Guts and chunks—not as glorious as the good books make it sound, is it?

Then . . . I fall over.

When I wake up—no telling how long I've been out—I'm barely able to move. When I finally flop myself over—pull my own feathers out of my chest—I take a deep breath in through my nose and my chest bubbles and gurgles a little.

I can smell sweet molasses from us both. And I turn my head toward her and her black eyes have turned bright blue and she has a smile on her face. *What the. . .?* And when I look, yeah there's crimson red blood and guts coming from her stomach, but out of her chest pumps the sticky black goo that I know all too well. "Molasses," I mutter. Then I turn my head back and look up at the roof. And it opens.

I would like to tell you that I lie here and cry into the sky—feel something human again—but the only thing I feel is emptiness and anger. And I listen to the screaming and screeching, as the fallen and the faithful claw and battle each other, and I close my eyes and try to shut it all out.

But my mind doesn't work that way—I don't stay relaxed for long —and I start grinding a little speck of grain in my craw. And it grows and it grows and then it's a sea of bright wheat. So bright that I'm squinting even though my eyes are closed. And as soon as I feel like I'm ready, I'm going to open them and then I'm going to see Rain and everything is going to be fine.

And I still don't understand. "Pointless," I mumble. And then I think to myself, *Do they even know what they do? Do they care?*

And when I open my eyes, there she is. No, it's not Rain, it's Life's body, floating up, glowing brighter than it did when she was. . . Is she alive? Was she? Are any of us? And her body floats toward the roof of the arena, and it grows brighter as it ascends. And then she looks at me through the bright and her voice whale-moans into my thoughts, "Goodbye. Good luck."

"That's it?" I ask. "Good *luck*?"

Once the Queen of Life, or Bread of Hearts, or whatever you want to call a vengeful, wrathful, psycho bitch from Heaven, is gone, a brighter, crystal-shining light descends through the roof. And this better be Rain, because otherwise this whole thing—

And thank—I have no clue who to thank for it, but she's there, hovering and star-bright between her pure white feathers and white sunglasses. *Now I'm in a sunglasses commercial or some other stupid shit*, I think. Or maybe it's that I'm bleeding out and hallucinating or dreaming or something?

But I can hear that the fighting has stopped and I grunt at the pain as I roll onto my side to look. And the faithful and the fallen are wing to warrior, frozen in mid-battle. Then, slowly at first, those that aren't limp on the floor of the great hall are staring at Rain. They start shading their eyes with their hands.

And then Rain speaks. But it's not my little angel's voice. Well, it is her voice, but older, more . . . commanding, "Behold," she says, "I shall tell you a mystery, my children. Then we shall sleep, and then we shall all be changed . . . but the same."

"Dammit," I mutter. It's gonna be more mumbo-jumbo bullshit. They've infected her, too. And I turn my head and look for Salvation, but I can't find her on the bloody, angel-strewn battlefield. I already know she's lying out there, dead. I just don't want to admit it.

And I wish I could just wake up in some med-mart with an aneurism and find out that Kelly had them operate on me to remove it—something that I could reconcile with the events I wish were a dream. But Rain flaps up next to me. My body, anyway, because I'm on the floor of the arena, bleeding, coughing blood, busy leaking my second life all over the diamonds and rubies on the field. And then I see my little angel.

And I see a golden angel coming down through the roof, and he's holding a great iron key on a huge chain in his hand.

And Rain points at me and says, "This is my father, Jump, the great dragon of judgment. And he is now under my power. He shall be bound for this two-thousand-year eternity in the lake of fire, beneath the dungeons of the arena, deep under the Hallowed Hall, atop The Great Mountain of the Eternities. And he who is Lived—the Dark Angel of Light—I shall cast into the dungeons."

And now I must be losing it—falling into some sort of coma—because I think my baby girl just said she was going to bring the Devil back to life. Why the. . .?

"My mother," Rain says, "the great Salvation of judgment, shall sit by his side and rule over him."

And that's the second person she is threatening to bring back to life, because Salvation is smoking dead somewhere on the floor of the arena. And now I hope I'm not hallucinating, because . . . my little girl sounds like she's turning into. . . I hope she doesn't turn out like the other one, but thinking about it, who else would have the innocence and compassion enough to take care of a bunch of zoo animals. I caw out a little laugh and spit some of my own blood. *Kids love animals*, I think. Then I smile. How much worse could it be than a couple of jealous, power-hungry lovers?

Rain looks back down at me, and then she holds her hand up in the air. Looks like she learned a little showmanship during her captivity, because the crowd starts to coo and caw—softly at first, then the sound starts to build. "And my judgment shall be the undead, the immortal," she says. Then she slices her fist so fast I don't even realize what she's done until I look at her holding my heart in her hand. But when I feel to my left breast there is no hole. *Just like him*, I think. But something is . . . wrong. I feel to the right of my chest and there's a huge, bleeding hole where my—

"I remove his right heart," Rain says, holding up my heart to an ever-deafening crowd, "as the right heart was removed from all of the Chosen One's children before him, and just as the Dark Angel of Light removed his wrong one."

I cough a little and try to speak. "My—"

Rain looks at me and motions her other finger to her lips. "Quiet, beast," she says. "In time you shall understand." And she turns her attention back to her followers. Leader, follower—in a crowd it's not too tough to figure out which is which. Because now, the cheeping and cooing and cawing are shaking the entire hall. "Your great mother was wrong. . ."

That little statement quiets them down a little. *Be careful*, I don't know why I think it—little shit just ripped out my . . . my other heart? Whatever is happening, this is—shit, she's changing the guard. This is an inaugural ceremony.

Rain says, "For to sacrifice one's right heart. . ." Then the sounds start building again. ". . .to acquire an immortal soul, is an arrogant and jealous god's folly. For no soul in all of the eternities can know peace without a just heart. Therefore . . . it is my first decree that no being in the next eternity shall shelter a wrong heart beneath their left bosom . . . without the balancing power of a just one under their right!"

And the crowd goes nuts for that little edict. Wrong hearts—doomed from the start. And I have no idea why, but the conditioned half of my brain starts cataloguing body parts. And I'm foggy and pretty banged up, but. . . *Arms, legs, eyes.* . . Shit, we even got two nuts just to make sure we can stuff more "apples" into the overbaked pie. So what does that. . .?

I'm no internal organs expert, but—hearts, dicks and assholes—not enough of the first, can't get rid of the second, way too many of the third. I guess we could use some genetic . . . restructuring.

Then again, maybe we are about to get it.

And I look back up at Rain and try to stand. Not happening, and I flop back down and cough black blood.

Without even looking at me, she points her free hand and I feel the light and bright surround me and tilt me to my feet. And I grab my chest, because . . . she's still got my heart! But when I do, I'm sealed back up. And I am not *ever* going to get used to that.

Then Rain points to the roof and she says, "The false truth of Life Is For Eternity . . . is dead. And in this eternity. . ."

And the faithful of Rain's new Heaven, and the faithless bastards of my new Hell all shout as if they've recited this part for centuries: "Long live Life!"

And then a bright, searing light streaks across the sky above the roof and I can feel the heat and see the fire and the flash—and then we are all . . . gone.

— LXIX —

I SIT UP from being hunched forward—such a long story to tell. And flames lap the sides of the fiery lake, illuminating their faces. A dozen or more little Purgatory angels, freshly judged and condemned to my cozy "new" Hell, stare back at me, wide-eyed and probably shitting themselves at the thought that this is their new existence.

"And *that*, children," I say to them, "is the truth of the end of all that Life-Is-For-Eternity crap. That is the story of how I killed God. Ah, the God old days—seems like I'm falling and dreaming more and more of them. Judgment under. . .? That was a long time ago—it's back under my power now."

I hear Salvation's voice, "Are they asleep yet?"

"No, they're still awake. Look at the little shits—they don't even believe me!"

"None of them ever do," says Salvation.

"Well, little purgatories," I say. "I would like to tell you that everything that happened was the Rain's honest truth, however. . . Now, do you remember what I told you about everything that comes after "however?" Good, because the rest. . . You know, I don't know if I can do the whole thing justice. Maybe I should just let Father Benito Octavio Benedetti tell you in his own words. Let me see. . . Where is it? Yes, yes, here we go. *Book of Blood*." And I open it to the first page. Then I look back at all the inquisitive faces. "Be careful, now. Fury says Father Faith is a miserable old cocksucker."

And I start reading.

Book of Blood
Benito Octavio Benedetti

Blood 1:1 And when I opened the seventh seal, I heard the voice of the seventh beast say, Come and see.

Blood 1:2 And I saw a great red book; and when I touched it the book spoke sweetness to my ears as the breath of angels; and it said. . .

Blood 1:3 And high on The Great Mountain of the Eternities, in the Hallowed Hall of the Word: the Destiny of Souls, the Bread of Life and the Dark Angel of Light did know of their loins.

Blood 1:4 And the seeds the Bread of Life planted were thus to be sown in blood.

Blood 1:5 And the Bread of Life's own seed was the seed of her children's destruction; and the seed was made a pariah of the chaos of man: and the child of their sin was to be cast out of the garden.

Blood 1:6 And so the seed was to be called The Fallen; for The Fallen denied faith in the book of the Chosen One.

Blood 1:7 And on his last day of man, the Dark Angel of Light, Lived, and Life did each tempt The Fallen with their own desires.

* * *

Blood 1:8 And The Fallen did spurn them in turn and choose of his own right heart.

Blood 1:9 And on his first day of judgment, the flesh of The Fallen became pierced: and he boiled in the blood of his own tears.

Blood 1:10 And the Salvation of The Fallen was raped and murdered.

Blood 1:11 And thus The Fallen became absent forgiveness, absent compassion, absent faith: for The Fallen was vengeance; and vengeance would harbor no mercy: and it was so.

Blood 2:1 And on his second day of judgment, The Fallen did speak his name and the Dark Angel of Light was compelled to spare an angel in the second Heaven.

Blood 2:2 And The Fallen before him did choose his name and he became an angel of both Heavens.

Blood 2:3 And darkness and light became the salvation of souls; for The Fallen was the will of the Word of the great books.

Blood 2:4 And thus The Fallen carried the task of destroying man; his lot was to author the end of Life Is For Eternity: and it was so.

Blood 2:5 And on the third day of his judgment, The Fallen was born in death; and he did bathe himself in the blood of his oppressors: and they did tremble at his resurrection.

Blood 2:6 And the Chosen One named a champion of the first Heaven; a soul of man: pure of hearts, and faithful of purpose.

Blood 2:7 And the Chosen One spoke the angel's name.

Blood 2:8 And the angel's name fell from the heavens as Rain. And the blinding light of the truth followed: and Rain hounded judgment through the anarchy of The End.

Blood 2:9 And the two Heavens sent Rain and judgment down upon the earth: and it was so.

Blood 2:10 And on the fourth day of his judgment, The Fallen bathed himself in the blood of man and woman and beast: and the great cleansing of the garden began.

Blood 2:11 And The Fallen cried and summoned forth the hounds of the two Heavens.

Blood 2:12 And the souls of the unjust and the just alike trembled in fear and despair.

Blood 2:13 And the hounds took the souls to the Great Mountain of the Eternities as the first sacrifice of The End.

Blood 2:14 And The Fallen caused the womb of Heaven to split open and Rain spilled forth from her guts.

Blood 2:14 And on the end of the fourth day, there was darkness.

Blood 2:15 And The Fallen rested atop the house of Faith: and it was so.

Blood 2:16 And on his fifth day of judgment, The Fallen did ascend toward the first Heaven: and Rain poured down on him.

Blood 2:17 And the bright light of truth pierced the flesh of The Fallen and tore at his armor and caused his wings to fold.

Blood 2:18 And I looked up, and beheld a brighter angel than any in the heavens ascend through the roof of the house of Faith: and Rain went with her.

Blood 2:19 And the blood of The Fallen had spilled at her hand as sweet nectar from the sap trees in the garden.

Blood 2:20 And The Fallen laid in stillness in the house of Faith. And judgment Under My Power was restored.

Blood 3:1 And on the sixth day, The Fallen spewed forth judgment, and Fury and Salvation descended upon earth; and he sent Rain and Faith toward the heavens.

Blood 3:2 And they all plummeted into the anarchy of The End.

* * *

Blood 3:3 And another great beginning of an Eternity came to pass: and it was so.

Blood 4:1 And on the seventh day of his judgment, The Fallen was possessed with vengeance.

Blood 4:2 And judgment summoned forth the faithful and the fallen of the two heavens.

Blood 4:3 And I heard a great wind of a thousand million wings beating toward the drum of judgment; and no angel slumbered lest their talons be bathed in the color of the blood of souls.

Blood 4:4 And Justice and Fury and Salvation slay every beast and burned every crop upon the earth. And the earth ran thick and red with the blood of beasts. And the land lay black in ash.

Blood 4:5 And the earth brought forth no grass, no herb yielding seed, no fruit tree yielding fruit.

Blood 4:6 And the angels boiled the waters of the earth and the sea and the great whales, and every living creature that moveth, which the waters brought forth abundantly, after their kind, and every winged fowl after his kind ceased.

Blood 4:7 And at the end of that seventh day, none stood in the garden: and it was so.

Blood 5:1 And The Fallen gathered his earthly forces and Faith and Fury and Salvation followed the Rain and ascended toward the mother and the father of the two Heavens.

Blood 5:2 And the Dark Angel of Light relinquished his reign in lightning and fire.

Blood 5:3 And all of the angels in all of the heavens took arms against each other. And father slay mother, and mother slay mother.

Blood 5:4 And judgment rose in death from the battlefield and inhabited the throne of the damned. And his Salvation was resurrected and ruled over him for eternity

Blood 5:5 And then there was a time of great nothingness—dark infinity.

Blood 5:6 And the light shined on The End and a new Chosen One understood The Beginning.

Blood 5:7 And Rain blanketed the earth for the next eternity; and it was good.

Blood 5:8 Let no god nor angel in the heavens nor being upon any earth hold tongue to speak against the Words.

Blood 5:9 For they shall all be born again . . . in fire.

* * *

Flames lap from the fiery lake, warming all in the pit, comforting the most damned for my tale.

"Are you still reading that book to them?" Salvation says to me. "Rain almighty, you need to put that thing down. You are going to go blind as Faith reading that thing to those innocent, little purgatories."

I look up from all the faces. "They aren't that innocent," I say to her. And I get a sly grin and look back. "Not anymore . . . are you, rookies? Oh, now . . . see, there you go with those faces. You look as confused as flame on a feather. Unravel that. But she might be right. All these burning rage stories before you roost. What? You don't wanna roost? Again with that shit? Read it again? But I've been telling you this same story . . . gotta be close to a thousand years. The end doesn't change . . . ever. Everyone just eats each other down there."

And I hear Salvation calling me again, "Your daughter is waiting, and I'm tired of being late."

"Late?" I say to her. "I'm never late. What's she talking about, I'm late?"

Fury laughs at me. She's always laughing at me now. "You're kidding, right?" she says. "That old cocksucker was right."

And I point at her. "Don't you go bitch-piling on top of me," I say to her. "Especially in front of—you know I'm never late."

Then that little shit. . . She laughs at me again. "Right to my face? You believe that?"

When I look at Fury, she tucks her wings tight and grins ear to ear.

I frown at her. "What was he right about?" I ask.

"Pretty much everything," Salvation says. "Now move it!" And she looks at Fury. "And you put those little rookies to roost. They can't handle any more of that truth and torture tonight. And we're out late —there's a fresh flight of souls."

"The show must go on," I mutter.

Fury nods and smiles—I know what that means.

"I'm coming," I say. Then I look at all of the little minds, screaming for answers. And I smile at Fury. "I'll leave you children in . . . angrier hands than mine. Careful, don't believe a word she says. She's meeeennn!"

By the time we leave and head up through our portal entrance to the Arena of Reckoning in the Hallowed Hall of the Unholy Word, atop The Great Mountain of this Eternity, I know Salvation was right —she's always right. "We're gonna be late," I say to her.

"She won't be happy with us."

"She'll get over it."

Salvation says, "She'll rain down on you again."

"Stop. . ."

"You better put on a good show," says Salvation.

"When have I not?"

"I don't know," she says. Then she grins as we walk. "Feels like you are . . . slipping."

"What the. . .? Slip—I'll slip you."

She's giggling at me as we enter the great arena to cheers and cooing and cawing from the gallery. And I think to myself, *So many different souls—never know what's coming next.*

One thing I do know, Fury's not putting anyone to bed.

The lakeside stories were a fiery favorite with the little purgatories.

Fury knew that. And all the hatchlings of the second Heaven sat beside the fiery lake, wide-eyed and silent as she spoke. She leaned in and whispered softly at first, with a devious smile, "Snuggle up here next to the fire and brimstone, you little bastards and bitches. Get good and cozy by the fiery lake." And then she opened her eyes wide and spoke a little louder, "You want another story? Auntie Fury has a story that not even Grandpa Jump knows. That's right, you little soul suckers. Careful though, because as mean as Life was. . . As horrible as the Dark Angel of death, Lived. . . This story will scare your flaming little tail feathers off!"

Fury always got a little crazy before a big fight night in the arena. But if she had to babysit these little rookies—if she was missing the fight up there—then she would have to do *something* to entertain herself. Scaring the shit out of little purgeys would have to do.

But first, no angel in the second Heaven was allowed to roost without praying first. Jump wrote that himself. Fury's eyes were wild now and she started. They all followed along, reciting the prayer of The Fallen:

With dreams and screams dark angels poke
And our feathers fire and our wings smoke
Because some dreams we leave and some we don't
And some we can't . . . and some we won't.

Then Fury started her tale, "Very good, little ones. I think you're like, finally getting the hang of this shit. Ready? Okay, here we go: Keep your talons sharp and your feathers hot, because this is a story that can't be forgot. So boil some blood and gather some guts. You'll need snacks for the story of how I almost . . . went nuts."

END OF TESTAMENT

Congratulations! You just finished *JUMP*, the first installment in Steve Windsor's *THE FALLEN* series.

Turn the page to find out about upcoming book releases for loyal fans of *THE FALLEN* series. >>>>>

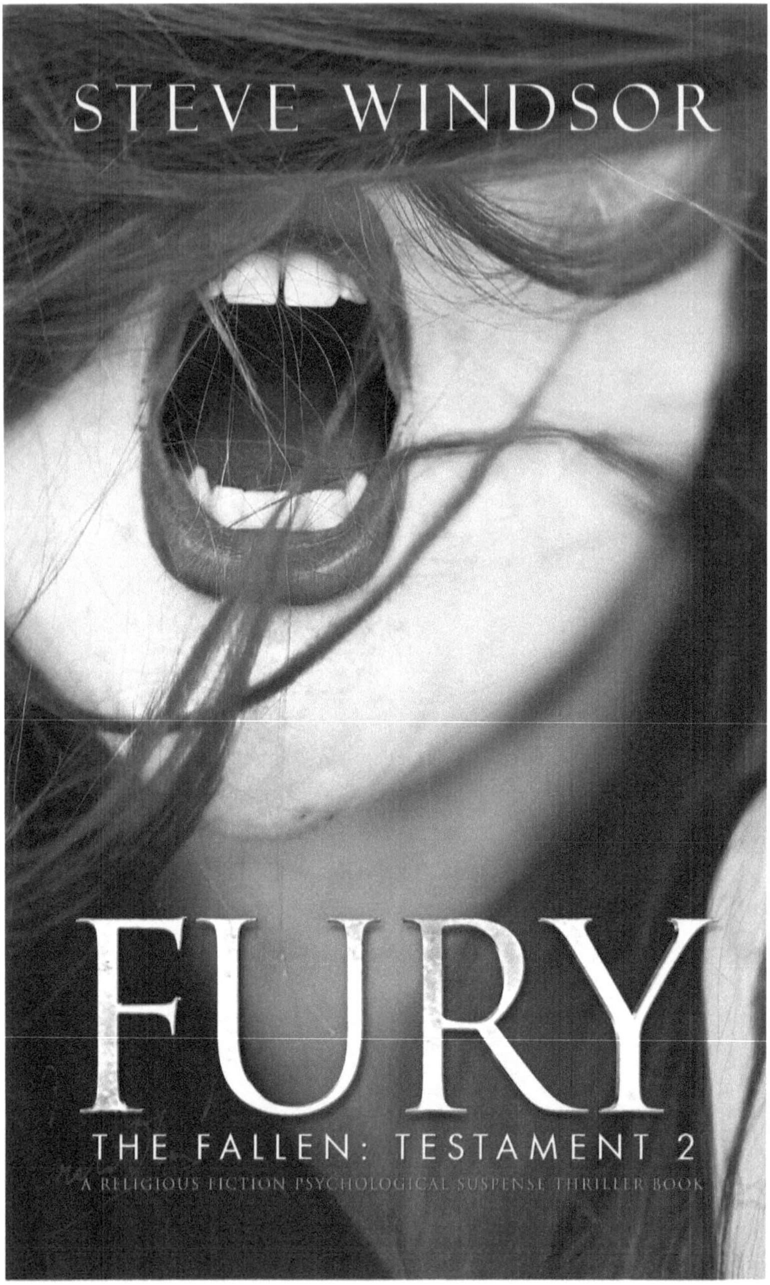
STEVE WINDSOR
FURY
THE FALLEN: TESTAMENT 2
A RELIGIOUS FICTION PSYCHOLOGICAL SUSPENSE THRILLER BOOK

Take a trip back from eternity ... for old times' sake!

Hold onto your wings! Have a Devil-may-care, good time with the gods in *FURY*, the second book in Steve Windsor's *THE FALLEN* series. An even more dazzling read, this hilarious close-up of a personality who cussed her way through one eternal conquest of Heaven and Hell will keep you riveted and clamoring for more. With Windsor's exceptionally concrete prose and dastardly, diabolical dialogue, you won't regret a repeat visit to his eternity of "everlasting impotence." If you've read *JUMP*, the introduction to this apocalyptic world, you'll love an intimate look at one of the stars of the "Great Mountain of the Eternities."

You won't get a judgmental showdown this time. The audience gets to leave the bleachers of the Arena of Reckoning and follow the acerbic-tongued angel and her friends through a trip not to eternity, but back from it for a required resurrection that could result in. . . redemption, retribution, rage. . . Whatever it's meant to be.

Mercedes King or "Fury," as she's now angelically known, is sent through the portal "back," and winds up falling back down the same Seattle high-rise to. . . Wait, didn't we see this before? Well, some of it. Read JUMP and then get back here quickly because you'll appreciate it far more.

Fury isn't traveling alone, which adds to the fun. There she is, holding forth with her little "purgatories"—beginner angels—at the fiery lake of Heaven, blaspheming her way through lessons-innumerable when she decides to do an otherworldly show-and-tell. Oh, and wait, we're in a different eternity now, led by a different god you'll recognize, and threatened by . . . well, other beings well-loved and well-hated.

It's all a power trip, motivated by words of wisdom such as this gem only a god of the two Heavens could love: "Sometimes it is much better to let someone live with their own failure . . . than to end their suffering for them." But you'll see plenty of learning here, along with the ever-present judgments back in Heaven that always get the reader the best seat in the house:

"The cawing and screeching and crowing and cackling seemed to last for hours."

Whoever winds up as the object of this gabble-babble, you're hearing every screech and loving every minute. And who can resist the reappearance of "granddad" Jump, the former Jake Blake, who features prominently and is still trying to get around to teaching his now "god"-daughter the "facts of the afterlife?"

All the others are back as well, and they don't disappoint for a celestial minute. So climb on the feathers of your favorite for a shocking conclusion and . . . hang on for more!

Ana - (Vixen ink Ambassador)

GET BOOK TWO

THE FALLEN series continues in *FURY : Testament 2*.
Sign up to get your copy of FURY before anyone else.

"Mercedes King is an eternally angry young lady. She's got more than enough reasons for it, but she has about seven trumpet blasts to get over that."

vixenink.com/fury-fallen

Oh, and one more thing >>>

*Conventional **wisdom says**,* there he goes again—my annoying inner voice—doling out helpful advice like a decapitated traffic agent, *you should **be polite** and ask them to **leave a review on Amazon**. Oh, now, **don't hesitate**.*

"Yeah, not happening," I remind him. "Salvation knows there's only a couple of things I 'ask' for. Reviews ain't one of—"

*The word is "**please**,"* Jake, he says, *try using it.*

There's an uncomfortable stillness. The only sound is the rain pelting my jacket, slithering its way down my arm to the end of the barrel of my big .60 cal. We both know that I'm deciding whether I should blow his head off or just shoot him in the guts.

I grumble a little, "Mmm." Then send pressure to my trigger finger.

I'll remind you, he says, interrupting my finger, *that if you do that they won't be able to follow FURY on her journey.*

I let up on my finger—I know he's right. "Fine. **Pretty-please**."

He knows that's as good as it gets. *Thank you.*

About the Author:

Steve Windsor is the author of the *THE FALLEN* series of religious suspense thrillers. *JUMP, FURY, FAITH, DOGG, HOLE, BURN, LIVED, LIFE, RAIN*, and *SALVATION*.

He lives with his wife and two daughters in the real world . . . and many, many other cool people in the imaginary world in his mind.

Connect with Steve:
EMAIL: steve@stevewindsor.com
FACEBOOK: vixenink.com/facebook-page

Thank you so much for reading *JUMP*.

"I write fiction novels, because the truth . . . is just way too scary."
—Steve Windsor